Praise for Dana Marie Bell's
The Hob

"*The Hob* has added layers of intrigue and secrets because Michaela is human and Robin goes 'undercover' as Ringo, but the chemistry off the two is fantastic. [...] ...perfect for a rainy day or a few hours away from the world."
~ *USA Today*

"I've always thought Shakespeare's *Midsummer Night's Dream* is a delightful piece of whimsy, but Dana Marie Bell takes it to a whole new level in her Gray Court series."
~ *The Good, The Bad and The Unread*

"This book had me laughing, gasping, and sighing with contentment through the very end. Dana Marie Bell has delivered pure comedic genius."
~ *Night Owl Reviews*

"Ms. Bell did a phenomenal job with this story. This story had humor. It had depth. I found myself laughing out loud several times."
~ *TwoLips Reviews*

"Author Dana Marie Bell can certainly hit all the notes that a woman is looking for, romance, fun, hot intimacy and scary moments."
~ *Fresh Fiction*

Look for these titles by
Dana Marie Bell

Now Available:

Halle Pumas
The Wallflower
Sweet Dreams
Cat of a Different Color
Steel Beauty
Only in My Dreams

Halle Shifters
Bear Necessities
Cynful

True Destiny
Very Much Alive
Eye of the Beholder
Howl for Me
Morgan's Fate

Gray Court
Dare to Believe
Noble Blood
Artistic Vision
The Hob

Poconos Pack
Finding Forgiveness
Mr. Red Riding Hoode

Heart's Desire
Shadow of the Wolf
Hecate's Own

Print Anthologies
Hunting Love
Mating Games
Animal Attraction

The Hob

Dana Marie Bell

Samhain Publishing, Ltd.
11821 Mason Montgomery Road, 4B
Cincinnati, OH 45249
www.samhainpublishing.com

The Hob
Copyright © 2014 by Dana Marie Bell
Print ISBN: 978-1-61921-638-9
Digital ISBN: 978-1-61921-381-4

Editing by Tera Kleinfelter
Cover by Angela Waters

This book is a work of fiction. The names, characters, places, and incidents are products of the writer's imagination or have been used fictitiously and are not to be construed as real. Any resemblance to persons, living or dead, actual events, locale or organizations is entirely coincidental.

All Rights Are Reserved. No part of this book may be used or reproduced in any manner whatsoever without written permission, except in the case of brief quotations embodied in critical articles and reviews.

First Samhain Publishing, Ltd. electronic publication: January 2013
First Samhain Publishing, Ltd. print publication: January 2014

Dedication

To Mom who, for the first time in her life, was rendered speechless. The memory still brings a tear to my eye, and will forever live in my heart.

To my Dad, who wanted to record it for posterity, but couldn't find the camera, damn it.

To my sister, for accomplishing this amazing feat we all thought impossible.

And to Dusty. Wish you'd been in the room, because Mom says it's never happening again. Ever.

To my readers: You can find a glossary of terms for the Gray Court (and my other series) at
www.danamariebell.com/Glossary.html.

Chapter One

"Hell and damnation. The man is becoming a master cock blocker."

Robin Goodfellow strode briskly down the marble encased corridor, his boot heels clacking on the dark hardwood beneath his feet. Being summoned by his king mid-seduction was becoming more and more common. If Robin got interrupted one more time his balls were going to fall off from lack of use.

Not that they hadn't been emptied recently. They had. Just not into a willing woman.

Whatever was going on, why he was having the most erotic dreams of a dark-haired lovely, Robin didn't know, but he was willing to bet it had something to do with the sculpture Shane Joloun Dunne, a hybrid with the power to see the future, had created. It graced Robin's private chambers, a taunting reminder that his bondmate was out there somewhere, waiting for him.

Ever since he'd placed it on his mantelpiece, he'd been dreaming of her. Dreaming and spending into his sheets.

Today, for the first time in months, he'd seduced someone, if only to get some damned relief. And even that was to be denied him as he answered his king's summons.

He paused briefly at the door to the library, captivated by the sight of a dark head of hair with a rooster-like ruff peeking over the edge of his black leather wingchair. Why she insisted on wearing her headbands that way he didn't know. Was it a sea nymph thing?

The moment she saw him she growled.

He bowed deeply, amused that such a homely face hid the heart of a lioness. "Lady Cassandra, how do you fare this fine day?"

Cassie grumbled and glared at him. She'd been with him for two months and had learned his ways. Surprisingly, like the Blackthorns and Dunnes, once she became used to him she was unafraid of him. "I thought he wasn't going to come here!"

It was a shame, really, that she did not belong to him. Robin could see past the too-long, almost homely face to the sweet, determined strength she bore like a badge of honor. Her hissed indignation as she sank lower into her seat had him chuckling in earnest.

"I swear, Robin, if he sees me I'm doomed." Bright turquoise eyes dominated her face, paler than usual.

"Hide then, if you must, but if you asked for sanctuary it would be granted." Robin would give his word, if need be, and tie her to his house. Not a thing he did lightly, but since she'd saved a dear friend of his Robin owed her.

The Hob *always* paid his debts.

She shot him a look so full of sorrow he tensed. "No. It wouldn't." She sank down in the chair. "I'll just stay here, if you don't mind."

One day he would get her to tell him what was wrong, but he'd learned not to push. To hear a siren sing her sorrow was to have even the staunchest heart break in half. "Not at all. Shall I shut the door?"

He could barely see the negative shake of her head over the top of the chair. "No, but thanks anyway."

"As you wish." Robin left the room, puzzled once more by the mystery of his guest. She intrigued him in a way that few did, and he found himself loathe to leave her side, even at the behest of his king. He hated to admit it, but the woman's dry wit and glowing smile had grown on him in the two months since she arrived, but Shane, acting as the Child of Dunne, had declared that Cassie was not to be his. Therefore, Robin was free to do as he wished despite her presence in his home, hence the pretty dryad who had just left his bed and home.

He'd served his lord for more centuries than he cared to count, and would continue to do so for centuries more, despite untimely interruptions and uncomfortably tight leather pants.

Still, having his fun interrupted had done nothing for his temper, something that showed in the formal bow and razor sharp grin he greeted his liege with at the front door.

He ignored the brief, indrawn breath behind him as he escorted Oberon past his library to his study. Cassie would disappear soon enough, eager to hide from the High King. Why she feared Oberon so was part of the mystery that surrounded her. Once more, he found himself intrigued, but he had little time to figure out the vagaries of the sea nymph. If Oberon had come to Robin rather than summoning him to the Gray Palace, the situation was not only dire but required the utmost discretion.

Robin closed the door, certain that Cassie would not dare eavesdrop on Robin and the High King. As to the dryad in his bedchamber, she was long gone, having used the portal therein for just such emergencies. Only Robin could activate that particular portal; not even Oberon could enter his bedchamber without an invitation.

"To what do I owe the pleasure of your presence, my lord?" Robin swept his long auburn hair behind him with an almost effeminate gesture, one that wouldn't fool Oberon for a second. Anyone daft enough to think that the Hob was weak would get what they deserved, and Oberon had never been a dimwit.

"I need someone I trust to go to Philadelphia." Oberon's waist-length silver hair gleamed in the reflected moonlight coming in through the huge wall of windows that showcased the rugged, snow-covered Rocky Mountains. He'd chosen a truly inhospitable place to put his Gray Palace, and had allowed Robin to build his home beside it. Robin loved it, loved the view of the mountains and the lake, the freedom to run as he wished, when he wished, as did several of his people.

"You need me to check out those rumors we've been hearing?" Robin accepted the glass of cognac Oberon handed him. He swirled the glass in his hand slowly, warming the amber liquid. They'd made themselves at home in each other's places far too long for him to be offended that Oberon had gotten into his liquor. Robin watched his liege through his lashes, observing the nearly imperceptible movements of frustration and annoyance that anyone not closely associated with his king would have missed.

"Titannia is up to something." Oberon faced the windows once more, and Robin hid a wince at his arctic tone. Oberon had adored his ex-wife, been devastated when she'd betrayed him. Her duplicity had cost him, emotionally and politically. He'd lost a piece of himself when the gods severed their bond, and he was darker for the loss. "Gloriana's nephew has been taken."

Well. Titannia had certainly upped the ante this time. "Shall I retrieve him, sire?"

"No. Not yet. For one, we don't know where she's stashed him."

Robin prayed she had not taken the boy to the Black Court, but chance would be a fine thing. Titannia would do anything to achieve power, even take a naive, innocent boy and twist him into her own image. Whoever she had been before the betrayal, she was undeniably evil now. Her pact with the demon had whittled away at her until Robin doubted she had anything left of her soul.

When Titannia betrayed Oberon it caused a rift in the Fae realm that would never be healed. Titannia, now the Dark Queen, ruled what had become known as the Unseelie, or Black Court. Gloriana, the White Queen, ruled over the Seelie, or White Court. By decree of the gods themselves, Oberon ruled over both Courts as the High King of the Gray Court, the final arbiter of justice when Titannia and Gloriana could no longer contain their hatred of one another. Oberon's task was to see to it that all-out war did not erupt between the kingdoms and ensure the safety of Fae-kind everywhere by maintaining the Seeming. The gods had decreed it; indeed, the gods were the only thing that had stayed Oberon's (and thus Robin's) hand at his faithless wife's throat. Their bond had still been in place, and though it had hurt Robin grievously, he had thought it would be better that Oberon die than Titannia live. Oberon had agreed, but had been spared the loss of his life at the price of Titannia's.

Both lived, and only one suffered for it.

Still, Titannia sought to overcome the decree handed down by the gods, turning this way and that to try and unseat both Oberon and Gloriana. This, the kidnapping of one of Gloriana's royal house, was but the latest move in a never-ending chess game that Robin was growing weary of. Perhaps Oberon would allow him to change the rules.

He'd always been fond of backgammon.

"Find out what Titannia is up to, but do not attempt to extract the boy unless all other hope is lost. Delegates have been sent to negotiate his release, arbitrated by one of our own." Oberon finally turned around. Robin wasn't surprised to see his king's eyes had turned silver-gray, almost white. They only changed that way when he discussed the Black Queen. "The negotiations cannot be interrupted for any reason. Titannia must return Gloriana's nephew before the next full moon or we'll have full-out war."

"I can retrieve the boy." Robin laughed. "It would be fun." He shot his liege a wicked glance.

Oberon sighed. "If it becomes necessary, yes. For now, I'd prefer to use diplomacy to achieve the same result."

"And Gloriana would owe you one?"

Oberon raised a weary eyebrow, his eyes returning to their normal, stormy gray. "I don't really care one way or the other, Robin. Just see to it the boy is returned, preferably unharmed."

Robin bowed his normal, mocking bow. "Do we know who holds the boy?"

"No one is sure. That is another reason I need you there. Find out where the boy is being held, and by whom. If necessary we *will* retrieve him ourselves."

Robin shook his head. "What does she think to gain by this?"

The stormy gray eyes turned silver once more. "I have no idea, but she won't succeed."

Robin took a sip of his cognac, thinking. "I can easily infiltrate the Black Court contingent if it's large enough. If she's decided to send only a few delegates, then things become...trickier."

"I leave it all in your capable hands." Oberon turned once more to the windows of Robin's study.

Robin interpreted this as a dismissal and began backing out of the room. Oberon would leave when he was ready, and welcome he was to the little warmth Robin had to offer.

After all, had it not been for Oberon, Robin would not exist.

"One more thing, Robin."

Robin halted at the soft tone of Oberon's voice. When Oberon spoke that way, all listened with respect, even Puck.

"You'll have assistance with this assignment."

Robin was certain he'd misheard. "My liege, I work alone. I always have."

"Not this time."

Oberon's back remained turned to him, but Robin could hear the faint smile in the king's voice. "All the times, my king." Even when he assisted his Blades, Robin worked alone.

"Do not defy me in this, Hobgoblin."

The Hob

Robin sighed. When the king called him that, he was displeased, a state of affairs Robin actively avoided. "May I ask why, my liege?" He was careful to keep his voice neutral.

Oberon waved his hand.

The chair, the white-on-white chair that Robin hadn't even noticed was there, shifted slightly, shocking him. The chair stood and stretched, its arms elongating, its legs growing, until before him stood one of the shape-shifting pookas. The pooka smiled at Robin, his shimmering, golden eyes with their horizontal, slit–shaped pupils watchful in his narrow, aristocratic face. He wasn't much taller than Robin's five foot ten inches, and he was graced with a fall of blond hair that would make a Sidhe lady weep. Ridged gray horns curled up from his forehead and blended into his hair. *This one must be a master shifter indeed, to hide itself from me.* He saw at once why such a talented shifter would be useful in his upcoming mission. If the delegation were smaller than hoped, who would notice one more chair? And if the pooka could fool the Hob, he could more than likely fool the Black Court idiots Titannia would be sending.

Then again, Robin had not been expecting a spy in his own study. The Black Court delegation would be on their guard for tricks, especially if they knew Robin would be there. And how could they not? He was Oberon's Blade.

"This is Lord Kael Oren. He will be coming with you. He is a cousin of the missing Prince Evan."

Oh, this should be fun! Not. Robin smiled at the other man. He remembered the scandal following Prince Edmond Yate's mating of a pooka commoner. The White Court had been utterly appalled that one of Gloriana's brothers had lowered himself so, forcing Gloriana to raise the girl's family to the peerage. Prince Edmond had told them all to go pound sand and declared that he was abdicating any right to the throne of the White Court to be with the woman the gods had declared was his.

Robin had sent them a lovely mating gift.

15

Robin bowed, graceful yet mocking, and saw his bow returned, mimicked nearly perfectly.

"Lord Robin." The pooka's tenor voice was soft and filled with amusement. He met Robin's gaze dead on, with only a slight twinge of fear, quickly masked.

Robin grinned, intrigued. *Maybe the boy has potential after all.* Robin was always on the lookout for potential Blades, men and women of integrity who guarded Oberon and did his will. This one could be a recruit, if he proved himself capable.

He turned his attention back to Oberon, one eyebrow cocked, the grin still lingering on his face.

Oberon merely shook his head. They knew each other well. Oberon would know how Robin would react to Kael. "If the prince is no longer with us, I expect you to dispense justice."

The green glow in Robin's eyes was swiftly hidden by his long lashes as he bowed to his king and friend. "Yes, my liege." He ignored Lord Kael's swiftly hidden shiver of unease.

This had the potential to be *fun.*

Oberon watched as Robin and Lord Kael left the room together. He smiled and lifted the glass to his lips.

Robin was hiding something from him.

It would have been the work of a moment to have the Hob come to the Gray Palace and meet Kael, but Robin had been acting suspiciously for two months now, and Oberon was determined to get to the bottom of it.

Oberon sighed and placed his glass back down on the bar. Robin was his closest friend, his greatest ally. They were like brothers. There was none he trusted more than the Hob. So what was it that Robin was hiding so assiduously from him? Oberon had not missed the sound of a feminine gasp as he walked past Robin's library, yet he knew Robin always sent his playthings away lest they overhear something they should not.

The Hob

Robin had not reacted to the female's presence, meaning he'd been aware of—but unconcerned about—her presence. Not even his Blades were treated with such trust.

Oberon was well aware that the few females Robin trusted to that extent were currently in Nebraska, helping Lord Jaden Blackthorn in dealing with the influx of those who wished to join the new Blackthorn Clan. So who was it that hid from him in Robin's library with Robin's full knowledge? And why had Robin not introduced his guest?

Oberon grimaced. For the first time in centuries he would have to keep a close eye on his Hob. The thought that Robin might play him false was almost too much to bear. He had had his fill of betrayal with Titannia.

He sent a swift prayer to the gods that Robin was not about to break what little was left of his heart.

Chapter Two

"Why are we staying at my place? Why couldn't we just rent a room in the hotel?" Kael had long since ceased to be amused, and it showed. "The Court can certainly afford it."

Robin held the steering wheel lightly and smothered his grin. "I told you, it's more inconspicuous this way. If for some reason someone decides to tamper with our room, your place is at least defensible. Besides, if worse comes to worst, Oberon has placed a mirror in your home." A defense Robin himself did not need, but a concession to the pooka, who could not move about the way Robin could. While Robin could have teleported them both, he was unfamiliar with Kael's home, and hadn't been to Philadelphia in decades. Besides, the trip gave him time to become better acquainted with the pooka he'd be sharing a home with for the next few days. Kael could have forced the issue, refusing to open his home to Robin, but despite his grumbling he'd been more than generous.

"Thus blowing my cover." Kael shot him a sour look. "I do have to continue living here, you know."

Robin sighed. "If it's that much of an issue, I will offer you sanctuary when the mission is done." Robin glanced in the rearview mirror, checking for traffic. He was distracted by his altered appearance.

He had to admit, he was charmed by the brown eyes he'd chosen for his current guise. They reminded him of Ruby, his favorite person in the world besides Oberon. Really, none would recognize the merry, redheaded scamp he preferred to be in the golden-skinned, dark-haired man he currently appeared to be.

"I have a job. I'm hoping to have a mortgage someday."

"Hmm." Robin could understand the desire for a home. He suffered from the same affliction. While he had the house, had filled it with color, life had not chosen to nest there.

Robin's house was still not a home, and he had no idea how to change that.

"Still, we could have rented a room. It would have been easier to monitor the delegates if we were all in the same place."

As Robin took the turn off of I-95 toward Center City, Philadelphia, he wondered if the pooka would ever stop complaining.

They were headed toward Kael's Center City apartment on Locust Street. It was roughly five minutes from the apartment to the hotel where the negotiations were to take place, making the location ideal. He'd have access to all of the amenities of Center City without having to worry about staying in the same hotel as the delegates. He patted the dashboard and smiled. The place even had free parking for his rental car.

Life was sweet. Now, if only he could get Kael to stop his incessant bitching. "Time for your big girl panties, Kael, my dear."

He slowed down once they hit Locust, following the flow of traffic. It was mid-morning, plenty of time to drop some things off at the apartment and do a little sightseeing before heading to the hotel.

"Are you going to make me sleep in the spare bedroom?"

Robin choked on a laugh. "I give you my word, I will not steal your sleeping space." If the spare room were truly inadequate, Robin would simply make other accommodations. Perhaps Paris? The City of Lights was beautiful this time of year. "I think we can manage."

Kael shot him a horrified look. "Not that I don't think you're attractive or anything, but my tastes tend to run more toward females."

Robin's eyes widened with hurt. "You mean you don't want me?"

"Yes."

Robin laughed with outright delight at the emphasis Kael had placed on that single word. *Not many would turn me down so flatly, out of fear of retribution. I was right. This will be fun.* He placed a hand on his chest, the gesture far more Robin than the persona he should have been adopting. "I'm hurt, Lord Kael."

"No, you're just bored."

Robin stopped laughing and glared at the pooka, aware a slight tinge of green had entered his eyes, but he beat it back, as he always did.

The sad part was, Kael was right. He was bored spitless. He had left Nebraska—and the very entertaining Dunnes—behind, putting him at loose ends until Cassie arrived at his home. Nothing he did, no one he attempted to sleep with, could fill the aching void left behind by the only family that had ever wholeheartedly accepted him. But distance was necessary, lest he attempt to steal that which did not belong to him, future bondmate or no.

Ah, sweet, loving Ruby. He missed her most of all, but she did not belong to him. It would kill her to leave her truebonded, Leo Dunne, and would devastate the Dunne family. Robin would sooner cut off his own arm than harm them.

But it would have been sweet to taste her at least once.

At least one good thing had come out of the fiasco at the Dunne farm last winter. Unfortunately, the White Court lost a powerful clan, the Malmaynes, to the Black.

But the Child of Dunne had not only fulfilled his duty, he'd shown Robin the future.

His future.

Shane Joloun Dunne had the blood of Seers running through his veins, faint but powerful. He sculpted his visions of the future, both possible and impossible. That power had nearly been turned against him by the trickery of the Malmaynes and one of Robin's own children. Fortunately, Shane had not only survived but found his own truebond in Akane Russo, hybrid daughter of the Seer, the last of her kind, and her dragon mate, now deceased. As one of Robin's most trusted Blades, Akane had been assigned to guard Shane from the machinations of the Malmaynes. She had failed, but through no fault of her own. Thanks to his powerful gift, Shane had known that the prophecy of the Child of Dunne could not be fulfilled unless he was captured. The hybrid had allowed himself to be taken and had suffered greatly for it, but had declared his task complete. He had refused to explain to Robin exactly what that task had been, but Robin suspected it had to do with Cassie and the mystery surrounding her.

Robin was fond of the young man, not least of which because he'd sculpted Robin's future. It had been the only thing to give him the strength to leave Ruby behind, truebond or no. Robin pulled into the parking garage of the apartment complex that was his new, temporary home and remembered the first time he'd seen the sculpture.

The sculpture Shane had created for him, and that now graced Robin's bedroom, was a ball made out of razor sharp, mirror-like metallic strips, with bits of jagged glass dotting them. The cutting metal edges stuck randomly out into space. Through the metal strips he could see a tiny figure standing, arms raised like a supplicant, one hand to her chest, one to the sky. Shane had reached one finger in, blooding the metal, and tipped that figure over. Thanks to the way he'd constructed the ball, the inside had reflected the jagged edges of the outside over and over until there was nothing left but chaos and death. The position of the figure's arms when standing was perfect for a figure lying on the ground as well.

If that figure fell...

Well. Best not think on that. Robin climbed out of the car and prayed that he found the woman in Shane's sculpture soon, or he would slowly go mad. The dreams were tearing him apart with need.

Kael stretched and groaned. "Gods, I'm glad I'm back."

Robin chuckled quietly. "Don't like flying, my friend?"

Kael snorted, amused. "Hardly. The seats are too tight, I always wind up near a screaming child, and the bathrooms are laughable. And that's *before* I get on the plane."

Oh, Robin was growing more and more fond of this one. "After you." Robin bowed with a grin, aware of the sound of another car pulling into the parking lot. He turned and saw the most mind-searing orange Jeep Wrangler he'd ever been privileged to lay eyes on pull into the parking spot next to his. The grin faded as the engine revved twice before cutting off.

Behind the wheel was a dainty female in hospital scrubs. She smiled over at them before reaching down to grab something off of the passenger side floor. He tilted his head, trying to get a better glimpse of the woman.

"Robin?"

He tilted his head the other way, staring at the tiny figure in the driver's seat. There was something about her, something that called to him. What was it? Robin sniffed, but all he could scent of was exhaust, rubber, human and pooka.

"Robin, we need to go."

Robin turned and nearly snarled at Kael, but the concern on the pooka's face stopped him. What had he been doing, staring at a human female?

A car door slammed shut. "Excuse me, is everything all right?" She practically bounced in place. "Hi, Kael."

Kael's tense posture visibly relaxed. "Michaela. Just getting home from work?" Kael smiled sweetly at the dainty, brown-haired sprite of a female. The girl barely reached Kael's shoulder. Robin guessed she'd be roughly chin height on him, were he in his normal form. As it was, she barely reached his shoulder as well. She was passably pretty, with a bottom lip fuller than the top and a square, soft jaw. Deep brown eyes gleamed with good humor over a larger-than-average nose. Scrubs, covered in the scent of illness and some hideous yellow bug-eyed *things* in brown pants and ties that grinned and

The Hob

capered about her person, obscured her figure. Sensible white shoes graced her feet, and her dark brown hair was bundled up in a tight ponytail. Her pale cheeks were flushed with wind and happiness.

Dear gods above. Robin felt faint for the first time in his life.

It was *her*.

It was the woman from his dreams, and she stood before him, tiny and vulnerable and tempting as sin.

That sweet smile turned on Robin. "You must be Kael's friend. I'm Michaela. Pleased to meet you." Michaela held out her hand. "I saw you standing there, looking like you were lost. Let me guess; Kael here is too much of a pain in the ass to show you where the elevator is."

She laughed as Kael took her hand and placed it on his arm. Robin wanted to rip Kael's arm off and beat the pooka to death with it. "Of course I was going to show him, once he was no longer blinded by your Jeep."

"Hey, no mocking the Punkinator." She wagged her finger at Kael before turning back to Robin with a sweet smile. "It took me a week to remember where it was when I first moved in." She shifted the heavy bag on her shoulder and pointed to a concrete column. She hmph'd. "Blind, my ass."

Kael stared at her with something akin to awe. "He's staying with me for a few days, and haven't we had this discussion before? Are you sure you should be speaking to a stranger so easily?"

The laid-back way Kael spoke to her made it clear they'd been friends for some time. His concern for the female was admirable, but still...

Robin fought off the urge as his eyes tried to shift to the green light that spelled death for any who crossed him. Kael had done nothing but be polite to the tiny woman, a friend of his to boot. Robin should have no quarrel with Kael's actions, but the way Robin was reacting to them was startling.

However, Kael had a point. Robin blinked down at the strange, little brown wren of a female. There was no way she could fend off two full-grown men, if they were so inclined to harm her. If Ruby had done such a thing he would have paddled her ass, mate or no. "Indeed."

Michaela smiled up at him serenely. "You won't hurt me."

Robin blinked again. His brows rose. Apparently the woman was certifiable. On the basis of Kael's supposed friendship, she trusted him? "Is that so?" Tempting though it was to accept her challenge, Robin was not a complete bastard. His little human was all right for the moment, but her insane belief that the world was a safe place was going to get her killed.

"Mm-hmm." She laughed. *Laughed,* as if the implied threat were nothing. She headed past the ugly concrete column, still chattering away like the perky little bird she resembled, but this time she looked up at Kael with a frown. "Oh, Kael? FYI, some new tenants moved in while you were gone. They gave me the heebee-jeebies." She shuddered delicately.

"Oh?" Robin exchanged a look with Kael. Perhaps they were sharing space with some Dark Court Sidhe after all. If so, it might be prudent to move their lodgings.

Her lodgings. Robin's instincts were telling him to get her the hell out of here, get her somewhere safe, but he couldn't. Not now. If he was right, if she truly was his bondmate, the last thing he wanted to do was draw attention to her while at a convention full of Dark Court fae. To do so would be to court disaster on an epic scale.

Kael's stance became protective, hovering over Michaela. "Did they bother you?"

"Nah." She wrinkled her nose, that pretty smile back on her face. She was absolutely adorable, and Robin wanted her on his arm, damn it. "I let them find their own way to the elevator."

She looked like a stiff breeze could pick her up easier than it did a sylph, but she bounced along beside them without a care in the world.

"You're awfully confident for someone the size of a flea bite."

Robin almost laughed at the insult Kael muttered.

Michaela did laugh. "I know, but I've got a few tricks up my sleeve if someone decides to get frisky." She made some idiotic motions with her hands and feet that Robin assumed were supposed to be some form of martial arts but looked more like a squirrel having seizures. "Take that, bad guys!"

Robin couldn't stop himself from patting her on the head. "You're cute."

She wagged her finger in the air. "And lethal. Don't forget lethal." She waved toward the elevator. "And here we are."

The amusement in her gaze let him know how seriously she was taking her own pronouncement.

Interesting. He hadn't been this hungry for a female since Ruby. He kept the predatory anticipation that filled him off his face, for fear he would frighten her away.

This one was available for consumption, and he would feast for many years to come.

But for now, he needed to earn her trust before he could claim her body. He kept his expression amused, rather than hungry. "I'm certain thousands live in fear of your mighty fists of death." Robin pressed the button to summon the elevator.

"Damn skippy." The dainty little thing sniffed and stuck her nose in the air as she stepped onto the elevator with all the grace of a Queen. Or she would have if she hadn't tripped over thin air, landing against the back of the elevator with a muffled, "Oomph."

"Can we keep her?" Kael stepped into the elevator and helped Michaela to her feet. "I even know what to feed her. Please?" He made puppy-dog eyes at Robin, and Robin reluctantly chuckled.

Hell. Robin sighed, more amused than he wanted to admit. He'd let the boy live. He was far too amusing to kill.

"Thanks." She blew her bangs out of her eyes and turned to Robin. "I'm sorry, I'm terrible with names. What did you say your name was again?"

Robin took her hand. "Ringo Midori, at your service, my lady." Robin raised her hand to his lips and chastely kissed the back, but he never once broke eye contact.

She blushed, her cheeks becoming fiery red. "I see now why you're friends. You two are bad, bad men, aren't you?"

Robin cocked an eyebrow, delighted when she laughed. The sound trickled down his spine, lodging in his cock. That uninhibited, utterly happy sound had him harder than anything a lover had done for him in centuries.

He needed to know more about her. Where she lived. Was she seeing anyone? What were her favorite foods? Was there anything she did not like a lover to do?

For make no mistake, Robin intended to have her before the mission was done.

The elevator dinged and Michaela sighed. "Damn. This is my floor." She reached up and patted Robin on the cheek. "Welcome to the building. It was nice meeting you."

"You, as well." Robin watched Michaela bounce her way down the hallway until the elevator doors blocked the sight. A strange silence descended as the elevator once more began to move.

"Ringo? Really?"

Robin shrugged. "He was my favorite Beatle." And if Kael forgot and started to say Robin, it would be easier to slip into the new name than if he'd named himself, say, David. He would not have taken such a precaution if he had been working with an experienced Blade, but Kael would eventually learn. Robin would see to it. In the meantime, it was better to be cautious.

Kael chuckled, then leaned back against the elevator wall. "She's single. And hot. I've thought about asking her out."

For a split second Kael's life hung in the balance. Rage filled Robin at the thought of Kael with Michaela, stroking that peaches and cream flesh. Wrapping that bouncing ponytail around his wrist as he rode her.

Robin took a deep breath and stared at the elevator numbers flashing above him. He was a split-second away from killing a man he had every intention of recruiting into the Blades, all over a fantasy. That was a reaction he would have to explore later. Much later. Alas, finding the young prince took precedence over Robin's reaction to the delectable little human.

Kael led the way to his apartment and opened the door. "It's not much, but it's home."

Robin looked around, curious as to why Kael lived in such a place when he was, at least technically, a member of Gloriana's family.

It was a fairly standard city apartment, with a galley kitchen, small dining area and slightly larger living area. The bedrooms were side by side toward the back. The entire thing couldn't be bigger than a thousand square feet. Already Robin felt stifled, boxed in. He missed his six-thousand-square-foot home in the mountains.

He would go insane if forced to live here indefinitely.

He struggled to find something nice to say about the place. "I like the furniture."

He did. It was what he might have picked if forced to live in such a small space. A pale cream sofa and glass tables lined one wall, cream-on-cream wallpaper in a harlequin pattern creating a focal point behind them. By the entryway, a large mirror leaning against the wall kept the small room light and airy. Two accent chairs in bright blue sat by the big window, a glass end table between them. Across from the sofa was an electric console fireplace with a large, flat-screen television perched atop it. In the tiny dining area a glass table for four created the illusion of space. Outside on the terrace dark wicker furniture with cream cushions dominated the space. Robin would be able to sit out and enjoy the city lights in comfort.

It was small, far smaller than he preferred, but Robin would live with it. For now. At least the pooka had good taste.

Kael frowned and stared at the large mirror. "Where's Oberon's mirror?"

Robin shook his head. The boy would learn. The mirror would be in the most obvious spot, but only those of the Gray would be able to use it. The mirror would recognize no other. "Follow me."

Robin led the way to the master bedroom. There, next to a very nice queen-size bed, was an ornately decorated mirror. Symbols etched in silver and gold graced the black frame, twining around it in a pattern only another fae would recognize. The mirror itself looked antique, the glass clouded.

"Oh. My room." Kael coughed, and Robin wondered if he feared the entire Gray Court traipsing about his apartment willy-nilly. "Well, then. In that case, let's unpack and settle in for the night."

"Good idea." The delegates had already arrived, but Robin knew they would not be getting together formally until tomorrow. The thought had crossed his mind to scout out the hotel ahead of time, but he was weary. He allowed Kael to show him to his room and stripped himself down, the lure of the soft bed far too strong.

Robin collapsed on top of the comforter and slipped quickly into sleep, thoughts of Michaela chasing him into his dreams.

Robin heard a giggle, a warm sound that filled him with eagerness. She was here somewhere, in Robin's house, sneaking about as if she could hide herself from the Hobgoblin.

"Come and find me."

So his beloved wished to play hide and seek, did she? Robin was more than willing to oblige. He ghosted through the house, *fully aware she could not sense his approach. He would take her, claim her, soothe her fears and make her sing for him.*

But first, he had to find her.

She was not in the great pool she'd come to love so much, nor in the gardens where she sat for hours and admired the mountains. She wasn't in the kitchen, badgering his staff and earning cookies with her huge eyes and gamine smile.

Would she hide there? In so obvious a place?

Robin snuck into his bedroom, and pondered anew the changes he'd made since he'd first dreamed of her. Where once his walls had been deep purple, his bed, a place of unbridled lust, she had taken it and made it a place that both appeased the beast within him and inflamed his desire. His walls were now painted a purplish-gray, still dark and decadent, but much calmer. For her, he had replaced the black satin sheets, the dark curtains, bringing light into the room with pale, cream sheets and curtains. Even the carpeting was lighter, a few shades off from the walls, creating a place she loved to roll around with him when he was feeling particularly frisky.

The four-poster bed was the one piece of furniture he'd insisted upon. She'd become bolder in their love play, allowing him to tie her down upon occasion.

Indeed, she'd tied him down once, and he'd discovered he enjoyed being at her mercy. She'd been a tender lover, careful of him as so few were, aware he could easily break free but trusting him not to do so.

He had not. After all, turnabout was fair play, and Robin enjoyed playing fair with his lover.

"Found you!" Soft arms encircled his waist. She buried her face in his hair and hugged him tight.

Robin chuckled. Trust her to be one of the few who could find him when he made an effort to be elusive. "So you did." He turned and pulled her into his arms, dazzled anew by her. "Gods above, you're beautiful."

She wrinkled her nose. "I know you are, but what am I?"

Robin shook his head. Always, she took his compliments and turned them back on him, teased him for his supposed vanity. He preened for her, and she sparkled with laughter. "Lucky?" She tickled him, and he grabbed her wrists, placing soft kisses on her palms. "Witch."

"Me?" She batted her lashes.

"You must be." He nibbled her fingers, delighted when her eyes darkened. "How else would you have bespelled the Hob?"

"With my sheer, unadulterated awesomeness."

It was said with such a straight face that Robin couldn't help but laugh. "I believe that last was a given."

"As long as we have that straight."

"We do, indeed, my dear." Robin bent and took his bondmate's mouth, eager to taste her once more.

Michaela whimpered as she woke. Damn it. Just as the dream was about to get good too. Stupid alarm clock. Stupid night shift.

Ugh. Stupid life.

She stumbled out of bed and into the bathroom, her body throbbing, eager to finish what her dream man had started. But she had to get ready for work. She had kids to take care of, kids who needed her.

She held up her toothbrush like a torch. "I am nurse. Hear me roar!"

Then she wiped the toothpaste off the mirror, thanking God her dream man wasn't real and couldn't see what a dork she was.

Chapter Three

"What the *fuck* is this?" Robin stared at the entrance to the Marriott. He turned and looked at Kael in disbelief as people, huge masses of people, streamed in and out of the building. A woman in nothing more than a bikini made out of leaves walked past him, distracting him.

Kael cocked one pale brow.

"What? She has nice eyes." There was no reason for the sudden guilt Robin felt. He'd barely met his bondmate, after all, and hadn't yet mated with her.

Still, from now on he would keep his gaze to himself. Robin rarely felt guilty about anything, and the sensation took him by surprise. It was unexpected, and unpleasant.

Kael grunted, whether in agreement or not Robin couldn't say. "I think it's a fairy convention."

Robin turned to where Kael casually pointed at a rather large, florally decorated sign situated right outside the front doors. He pinched the bridge of his nose. He could think of only one person who would've chosen this is as the place to negotiate her nephew's release. Laughter bubbled up inside him, seeking release. It was a truly evil mind that had thought up *this* as a neutral location. "Gloriana's idea?"

"Who else? Ugh. *Fairies*."

The utter disgust in Kael's voice was his undoing. Robin threw his head back and howled. Truly, Gloriana could not have picked a better venue. The Black Court delegation would be climbing the walls within seconds. The laughter was welcome after his aborted dream last night.

Just a few moments more, and he'd have had her. But something had interrupted his dream, waking him abruptly. He'd been in a foul mood ever since.

Trust humanity to find a way to amuse the Hob. Kael glared at Robin. "I see nothing funny in this."

Robin snorted, his shoulders shaking.

"How are we supposed to hide in a group of humans this big?"

"You have got to be kidding me." Robin snorted, still laughing. The two of them were masters at hiding in plain sight. And here, even if Kael dropped his Seeming, he'd fit right in.

Robin, not so much.

"Did you see those idiots with the strap-on fairy wings? I mean, really. *Butterfly wings?* A real fairy wouldn't be caught dead with wings like that." He completely ignored the woman with the purple monarch butterfly wings glaring at him.

The laughter was turning into outright guffaws at Kael's continued disgust. The man was entertaining as hell.

"It isn't funny."

Oh, yes it was. Robin bent double, clutching his knees to hold himself upright. He could just picture some Black Court Sidhe prancing amongst mortals in strap-on wings. He'd have to videotape it just so Oberon could also watch the fun. Perhaps Gloriana was finally developing a sense of humor.

"Don't even *think* you're strapping fake wings on *my* ass. And don't even think about solid-gold Lycra boy over there." Kael pointed to a man in a skintight gold bodysuit, his face, hands and hair spray painted gold to match.

"I think you'd look stunning."

Kael snarled. "I'm not the one who's willing to grow a vagina. You wear it if you like it so much."

Robin laughed so hard he nearly stopped breathing. He was definitely recruiting Lord Kael for the Blades, if only for his entertainment value.

Kael sighed, grabbed Robin's arm and turned him around, navigating around a slightly pudgy faux fairy in iridescent dragonfly wings to enter the hotel. The fact that Kael felt comfortable enough with Robin to manhandle him nearly stopped his laughter. Unfortunately, some human male in far too much body glitter and far too little clothing chose that moment to walk by. His companion, a burly man dressed as, of all things, a large furry pooka, had Kael literally growling, setting Robin off once more.

Kael sighed. "C'mon. I don't know about you, but I need some caffeine. I can't deal with this shit before coffee."

Kael managed to keep Robin upright until the last of the laughter worked its way out of his system.

This assignment had a great deal more potential for fun than he'd first thought.

Michaela sipped at her salted caramel hot chocolate and listened to the discussion her two friends were having. Why they insisted on picking on her over her crush on Robin Goodfellow she'd never know. She'd been dreaming about him since she was a little girl, fascinated by bright blue eyes and impossibly long hair. She'd pretty much devoured anything remotely related to Puck. She'd even liked the way the character was brought to life by Stanley Tucci in the movie version of *A Midsummer Night's Dream* with Christian Bale and Calista Flockhart.

Her friends just wouldn't let it alone. Did she bother them over their obsession with Jason Momoa? No, she did not.

Okay, so the dude was hot. But she could so totally tease them if she wanted, she just chose not to.

"Face it, Puck was a serious bastard of the first order. If you look at what he did just in Shakespeare's plays, you'd realize that. He gives a man a donkey head, for fuck's sake." Stella began ticking points off on her fingers. "In Jonson's work he forced people to follow him, leading them away from their homes, probably killing them in the wild."

"Pfft. In the wild. Please." Michaela rolled her eyes. They were talking Lancashire, not the Serengeti.

Stella continued as if Michaela hadn't interrupted. "He stole kisses and food, would strip their bedclothes from them, pinched them, punched them and threw them out of bed." She wrinkled her nose. "Seriously, he's a prick."

Amanda nodded in agreement. "It's true. Just read the ballads."

Michaela rolled her eyes. Like she hadn't memorized the darn things. "You're forgetting something."

"And that would be?" Stella leaned back and crossed her arms. Amanda gave her that annoyingly superior look.

No matter what Michaela said they were going to stick with their belief that Puck was nothing more than an evil little hobgoblin, but she had to try. This wasn't the first time they'd had this argument, and it wouldn't be the last.

The guy had a bad rap, but it wasn't entirely his fault. Most of what he'd done had been to people who'd deserved it, but Stella and Amanda had been teasing her over her obsession for too long now to acknowledge that. She began ticking her own points off, just as she always did. "According to the very same ballads, Puck would card wool to help the less fortunate, help with the farm work, get lazy workers to do their jobs, lend money to the needy and expose nasty gossips to those they'd betrayed. Even Bottom's misfortune was due not to Puck's mischief but orders from Oberon." She shrugged. "He just got it a little wrong."

Stella sniffed. "You can't deny that Puck did an awful lot of bad things without orders from Oberon."

Michaela wagged her finger at Stella. "The thing is, when he did them, did he do them because the person deserved it or not?"

The Hob

"Not always. You've read the ballads, you should know better than us." Amanda picked up her empty cup and frowned. "Damn. All out of my skinny mocha. Anyone want seconds?"

"Not me. It goes right to my hips." Stella patted her well-rounded bottom. Her boyfriend loved Stella's hips and would have already bought her another one, silencing her protests with a kiss. Frank was good for Stella, and Stella adored him. It did Michaela's heart good to see one of her friends settled with a wonderful man.

Michaela held up her cup. "I'm good."

"Be right back, then." Amanda stood and threw her cup in the recycling bin before getting back in line.

Stella kept up the argument. She was never one to let something die. "I'm telling you, Puck was a shithead."

Michaela frowned. "No. He wasn't." The final act of the play, where Puck asks forgiveness of the audience, had been both sad and roguish at the same time. She was enchanted every time she saw it.

She wrapped her hands around her cup and began to recite one of the ballads.

"*Yet now and then, the maids to please,*
I card at midnight up their wooll:
And while they sleep, snort, fart and fease,
With wheel to threds their flax I pull:
I grind at mill
Their malt [up] still,
I dresse their hemp, I spin their towe;
If any wake,
And would me take,
I wend me, laughing, ho, ho, ho!"

Stella laughed. "You are *not* quoting Ben Jonson at me."

Stella was a literature major, but Michaela was a connoisseur of all things Goodfellow. There was no way Stella would win this fight. "Yes. Yes, I am." Michaela sipped her hot chocolate and smirked at Stella over the rim. *Take that, hater.*

Stella's eyes narrowed. The woman loved a challenge. "What about the times he messed with people's weddings just for fun?

"*He welcome was unto this feast,*
And merry they were all;
He play'd and sung sweet songs all day,
At night to sports did fall.
He first did put the candles out,
And being in the dark,
Some would he strike, and some would pinch,
And then sing like a lark.
The candles being light againe,
And things well and quiet,
A goodly posset was brought in
To med their former diet.
Then Robin for to have the same
Did turn him to a beare;
Straight at that sight the people all
Did run away for feare."

Michaela bit her lip to keep from laughing. "He was hungry."

"Hungry. Uh–huh."

Michaela grinned. "What about the time he saved a woman from her lecherous uncle by tricking said uncle into writing down his consent for her marriage to her true love? Remember, Oberon gave Robin a scroll that said he was not to harm any who didn't truly deserve it."

"Oh, please. He played pranks on everyone, never mind if they deserved it or not." Amanda flopped back down in her seat and sipped her skinny. "Besides, it's only when Oberon is listed

The Hob

as Puck's father that he gets that scroll. All the others, he's just another hobgoblin."

"Then why was he so closely linked with Robin Hood?" Michaela chalked that one up to a victory.

At least until the girls burst into laughter. "You can't actually believe that."

Amanda was laughing so hard she almost dropped her skinny. "That's been disproven by *numerous* scholars."

Michaela's grin didn't slip. If anything, it became sweeter.

"*Amongst the rest, was a good fellow devil,*

So-called in kindness, 'cause he did no evil,

Known by the name of Robin (as we hear)

And that his eyes as bigge as sawcers were,

Who came a nights, and would make kitchens cleane

And in the bed bepinch a lazie queane..."

"And now you're quoting Thomas Rowland. Seriously, your obsession with Puck is getting ridiculous." Stella twirled her empty cup between her hands.

"You're the one writing a thesis on how evil he truly was, and that was why he was equated with Satan." Michaela threw her napkin at Stella's head. She was only doing it just to prove her point once and for all. "He wasn't. He was a good guy."

"He was a rotten bastard who pinched women's butts, which makes him a skanky, sexist asshole." Amanda stood, her skinny mocha in her hand. "Listen, I'd love to sit here and argue with you some more about Puck the Magic Grab-hands, but I've got to get to work."

"Me too." Stella threw her empty cup in the trash and shook her head. "You know what you need, Mick?"

"Here we go." Michaela rolled her eyes. Stella knew how much she hated being called Mick. She only did it when she was losing an argument.

"You need a real man in your bed, not some goat-faced, fuzzy fantasy."

"Oh man. I never thought of that. Mick is a fuzzy." Amanda's eyes widened dramatically. "Please tell me you don't get turned on by My Little Ponies."

Michaela sighed and banged her head on the table. "I hate you all."

"Oh my God. I bet she has a thing for Twilight Sparkle." Amanda's voice shook, and Michaela knew the bitch was trying desperately not to laugh. "Or maybe Rarity. She always did go for the pretty ones."

Stella tilted her head. "Wouldn't that make her a lesbian fuzzy?"

Amanda choked on her last sip of mocha. "You're a lesbian too?"

Michaela pointed toward the front door without even raising her head. "Go!"

"You think you know your friends," Amanda muttered, making her way to the door.

"Later, Mick."

"Bye, guys." Michaela raised her head and waved to her friends as they headed out the door. "And I am not a fuzzy!"

"I'm glad to hear that."

Oh, shit. Kael and his totally hot friend were standing next to her table. The friend was silently laughing, his hand covering his mouth in an oddly familiar gesture. Kael had his hand around the dark-haired man's arm, holding him up.

Shit. They must be a couple. She hadn't suspected Kael was gay. He eyed her up whenever they met, no matter how subtle he thought he was being, but his hold on the other man was proprietary.

Damn. There went her daydreams of getting biblical with Tall, Dark and Dreamy.

She had to admit, they were certainly gorgeous together. There was no doubt of that. The dark-haired man's golden skin and dark, almond-shaped eyes were the perfect contrast to Kael's blond, all-American good looks.

It was weird, because Michaela tended to like guys with lighter hair and eyes, like Kael, but her gaze was constantly drawn to the darker of the two. It had been that way earlier in the parking garage too. She just hoped she hadn't been too obvious in her attraction, especially if the man was taken. Michaela didn't poach, not even when the object of her unrequited lust steered toward the fairer sex.

Out the window behind them Michaela caught a glimpse of one of the convention goers dressed as some kind of walking tree. She tsk'd loudly. "Poor guy. He's going to wind up with splinters in some interesting places."

The brunet, still vibrating with laughter, collapsed into the chair Amanda had recently vacated, placing him right next to Michaela. "In truth, it gives new meaning to the term woody."

Kael pinched the bridge of his nose. "Not enough caffeine in the gods' bedamned world." He sighed. "Ringo?"

"Iced caramel macchiato."

"Got it." Kael walked away, shaking his head.

Michaela bit the bullet. She would remember his name this time if it killed her. "I'm sorry, what did Kael just say your name was?"

He tilted his head and smiled. Something about that smile sent shivers down her spine. His eyes had odd flecks of blue in them, like chips of blue topaz in rich, dark earth. He tilted his head in an oddly old-fashioned gesture, almost like a bow. "Ringo Midori, at your service."

Wait. She knew what those words meant from all the manga she read. "That name's Japanese. That would make your name Midori no Ringo." She laughed. "Oh, man. Your parents named you *green apple*?"

One dark brow quirked upwards in surprise. "I was an interesting looking baby." She thought for a second she detected respect in his gaze before the laughter returned. "You speak Japanese?"

"Nope. I read a crapload of manga, though."

"Manga?" Kael settled into his chair and handed Ringo a cup.

"Yup. I love yaoi."

The cup Ringo had begun to lift to his lips paused. "Aren't they Japanese man-love comics?"

"Ever hear of Naono Bohra? She's one of my favorites." Michaela waited to see what would happen. Most guys had one of two reactions.

Sure enough, Kael made a face. "Not my cup of tea."

Ringo just smirked and sipped his macchiato.

Michaela didn't understand why she felt so comfortable talking to these two, but her instincts hadn't steered her wrong yet. After all, Kael had proven more than once that he was a nice man, and so far Ringo was proving to be fun-loving. She decided to go with it and tease the hell out of Kael. She propped her chin on her hand and fluttered her lashes at him. "So you're not looking for a big, strong *seme*?"

Ringo almost choked on his drink. He obviously understood what the word meant. Kael, however, appeared lost. He turned to Ringo. "I don't want to know, do I?"

Ringo leaned back in his chair. "No, Kael. It's best if you remain ignorant."

Hmm. Maybe they weren't a couple after all.

"Then color me blissful." Kael sipped his drink and watched the fake fairies dancing outside the window. One gentleman in particular seemed to think that a strategically placed fig leaf meant he didn't need briefs. Too bad he hadn't secured the leaf properly. Kael whimpered. "Remind me to bleach my eyes later."

She winked at Ringo, blushing when his gorgeous eyes narrowed. For a split second, she could have sworn they turned blue, but it must be some trick of the light. "Are you going to the fairy con?"

Ringo and Kael exchanged a look she could read quite well. She worked around children every day.

The two of them were up to something.

"Yes, indeed. Are you?" The speculation in Ringo's gaze would have been flattering if not for the sharp look Kael sent him. What was going on, and why didn't Kael want Ringo admitting they were going to the con?

"Oh, yeah. I've been looking forward to it." Michaela almost bounced in her seat, she was so excited. She'd managed to finagle the graveyard shift at the hospital just so she could attend the con. She'd be tired, but it would be worth it, and the kids would love the pictures she was planning on bringing them. "I have the prettiest pair of light-up butterfly wings. I'm wearing them to the fairy ball." The gown had cost a pretty penny, too, but it would totally be worth it.

Ringo sputtered, nearly spraying them with macchiato. "Fairy ball?"

Kael groaned and dropped his head in his hands. "Butterfly wings," Kael moaned. "Not more butterfly wings."

Ringo's lips twitched. "They light up too."

Kael sobbed.

Michaela just stared at them. "You have something against butterflies?"

"No." Kael made a face. "It's...complicated."

All righty then. Maybe he had mottephobia, fear of moths and butterflies, and was too ashamed to admit it. If so, he'd have one hell of a time at the convention. Almost all the women had butterfly wings strapped to their backs.

"So I guess you'll be going as something else, then." With his thin build, golden eyes and blond locks, he'd make an excellent— "Oh, I know! You're going dressed as Puck!"

This time, Ringo did spray the table.

Chapter Four

"You heard?"

Robin watched Michaela leave the coffee shop. He still couldn't understand why she'd been so vehement in her defense of him. The passion in her voice had both amused and humbled him. "Yes." He tilted his head. "Tell me about her."

Kael took a deep breath and leaned back in his chair. "She's twenty-eight, works in medicine, but I'm not sure where or in what capacity. She's human, as far as I can tell. She has several friends she spends time with, but no boyfriend. Either that or she's dating multiple men at once."

Robin did not like that thought one little bit. Green fire danced in his eyes before he could subdue it. "Anything else I should know?"

"She goes away on the weekends sometimes with her friends. Sometimes she brings equipment, like skis or a snowboard, others she doesn't. And you heard her—she's got a thing for Puck."

Robin smiled. That, he could live with. It was the thought of other men that would drive him insane.

Kael's amused expression deepened, became wicked. "She thinks I should dress as you."

Robin felt his eyes flare with green light. He quickly masked it by closing his eyes. It wouldn't do to have the Unseelie alerted to his presence so quickly. "So she did."

"Robin?"

Robin shot the boy an inquiring look.

"Go after her."

He smirked. He'd caught sight of an unknown Sidhe sidling up to the coffee bar. Chasing after Michaela would not be wise. Black Court, Gray or White, the Sidhe were indistinguishable until they chose to reveal their allegiance. "While her defense was flattering, I hardly think we have the time to—" But Kael wasn't looking at him. Instead, he was sitting straight up in his chair, his gaze glued to something outside the window. Something that had the pooka on high alert. "What?"

"I saw someone I recognized following her."

Hell and damnation. That could mean only one thing. One of the Black Court delegates had seen the girl speaking with Kael and marked her as prey. If they recognized him as Prince Evan's cousin their cover was already blown, despite the fact Kael lived and worked in the city. They would see his presence as a direct result of their kidnapping of his cousin and respond accordingly.

Michaela would be nothing more than a statistic to the humans. To the Black Court, she'd be something worse. A bargaining chip, one they would ruthlessly use and cast aside if it proved less than valuable to them.

Robin stood, threading his way through the sudden crowd of convention goers streaming in for a hot cup of coffee. Why was it whenever he had the need to move quickly someone, or something, blocked his way?

By the time Robin made it out the door, his quarry was gone, lost in a sea of humanity. He glanced at his watch and realized the time. Rush hour in the city. With a muttered curse he headed the way Michaela had, hoping he would find her on the way to her apartment building. If the Black Court got hold of the female her chances of survival were slim at best. Her bright smile would be dimmed forever.

That would be a tragedy, one Robin fully intended to avert.

"OW! Hands off, fucker!"

Robin froze. Was that—?

There. Down that small side street, with no other pedestrians, Michaela struggled against the pull of a tall, dark-haired man with shoulders so wide he took up almost the entire pavement. Robin scented the wind and snarled.

Redcaps. The aroma of mushrooms and earth was unmistakable.

"Hey!"

Robin watched, appalled, as Kael dashed to Michaela's rescue. The redcap whipped around, throwing Michaela into the street so hard Robin could hear her hit the ground even over the sounds of the city. He would be surprised if there were no bones broken.

His eyes flared green. Robin dug out his sunglasses, hiding behind them, as he began to stroll forward.

The redcap would pay for harming her.

Kael threw a punch at the redcap that it easily avoided. Idiot boy. Redcaps never traveled alone, and certainly never attacked alone. Kael would be dead within moments, brutally torn apart before Michaela's horrified eyes.

Robin quirked his brow, and behind him the lights changed. A car, unable to stop in time, slammed into another one in a shower of steam and the crunch of fiberglass. The redcap, attention diverted, didn't stop the blow Kael threw this time, the pooka's fist landing on its jaw.

The redcap's head barely moved.

Robin sighed. The boy would have to learn quickly, it seemed.

Robin sauntered down the pavement, hands in his pockets. He yawned, and a door sprang open, to the astonished cursing of the human chefs hidden behind it but knocking into the redcap, startling it. Robin kicked at a piece of paper and the redcap howled, clutching the thumb that suddenly bent backward.

Robin stood over Michaela and held out his hand. "Are you hurt?"

The Hob

She winced. "I think my wrist is sprained. Other than that, just some minor scrapes and contusions." She took his hand and Robin pulled her to her feet.

Just as she went to brush her hair out of her face her eyes went wide, her mouth dropped open, and Robin smiled. He'd wondered when the other redcap would show up. He winked at Michaela, pleased when another howl of pain shattered the air. The redcap behind him was hopping up and down and clutching its foot. Robin tilted his head, amused, and the redcap tripped over the curb, landing on its ass with another yowl.

"Oh, shit. Your friend's in trouble."

Indeed, Kael was. The redcap had his hand around Kael's throat and was choking the life from him. Before Robin could move, Michaela pulled something out of her oversized purse without even looking. How women could do that, just reach into a bag like that and find exactly what they needed without thought, defied logic.

Even to the Hob, the bloody things were a mystery.

"Hey, asshole!"

Robin's breath hitched as Michaela dashed past him. What was she *thinking*? He took a step toward her, ready to rip the redcap in half if he dared lay a finger on her. None should so much as make her frown.

Before he could reach her she held up her hand, spraying something in the redcap's face that had him screeching like a troll giving birth. Kael, released, reeled back, sucking in air and coughing.

Leaving Michaela open for the blow the redcap almost landed.

Almost.

Robin grinned up at the redcap as he squeezed its fist, breaking every single bone and joint with a brutal crunching sound. His eyes were a shining, iridescent green, and he didn't care. Either the sunglasses shielded them or they didn't. "Didn't your mother ever teach you not to hit girls?"

The redcap fell to its knees, in too much agony to even scream.

The sound of limping footsteps had him glaring in the direction of the redcap's fleeing partner. A car blew past the entrance to the side street, sending the redcap flying.

"Crap." Michaela took off once more, this time in the direction of the accident, a determined expression on her face.

Robin was stunned. The woman was insane. There was no other explanation.

Robin didn't even hesitate. He eliminated the redcap at his feet, and then raced after Michaela as if his hair was on fire, leaving Kael to destroy the remains however he saw fit.

Michaela dashed through the crowd and landed on her knees at the victim's side. "Call an ambulance!" She quickly assessed the damage, praying the ambulance would arrive in time to save him. It didn't matter to her that just moments ago he'd been attacking her and her friends. His life was in danger, and Michaela would do her best to save it.

"He just ran right in front of me." The panicked tone of voice made it clear that the speaker was the driver of the vehicle who had hit her patient. Michaela didn't even look up. She didn't have time. She began CPR, counting out thirty compressions before she pinched his nose, tilted his head back, and breathed for him. She kept it going despite the ache in her wrist causing her to see spots before her eyes.

Definitely a bad sprain, one she'd have to wrap. She'd have to find a nice colorful bandage the kids would enjoy.

Time to breathe for him again. She barely noticed the protective stance Ringo had taken up behind her and to one side, or the sound of Kael keeping the crowd back. She had a patient under her hands and that was all that mattered.

"They want to talk to you."

Michaela nodded absently at the stranger and accepted the cell phone. She balanced it between her shoulder and her ear as she kept the compressions going. "This is Michaela Exton, I'm an RN with Philadelphia General Hospital. I've got a patient on the ground, nonresponsive. Performing CPR. Vic ran out into traffic and was hit by a car. I need the ambulance to come in hot." She handed the cell phone back to the stranger. "Thanks." She breathed for him again, two quick breaths that barely moved his barrel chest.

She bit back the urge to spit when she was done. What was that funky taste in his mouth? It was like old mushrooms. Blech. She'd have to avoid ordering mushrooms on her pizza later.

She heard sirens in the distance and knew help was almost there. Even better, the man beneath her began to breathe on his own. Michaela took his pulse, and while it was not as steady as she would've liked it *was* there. If they could stabilize him in the ambulance he stood a good chance of surviving.

"Why?"

Michaela looked up at Ringo, most of her attention still on her patient, monitoring his breathing and heart rate. "Why what?"

"Why did you save him?"

She didn't like it, but she understood why he asked. Most other people wouldn't have hesitated to leave their attacker to his fate, but Michaela just wasn't built that way. "This is who I am." She looked down at her patient, smiling when she saw his eyes were open. She stroked his cheek, knowing that simple human touch would reassure him despite the pain he must be in. "Hey. My name's Michaela and I'm a nurse. You're going to be just fine, okay?"

The man studied her for a moment, then relaxed and nuzzled his face into her palm. He shut his eyes, his breathing harsh with distress.

Michaela tried to soothe him as best she could, stroking his hair and shushing him as he whimpered.

"That's going to the top of my list for oddest things I've seen today." Kael knelt beside her. "Do you need to go to the hospital?"

Michaela shot him a horrified look. "Of course he does. He's been hit by a car."

Kael rolled his eyes. "Not him. You."

Michaela winced as the pain of her sprained wrist registered once more. "It's not broken. I'll ice it and wrap it once I get back to my apartment."

Ringo tilted his head, his sunglasses reflecting the glow of the car's headlights. "You are a strange woman, Michaela Exton."

Michaela hummed her agreement. It wasn't like she hadn't heard that one before.

"Michaela? Is that you?"

Michaela glanced up to see one of her weekend buddies climbing out of the ambulance. "Hey, Will."

He knelt by the injured man and grinned at her. "We on for this weekend?"

Damn. She'd forgotten about that. "I'm going to the fairy con, so I'm going to have to pass. Next weekend?"

"You're on. This time your ass is mine."

Ringo took a step closer to her, almost close enough to interfere with Will as he tried to take the vic's vitals.

The hood of the car behind her flew into the air, setting off the car alarm. Michaela jumped, and she was used to dealing with loud noises.

"What the hell?" Will glared at the car before turning to the patient once more. "Damn foreign cars."

"Michaela. Trust you to be in the middle of trouble." Will's partner Ed joined Will by the victim. "Vitals?"

Michaela rattled off what she knew while Will took his own readings. He corrected her as needed, but otherwise let her speak.

"I think we have some internal injuries. Let's get him loaded." Will grinned at Michaela. "You're seriously giving up a weekend with us for a fairy con?"

Ed looked horrified. "No way. You promised us Camelback and good powder, remember?"

Ringo coughed.

One of the streetlights toppled over with a groaning screech of metal.

"Shit!" Ed took off, checking to see if anyone was hurt.

Will shook his head. "Maybe there are some bad luck fairies at the con." He smiled sweetly. "In that case, you need to come with us and avoid the bad juju."

"Aw, shit." Kael's soft curse was almost drowned out as all four tires on the ambulance went flat with a loud, wheezing *pfffft*. "Uh, Ringo? Can I talk to you for a moment?"

Ringo backed away, joining Kael on the sidewalk for what looked like a very intense discussion.

"Shit."

Michaela stared, dumbfounded, at the ambulance. "I think I'll skip the snowboarding for a little while."

Will blinked and backed away from her. "Yeah. Camelback Mountain can wait a couple of weeks." He ran and got a board from the back of the ambulance. "I need to get this guy on the board. Ed! Call for another ambulance." He shot a rueful glance at the flat tires. "And a tow truck."

Michaela shook her head. Most of the people on the sidewalk had their phones out, snapping pictures and typing furiously.

I guess some days are meant for Twitter.

Chapter Five

"I still don't understand what the hell you were thinking yesterday."

Robin gritted his teeth and ignored Kael. The pooka had been nagging at him since they'd seen Michaela to her door the previous evening, turning down her invitation for pizza to return to Kael's apartment. Was that not supposed to be his line? He wasn't the young, foolish lord who'd leapt, unprepared, into battle with a redcap.

In truth, he'd been in a foul mood ever since the human had saved the redcap. If he had his way the creature would be eating its own anus, but Michaela had done her level best to give it a chance. He frowned, ignoring the squeal of an alarm behind him, at the memory of her sweet, full lips pressing against the creature's mouth. It didn't matter that she hadn't been tasting the creature.

All that mattered was that her lips had not yet touched Robin's own.

"Um, Robin? I think you need to calm down. Unless you really did have it in for that poor artist's display case, in which case feel free to continue."

Robin took a deep breath. His power was slipping out of his control, his eyes glowing with green, feral light, his nails black and sharp. If he didn't get it under control, bad things would begin to happen. The humans here didn't deserve the sharp edge of his anger. He would reserve it for the Black Court lackeys Titannia had sent.

The very fact that he was losing his control did not bode well for the conference. The last time Robin had failed to rein in

The Hob

his anger...well. Scientists were still arguing over the cause of the 1908 explosion over the Tunguska region of Russia. They believed a meteor or comet fragment exploded roughly three miles above the spot that had been decimated.

They were wrong.

Robin hid his wince. What had happened at Tunguska had been unfortunate. He and Oberon had argued, and the result had the impact of roughly ten to fifteen megatons of TNT. Nothing had survived intact, something he mourned to this day. The fallout from that explosion had been seen around the world, causing strange lights that could be seen as far away as England. People there reported that it was bright enough to read the newspaper by. When an expedition was finally sent by the Russians in 1927, the pictures of the devastation had been humbling, even to one such as him. Oberon and Robin were usually careful to not allow their tempers to get the best of them. Tunguska was a vivid reminder of why.

The topic of a queen for his king was officially closed. Oberon would not budge, and Robin would no longer nudge, no matter how badly his king needed to get laid.

"At least the Seeming will take care of any curiosity about him."

Robin growled. As if he cared that the gift of the gods would protect a redcap. While human medicine had advanced in leaps and bounds, it had not yet penetrated the Seeming. Fae, in their human form, appeared fully human even to the most advanced human instruments. Robin wasn't certain how the gods had accomplished that feat, but not even he was brave enough to ask. He'd lived far too long, seen far too much to question the miracle that had been granted to the fae.

Robin took a deep breath to calm himself. He peered around, gratified to see no one had noticed his lapse. "Who is representing Gloriana?"

Kael pulled out his cell phone. "Lord Rudolph Adair, Lady Annabelle Beauchene, Lord Wesley Martel and Prince Gregory Yates, Evan's older brother."

"So the Adairs have sent one of their minor lords, but the Beauchene clan sent their Lady. Interesting." Robin rubbed his chin. "I'm unfamiliar with the Martel clan representative." Something that would soon be remedied. Robin quietly noted that each of the White Court delegates, other than Prince Gregory, was Sidhe, an oversight on Gloriana's part. She relied too heavily on the children of the Tuatha Dè at times, a habit that would eventually cost her.

"He's the youngest of the delegates on either side, a newcomer who has his uncle's favor."

And with the power vacuum left behind by the turn of the Malmaynes to the Black, the Adair, Beauchene and Martel Clans were poised to gain more prominence in the White. Interesting. Perhaps Gloriana was testing their mettle. "And the Black delegation?"

Kael frowned and scrolled down. "It looks like Lord Aaron Wyght, Lady Cecelia Malmayne—" and didn't that name give Robin a start, "—Lawrence McNeil and..." Kael paused, then began cursing under his breath.

"Who?" Robin was curious. Facing a redcap hadn't unsettled the pooka, but a name on his cell phone had him pale and swearing.

"Lord Raven MacSweeney."

Robin gritted his teeth to keep his own curses from escaping. He'd had Blades who'd run afoul of Lord Raven MacSweeney, the Fear Dearc, though he himself had yet to meet the reclusive fae. It was said the man bore a striking resemblance to Titannia's dark beauty and that his powers rivaled Robin's. He held the power to summon ravens at will, using them to blind his enemies, thus earning the nickname the Raven Lord. Indeed, none knew for certain if Raven was truly his first name, or the name he'd chosen for himself.

The Hob

No doubt the comparison to Robin was a result of the Dark Queen's wish to mock him, but Robin had no choice but to take the reports of his Blades as truth.

"If he's here, we've got problems." Kael looked worried for the first time since Robin had met him. "He'll use any perceived weakness against us."

"Meaning Michaela." Robin understood Kael's unspoken message, but it was already too late. Robin's actions had already marked the female, rendering her vulnerable. Too many had seen him save Michaela, a woman who had no power over him, from the redcaps. He wasn't certain how many may have been Black Court, slipping away when the ambulance arrived.

Robin should have left her to her fate, saving his cover rather than her life, an act he'd been forced into countless times over the long centuries. This time he'd found himself unable to stand aside. He could not allow his bondmate to come to harm, not even on Oberon's orders.

Michaela had needed him, and Robin had responded.

He'd have to see to it that she was protected at all costs. He could not afford to be distracted now, not with Evan's life on the line.

Balls. This is going to get complicated. And when Oberon finds out... He shuddered. It did not bear thinking about.

"What do we do with her?" Kael smiled at the woman behind the registration desk.

"Name?" The tired-looking female smiled up at Kael. The boy was attractive. More than one female had turned her eye to him, and not a few males as well. If he wished, he could have his pick of the available and, possibly, the less than available.

"Kael Capall."

Robin also gave his fake name. The two men were handed their passes and maps of the convention, passing numerous fake (and a surprising number of real) fae on their way to the room where the negotiations were to take place. "We place a guard on her."

Akane might be tired of life in Nebraska with her mate. Perhaps he would call for her. She was one of his best Blades, and her unique clairvoyant powers would allow her to keep an eye on Michaela without having to be in the room with her. However, the young dragon was pregnant with her first child, and Robin was loathe to take her from her mate's side. Akane would begin nesting soon, and Robin wished Shane joy in dealing with *that*.

Etienne would balk at guarding a human, even with direct orders from Robin. The Sidhe was becoming problematic, attempting to pick and choose his partners rather than work with the ones Robin gave him. Robin was going to have to deal with him soon, before he placed a "lesser" Blade in danger due to his prejudice. Too bad the Sidhe was a slick manipulator, one of the best at slipping into a subject's mind and ferreting out his secrets without being caught.

Hell. Perhaps Robin should have taken him on this mission to keep an eye on the delegates. He was picky, but he was *good*.

That left Jaden, who was busy with his new clan and the repercussions of Duncan's loss of the Malmaynes. The rest of his top agents were currently out on assignment and pulling undercover agents out of the Black or White Courts was not an option. "A Blade guard might attract more attention than we want to deal with."

"But if the rumors are true, only a Blade can deal with MacSweeney."

"Then a Blade shall deal with him." Even if Robin had to guard her himself.

Michaela adjusted her wings and stepped up to the registration desk. She was so excited she could barely stop herself from bouncing.

"Name?"

"Michaela Exton."

The Hob

The woman handed over her badge with a smile and waved to the next person in line. Michaela started to move out of the way, eager to begin her day. She flipped through the convention booklet, scanning the list of workshops eagerly. She had tons of workshops she wanted to attend, especially that one with the author who wrote about—

Papers flew everywhere as Michaela ran into someone. "Oof." Michaela stepped back and rubbed her nose. The dude had a seriously hard chest. "Owie."

"Watch where you're going."

The angry male voice reminded her of someone. The tone, the cadence of the words was familiar somehow.

"I'm so sorry." Michaela shot the man her best apologetic smile. *Wow, another hottie.* The dark-haired man, even with the scowl gracing his face, was dazzling. "Here, let me help you with that." She got down on her knees and began gathering pages, stunned at the beautiful drawings. "Oh, wow. These are *really* good." The subject matter was a little macabre for her taste, but the pictures themselves were absolutely gorgeous. In one, a dark vampiress wept blood tears over her victim. In another, an army of fairies with black-on-black wings hovered over fields of blood red roses, bright silver swords shining in their hands. "Crap. You're one of the fantasy artists for the con, aren't you?"

The man blinked, looking shocked. "Uh—"

"An aspiring artist, then?" Michaela handled the papers with even more care. If the dark-haired man with the gorgeous blue eyes were truly a starving artist then she held not just his livelihood but all his hopes and dreams in her hands. "You shouldn't have any trouble getting an agent with these. I mean, they're some of the best I've ever seen."

The man knelt, his expression still wary, but something dangerous glittered in those bright blue eyes. "You think so?"

"Yes, I do." She picked up one of a hauntingly beautiful male, long silver hair nearly hiding his features. Mist rose around him in an icy aura that sent shivers down her spine. He

55

looked both pissed and mournful at the same time. She got the feeling just looking at it that someone was about to get his or her ass seriously kicked. She held it up, careful not to crinkle the corners. "I could so see this on the cover of a fantasy book. Show this to an author and I bet they'll have a story idea in their head in two seconds flat."

The man smiled and Michaela shivered. Something wasn't quite right with him, some deeply hidden…sadness? Anger? She couldn't tell, but the gentle way he touched her hand as he took the pictures calmed her fears. Whoever he was, he meant her no harm. Michaela was certain of it, that odd sixth sense she relied on kicking in. "Thank you."

"You're welcome." She frowned. Those long, slender artist's fingers were damaged. She noticed some bruising on his knuckles, some dried blood. The wound was recent too, still oozing. She took hold of his hand and flexed his fingers, ignoring his attempts to pull his hand away. "Is there any pain when I do this?"

"It's fine." He tried once more to pull his hand away but Michaela wasn't having any of it.

"I'm a nurse, so let me be the judge of that." She tsk'd as she realized how he'd more than likely gotten those wounds. The knuckles were obviously swollen. "You shouldn't be fighting. What if you permanently damaged your hands? What would you do if you couldn't draw anymore? That would be a shame." She stood and, still holding on to him, tugged him to his feet. "C'mon. Let's get that cleaned up and make sure there's no other damage."

He was staring at her as if she were the strangest creature to ever walk the earth. "You're not afraid of me."

She glanced up at him in surprise. She tilted her head and studied him intently. None of the wariness she'd had when that big goon had assaulted her yesterday triggered with this man. If there had been even a hint of it she would have handed him his artwork and lost herself in the crowd. "Are you a psycho axe murderer?"

His lips curled with sardonic amusement. "Would I tell you if I was?"

Michaela laughed. Really, if Stella and Amanda could see her now they'd have a fucking conniption. Bad enough she'd trusted Ringo and Kael, and those two were neighbors. Neighbors who'd saved her from possible, no, probable, rape and murder. This man had a vibe similar to Ringo's, so Michaela was going to trust her instincts and take care of him. "True. This is sort of the way Ted Bundy met women, isn't it?"

The man shook his head. "You are far too trusting."

"Funny, you're not the only one to say that to me recently."

"Oh?" His hand cupped her elbow and steered her out of the crush of people to a quiet corner. "I'm afraid I didn't catch your name."

"I'm sorry. I'm Michaela."

His eyes widened just a fraction before the pleasant smile returned. "Michaela. My name is Raven MacSweeney." He lifted her hand and brushed his lips delicately over the back. "It's my pleasure to meet you."

Oddly enough, the touch of Raven's lips, while pleasant, didn't send nearly the rush of *want* through her that the feel of Ringo's lips had. Now there was a man who could kiss any part of her he wanted.

And he was real, unlike her dreams of Robin. She'd eventually have to give up her dream-man and find a real one, and Ringo was a delicious place to start. "A pleasure to meet you too." She pulled her hand free and took hold of his once more. "Now, let's see about those wounds of yours."

"As you wish."

From the sensuous smile on his face, Michaela bet he was willing to show her other places that hurt too. It was a shame, really. If Ringo had flirted with her the way Raven was, she'd already be in his room, checking out his etchings.

Ah, well. At least she'd made a new friend today. That was something, at least. As far as Michaela was concerned, you could never have too many friends.

Robin damn near tripped over Kael as the pooka stopped dead in his tracks. He turned to see what Kael was staring at and nearly growled out loud.

It was Michaela, her dark head bent over a strange fae's hand. There was something about the dark-haired man with the vivid blue eyes that had Robin studying him closely. The aura of carefully banked danger was familiar to him. Robin took a deep breath, attempting to scent the male's essence.

Before he could, Michaela moved, sending her essence his way. The sweetness of the human female nearly overwhelmed him. Somewhere in her deepest past, Michaela's ancestors had played with the fae, borne children for them. What species of fae they might have been had been lost to time, as not even Robin could discern it beneath the overwhelming scent of her humanity. Perhaps Oberon could, given time. Even Robin did not know the full extent of his lord's power, but he doubted such was beyond him.

The woman became more and more intriguing the closer he came to her.

However, her taste left something to be desired. Her strap-on wings were truly hideous. Where had the woman had found that particular shade of rotted pumpkin?

"Holy *fuck*."

"Kael?"

Kael was pale, his breathing erratic. "That man holding hands with Michaela? That's Raven MacSweeney."

Robin's head swiveled so fast his neck popped. "That's the Fear Dearc?" *Gods save me. The woman will be the death of me.*

"How?"

Robin nodded, his gaze glued to Michaela. He understood what had gone unsaid. The woman had an uncanny knack for finding trouble. MacSweeney bent his head, listening intently to something Michaela said, a gentle expression on his face at odds with his ruthless reputation.

Robin blinked, nonplussed. If asked a question at that moment, he wasn't certain he'd be able to give a coherent answer. She'd literally shocked him speechless.

Somehow, once again, she'd tamed a beast to her palm.

Intriguing.

"How does she *do* that?" Kael gasped like a landed fish. "It's a wonder she's survived this long."

Robin growled as Michaela gifted the Fear Dearc with one of her sweet smiles. Amazingly, the Fear Dearc merely smiled back, speaking too softly to be heard over the crowd. Whatever he said caused Michaela to laugh, and that Robin did hear. The sound slithered through him, took up residence in his balls, hardened his cock.

Robin had never met anyone who had such an instant effect on him. And if the Fear Dearc didn't get his slimy, Black Court hands off of her *this instant* Robin was going to explode.

Literally.

Fortunately for the Marriott, Michaela took a step back from the man. Perhaps she finally sensed the danger she was in. If so, he...

No. Robin was not that fortunate, was he? When she reached up and patted Raven's cheek, every light bulb on the convention floor exploded in a shower of glittering, smoky glass. Gasps arose around him as the room went dark.

Well. If the Black Court delegates were unaware of his presence before, they certainly knew of it now.

Kael sighed. "So much for a quiet entrance."

"Come. We must get you to the conference room before the delegates arrive." Robin hoped Kael would hear something, anything, from either side that would indicate Prince Evan's whereabouts. That was the true mission.

Michaela was, may the gods help her, on her own.

For now.

Chapter Six

Lady Cecelia Malmayne sat, not a blonde hair out of place, between the Fear Dearc and Lord Wyght. McNeil, a grimace on his face at odds with his handsome, easygoing appearance, sat next to MacSweeney, their dark heads close as they conferred. Robin was surprised that an *each uisge* was part of the Black Court's delegation. Their appetite was legendary. Placing them in close proximity to so many humans could lead to one hell of an incident.

The only saving grace was the lack of water. If this hotel had been on the waterfront, there would have been a bloodbath. *Each uisges* always took their prey to water, devouring them there and leaving nothing behind, not even bones. While the Delaware River was not *that* far away, he doubted the *each uisge* would put itself out, especially in a city as large as Philadelphia. To do so would to risk exposing them to the mortals that surrounded them. Not even the Black Court bitch would condone that.

Robin pulled back from the door before any of the delegates could see him. He might be wearing the guise of Ringo, but he was wary that some might still sense his power. Kael was already in place, once again disguised as a chair. The pert bottom of Lady Beauchene was currently gracing him, surely giving the fellow a thrill.

So far none of the delegates had indicated that they were aware of Robin's or Kael's presence, but he hardly expected them to do so. Each delegation chatted amongst themselves with false amity, patiently awaiting the arrival of the arbiter Oberon had sent.

He was not long in coming. Robin watched in shock as Lord Duncan Malmayne-Blackthorn sauntered toward the conference room, his golden good looks nearly eclipsing the red-haired female at his side. "I still think you should have remained in the room."

Lady Moira Malmayne-Blackthorn, nee Dunne, sister of Leo and Shane Dunne, growled at her Sidhe mate with all the ferocity of her leprechaun blood. "And I told you where you could stuff that idea. You think Jaden and I would allow you into a room alone with Cecelia?"

Duncan rolled his silver-gray eyes. "I'll hardly be alone, *amoureaux*."

"Neither will she."

It had been a while since Robin had seen someone speak through clenched teeth. Robin hid his smirk behind his hand. His week had just gotten a little bit brighter.

Wait. If Duncan and Moira were here, then Jaden Blackthorn, newly minted Lord of the Blackthorn clan, could not be far away. His Blade would never allow his mates so far out of his sight without direct orders from either Robin or Oberon, which meant Robin could safely assign the Blade to guard Michaela with impunity.

He stepped aside and allowed Duncan and Moira to pass into the conference room without greeting them. He would let his presence be known to them later.

Right now, he had a vampire to talk to. Using his blood connection to the young vampire, Robin found him in the lounge, staring at the conference goers with an expression of unholy glee.

"I thought you were nearby."

Robin twitched. The Blackthorn-Dunnes continually surprised him. He bowed, allowing some green to flash through his currently brown eyes. "Jaden."

"Robin." Jaden grinned and waved toward a seat. "Cop a squat and have a cup of coffee with me." He tilted his head, one midnight brow rising nearly into his hair. "I gather you're here for the Yates boy?"

Robin returned Jaden's grin. "I'm here to find out what our dear Dark Queen is up to with this mad start of hers."

Jaden practically bounced in his seat. "Oh. Can I help? Can I? Huh? Huh? Pleeease? I'm *so* bored."

Robin laughed, delighted. "Yes, you may."

"Yes!" Jaden rubbed his hands together. "Akane's gonna be *so* jealous."

"I have something special in mind for you, in fact."

Jaden leaned forward eagerly. "Do tell."

"I need you to guard someone."

Jaden whimpered.

"Someone Raven MacSweeney has taken an interest in."

At that, Jaden's pained expression disappeared. He sat up slowly, that quick mind of his already going over the implications. "Oh? The Fear Dearc has a girlfriend?"

The handle of Jaden's coffee cup snapped off, overturning the cup and spilling hot coffee all over his hand. Jaden yelped and grabbed a napkin, wiping the burning liquid off his hand. He glared at Robin. "What the hell?"

Robin sat back in his chair and took a deep breath. It wouldn't do to allow the vampire to see him shaken. Just the thought of Michaela with MacSweeney was enough to set him off.

Something was going on. Something Robin would have to deal with personally. "Perhaps I should give you my assignment and take the girl on myself."

"The girl?" Jaden's sudden stillness gave him pause. "Not MacSweeney?" The knowing look Jaden shot him had a tinge of fear. "Could she be the one?"

"Fate is a cruel mistress with very bad timing."

Jaden's brows rose. "I'll take that as a yes. Fate has an odd way of giving you what you need when you least expect it."

Jaden smiled grimly, his gaze turning inward as he spoke to his bondmates. "Duncan and Moira say hello, and they're willing to help protect your female. When she's near the Fear Dearc, Duncan will keep an eye on her. Moira's going to try and find her and make nice. I'll watch over her when I'm not protecting Duncan."

He hadn't even had to order Jaden to watch Michaela. He'd volunteered, as had his bondmates. "Are they certain? The Fear Dearc is not one to fool around with, and Michaela is mortal. She would be of no help to Moira in a fight."

Jaden waved his hand. "You watched over my bondmates when I couldn't. It only seems fair we watch over yours. Besides, Moira's dying to meet her. Hell, she's already on her way out of the room. Duncan agreed she should go, and for once she didn't argue too hard."

Robin was, once again, touched by the generosity of the Dunne-Blackthorn family. There was only one response he could give, and he would, gladly. "You have my thanks."

Jaden lifted his broken cup, grimacing at its emptiness. The vampire had already healed the minor burn to his hand. "You're welcome." He set his cup down and stood. "Moira's made contact." He grimaced. "She wants a pair of strap-on wings for some strange reason."

Robin shuddered delicately.

"She also has a plan." Jaden gave Robin a mock sympathetic look. "Be afraid."

Robin sighed and followed the vampire. Perhaps assigning the Blackthorns to watch Michaela hadn't been his best idea. The thought of Michaela and Moira conspiring together had his gut clenching in terror.

Alone, the women were a force of nature. Together?

Robin was in deep trouble.

"Excuse me, can you point me toward the ladies?"

Michaela pointed without even looking up.

"Ah. Thank you. Um. I was wondering, is your name Michaela?"

"Yes. How did you know?"

The woman looked relieved. "Do you know a man named Robin?"

Michaela started. "No." But boy, did she wish she did, especially if it was *her* Robin. Too bad he was the figment of an overactive imagination.

Damn.

The redhead in front of her made a face. "Oh." She bit her lip. "I'm looking for someone, actually. Long red hair, blue eyes, looks like someone off the cover of a romance novel. His name is Robin."

Michaela would have remembered someone like that. Hell, she would have been all over him. That description matched her Robin to a tee. She had a serious thing for redheads. It was Ringo's only fault, but one she was willing to overlook due to his utter hotness and the fact that he seemed to want her too. "The closest I've seen is a guy in a cosplay wig dressed as InuYasha, but that wig was white. Sorry."

"That's okay." The woman pointed toward Michaela's wings. "I like them. Do they light up?"

Michaela smiled. She *loved* her bright orange and black wings. "Yup. Want to see?"

"Yes, please."

Michaela pressed a button on her special belt, twirling around when the woman gasped.

"Where did you get those?"

Michaela shrugged. "Internet."

The woman laughed. "My name's Moira Malmayne-Blackthorn."

"Pleased to meet you, Moira."

"Same to you."

"Are you here for the convention?"

Moira grimaced. "Nah. Business trip for one of my husbands."

One of? "You…have two husbands."

Moira nodded, but her open, friendly expression had begun to close off.

"How do you handle that? I mean, my mom had a hard enough time getting *one* guy to remember to lower the toilet seat. Then my brothers came, and she swears she became a duck from her butt landing in all that cold water at two a.m."

Moira barked out a laugh, her expression easy once more. "It's not easy keeping them in line, let me tell you. They have a habit of finding trouble wherever we go." Moira shuffled her feet. "Actually, I have a confession to make."

Michaela's brows rose.

"My friend wants an introduction, so I was tasked with coming over to meet you, see if maybe you were single?"

Michaela wished she could give Moira the answer she wanted. "I'm single, but—"

"Then wait right there." Moira dashed off before Michaela could finish her answer.

Michaela was just too damn busy to date. Being a pediatric oncology nurse at PGH consumed all her time. What little time she had left she used to pursue her hobbies, like snowboarding and MX biking. She was even taking classes in mixed martial arts, although she found herself on her ass more there than she ever did when she was learning to snowboard.

Michaela shook her head and decided to leave before Moira could find her again. The last thing she needed was some stranger trying to set her up on a blind date. She flipped open her program, then glanced at her watch. Maybe she could still make the class on fairy gardening. Someday she'd be able to afford a house with a garden, and she'd want to know what flowers to plant. Even though fairies weren't real, the possibility that she *might* attract one was too good to ignore. She barely looked up as someone moved to block her path. "'Scuse me."

"Leaving so soon? And Moira thought you would be interested in saying hello."

Ringo? Michaela glanced up into deep brown eyes filled with laughter. "Hey, you made it!" She was unable to contain her smile. Somehow, the day seemed just a little bit brighter.

Good-bye, Robin. Hello, Ringo.

"I did indeed." Ringo took her hand and led her back to the smiling redhead. A tall, dark and handsome man stood next to Moira, his arm wrapped securely around her waist. "I'd like to introduce you to Jaden Blackthorn. Jaden, this is Michaela."

"Charmed." Jaden bowed, his movements eerily similar to Ringo's.

In fact, Jaden was sporting a grin very similar to Ringo's. Despite his obvious American Indian heritage and Ringo's more mixed, Eurasian looks, she couldn't help asking the obvious question. "Are you two related?"

Moira jolted as if stung, but Jaden answered easily. "Cousins." He frowned through his smile. "Most people don't pick up on it that quickly."

"You move the same." She turned to Ringo and placed her hand on his arm. "Hey, I need to get going if I'm going to catch the fairy gardening workshop." She ignored Jaden's muffled laugh and concentrated on Ringo. "Want to grab lunch later?" She could sleep tomorrow, right?

Ringo took her hand and kissed her wrist. It took everything in her not to shiver. "I would love to."

"Cool. There's this little hole-in-the-wall that has the best pizza just a block or two away." She frowned. "You do like pizza, right?" Because a man who didn't love pizza was not the man for her.

"I adore it."

Michaela relaxed. "Excellent." She turned to Moira and her husband. "Do you three want to join us?"

"Ah." Moira exchanged a quick look with Jaden. "We'll have to talk to Duncan, but if Ringo has no objection, we'd love to."

Michaela heard the odd emphasis Moira put on Ringo's name but decided to let it pass, at least for now. He'd explain it when he was ready. Why he would lie about his name she didn't know, but his vibe hadn't changed. Ringo was no danger to her. If anything, she felt a hundred times safer when he was nearby.

Speaking of feeling safe... "Hey, do you have any idea what happened earlier? All the bulbs blew out."

Moira nodded, looking suddenly pale. "It was freaky."

"I swear I'm going to be brushing bulb glass out of my hair for weeks."

Moira eyed Michaela's long brown hair and nodded in sympathy, absently fingering her curls. "I know what you mean."

"Didn't you need to hit the ladies?"

Moira nodded furiously. "Like babies need boobies."

Jaden doubled over, laughter erupting from him.

Moira merely rolled her eyes at him. "I'll be right back, *a ghra*."

"That sounds sweet. What does it mean?" Michaela followed Moira toward the ladies' room. She was going to miss the flower gardening workshop, but that was okay. Her new friend was married to Ringo's cousin and seemed to know some of his secrets.

Moira blew Jaden a kiss, which he returned despite his continuing laughter. "It means 'my love'."

Michaela couldn't help it. She risked a glance at Ringo only to find him watching her, an odd expression on his face. She nearly tripped over her own feet when she realized what it was.

Longing.

The Hob

Robin waited until Jaden was done laughing before gently placing his hand on the nape of his Blade's neck. "What were you thinking?"

Jaden gulped, his laughter suddenly gone. Good. Despite his affection for the boy, it wouldn't do to let him think he could get away with something as vital as mucking about in the Hob's plans. "That she'd trust us more if she knew we were associated with you, since you mentioned you'd already met her."

Robin paused a beat, letting Jaden's fear ramp up. Had he mentioned that? He couldn't remember. While he was not entirely displeased by Jaden's actions or logic, openly making friends with Michaela right where the delegation sat had not been in his game plan. It was not the best way to keep her safe, but it was too late now, had possibly been too late when she'd been attacked by the redcaps.

That and his honest, if misguided, intentions were what saved Jaden's life.

He scraped his nail across Jaden's neck, drawing a minimal amount of blood, just enough to express his dissatisfaction. "I had thought to keep our surveillance secret."

"If we're right and she's yours, she'll need something a little more upfront. If we don't let it be known right off the bat that she's protected and off-limits, someone might make a move on her before we can get to her in order to hurt you."

Robin tilted his head, acknowledging Jaden's facts without outright saying he might be right. It was a tricky thing, protecting the truebonds of the powerful.

Robin bit back a gasp.

Truebond? He had been certain she was his bondmate, but a truebond? A truebond was a bond so deep, none but the gods themselves could break it.

He stared at the small room Michaela had disappeared into and bit back a growl as Cecelia Malmayne sauntered in, neat as you please. The urge to run in and rip her blonde head from her neck before she could give Michaela so much as a shiver of unease was intense.

It was official. Robin was fucked, and not in the good way. And to make his day even more interesting, the mirror in his pocket began to vibrate.

Oberon wanted his report, and Robin had literally nothing to give him but an insane brunette who might or might not be his truebond.

Chapter Seven

"How go the negotiations?"

Oberon waited a beat while Robin, strange looking with brown eyes and hair, tilted his head in thought. "Kael is still in the room. It appears the preliminary pleasantries are over, but I have been unable to enter. I have, however, managed to make contact with Jaden and Moira Blackthorn. They've promised to keep me apprised of the goings-on via Duncan, so in essence we have two spies within."

Oberon nodded, pleased. That had been his intention in sending Lord Duncan, a man who was mated to a Knight of Oberon and was himself a negotiator of some note. Jaden and Moira's ease in Robin's presence would also be of benefit to Robin in his investigations, as they would easily follow Robin's lead without question or fear. They would also act on their own as needed, something other Blades forced to work with Robin might balk at for fear of incurring his wrath.

The founding members of Clan Blackthorn were an odd family, but they'd adopted Robin as one of their own and would guard him fiercely. He wondered if Robin was aware of that or not.

"Apparently, one of the delegates is a bit of an issue, but I do not foresee any problems. We've made note of his name, and I will keep tabs on him personally."

"Which delegate?" Last Oberon had seen, the list contained the usual names.

"The Fear Dearc."

Oberon froze. "Lord Raven MacSweeney is there?" That could be problematic, as the Fear Dearc had a reputation similar to Robin's, and almost as sinister.

Robin's head tilted further in a gesture that was almost bird-like. "Was his name not supposed to be there?"

"No." Oberon waved his hand and the original list appeared in the mirror they spoke through. "It was supposed to be Song Kuan-Yin, a siren." Oberon frowned. "Perhaps that was the issue, then."

"Oh?"

Robin's innocent expression didn't fool him. The word *siren* had his Hob's ears practically standing at attention. "The King and Queen of Atlantis have lost one of their daughters."

"Ah. I see. I am sorry for their loss."

Oberon's brow rose. Robin's regret was less than sincere, but it would take someone who'd known him as long as Oberon had to pick up on it. "She is not dead. She ran away from an arranged marriage to one of the princes of Pacifica. The ensuing merger would grant both sides much power, but apparently the princess decided she did not want to comply with her parents' wishes and fled."

Robin grinned, and it was vicious. "The last arranged marriage a child fled resulted in the Child of Dunne. Perhaps a consultation with the Seer is in order?"

Oberon scowled. He had no time for this. His dreams had been...strange, of late, and he was weary. "This is no laughing matter, Robin. Should Princess Cassandra not return to her family, war could break out." And while Oberon could send someone to negotiate a peace between the two nations, unless directly asked there was little he could do. His main objective was, and always would be, to prevent war between the Black and the White courts. Minor courts, even ones as large as Atlantis and Pacifica, were on their own unless they directly impacted Titania or Gloriana, or they appealed to Oberon for

The Hob

aid. Atlantis owed shaky, often ignored fealty to Gloriana. Pacifica was sworn to Titannia.

"Who are you sending?"

His Hob knew him well. Oberon would keep an eye on the situation, asked or no. "We have few deep-sea nymphs trained as Blades."

"I would suggest Dylan."

A selkie? In the court of Atlantis? That would be amusing now, wouldn't it? The Atlanteans could be even more prejudiced than the Sidhe when it came to the "lesser" fae. "He wouldn't have access to the higher courts."

Robin frowned in thought. "I'll send him, nevertheless. I might be able to grant him access where normally he'd have none."

"Hobgoblin."

Robin started, his attention once more totally on Oberon.

"How will you gain that access?"

Robin started and looked over his shoulder. "I will answer that anon, my liege. For now, forgive me." He bowed. "It seems I have a date."

The mirror went dark, and Oberon blinked. "A date?"

What was Robin thinking? Oberon stepped away from the mirror, unsure if he was irritated or intrigued. Boredom was a daily companion, and Robin's little dance offered to bring some much-needed distraction.

Perhaps a consultation with the Seer was, indeed, in order.

Robin adjusted his breasts and smiled, checking his teeth for lipstick. Never was he gladder to be male than when he forced himself to be female. How did women live with underwire bras and lip gloss on a permanent basis? He swore to himself that next time he would disguise himself as a tomboy. They, at least, wore comfortable clothes. And since it required less energy to simply change clothes than to cause the ones he wore to conform to his wishes, Robin always traveled with an unusual array of attire.

He missed the hippies and their bra-burning ways. It had to be the most comfortable decade of his existence.

He zipped up his high-heeled boots and leaned forward to check his horns one last time, noting absently the overabundance of charms revealed by his low-cut halter top. He'd use those assets to his best advantage as often as needed, with no qualms. He'd gotten more information through the use of low-cut blouses than almost any other method he'd tried.

Women were right. Men were foolish creatures indeed.

Kael was going to have a fit when he saw Robin, but if he was going to recruit the boy he'd need to get him used to seeing Robin in disguise. Robin might prefer to be male and often disguised himself as such, but changing his gender often threw his prey off balance. The pooka would more than likely wind up using his own shape-shifting abilities to don the appearance of other sexes and races himself. The charade was all part of the job.

He tucked the lipstick into the oversized purse and added the final touch, a pair of diamond studs in his ears. He eyed his appearance critically, satisfied with what he'd achieved. While Robin could change his gender or race at will, it took a great deal less power to put on a dress and apply makeup.

Robin had shrunk six inches and gained fifteen pounds, making him a well-rounded female. He fluffed out his curly, blonde hair and batted his big, deliberately vacant blue eyes. He chuckled softly to himself.

He looked both pretty and daft. It should be enough.

He intended to join the con tomorrow as a large, black male, and the day after that? It would depend. If either of his disguises made contact with a delegate, he would use that to further his agenda.

He checked his watch and grimaced. He wouldn't have much time to case the convention. Robin would have to make sure he was back to male (and gloss-free) in time for his date with Michaela. Robin's expression softened. She was an odd little thing, with her big, innocent brown eyes and her easy acceptance of the world around her. There was something about her that drew him, made him want to protect her. If she truly was the one for him...

Robin shivered, terrified. The way she dealt with the most insane of situations petrified him. She'd run up to a redcap and *pepper sprayed* it to save a pooka, and nearly charmed the pants off one of Titannia's top lieutenants, the Fear Dearc. Gods forbid she actually spoke to Cecelia Malmayne in that bathroom. She'd probably arranged to go get her nails done with her.

Robin paled as thoughts of what his future would hold appeared before his eyes in horrifying detail. What would happen when he let her loose in the Courts? He shuddered at the thought; certain catastrophe would follow in her wake. Would she have Titannia and Gloriana over for tea? Meddle in Oberon's love life?

Redecorate the Gray Palace?

Or worse, interfere with Robin's work in the guise of "helping" him, thus placing herself in danger too great for her wiles to get her out of?

Ugh. And the very thing he'd been attempting to avoid had already occurred. She'd gotten him so wrapped up in thoughts of her he was distracted from his very real, very dangerous mission. If he did not pull his head out of his ass, Prince Evan could die.

Robin grabbed the compact mirror disguised as a cell phone and stuffed it into his purse. Only Oberon knew the trick of creating them. It was an art long lost, along with the Tuatha Dè Dannan, and Oberon was loathe to give them to any but those he trusted implicitly. As far as Robin knew, he was the only other recipient of a mirror since the war that split the Grand Court.

Robin swirled, his matter dissipating into the ether, reappearing in a swirl of dark mist in a stall in the ladies' room just outside the fairy convention. He took a deep breath and opened the door, smiling at the startled woman staring at him in the mirror. Considering she was dressed like a troll doll, with bright green hair standing straight up from her head and a fur-lined cloak that had to be too hot to be comfortable, she had a lot of nerve.

Robin fluffed out his blonde hair one last time and strode for the door. He had a convention to attend and numerous fae to spy on. He would find out what Titannia was up to, come hell or high water. He did his best to ignore the insane humans around him, desperately trying to tap into their own sense of the fae. Since the decree of the gods to hide their existence from humans, the mania to find something, anything supernatural in the world had driven humans to highs and lows of insanity. Between the hunting of "devil worshippers" and the Salem witch trials, to the fake fairy pictures of the early 20th century and faery Wicca, humanity was obsessed with the fae, and not always in a good way. This, however...

A man in a set of mechanic's overalls with wings made of wires and gears glided past Robin, deep in conversation with a much more conventional-looking female dressed in sparkly pink. There was a set of welder's goggles perched on top of the backward baseball cap he wore, bending fake pointed ears. Black tinted nails completed the man's look. Robin nearly laughed out loud. Too bad Big Red wasn't here with him. The gremlin would have surely enjoyed the sight.

Red would have figured out a way to make the man fly.

Robin snickered. That sounded much dirtier than what he'd meant.

Red was brilliant, and one of his favorite Blades. Hell, he'd been the one to find the information that helped take down the leader Malmayne clan. Big Red was Robin's go-to man when it came to anything computer related.

"Did you hear? They pulled someone out of the Delaware this morning."

Robin half-listened to the humans muttering around him. He was too busy trying to find any of the Black Court fae wandering the halls. The bitch queen wouldn't send just anyone to these negotiations. No, if Robin were to guess, their purpose was far more sinister than simply watching humans pretend to be fairies.

"They say it looked like it was attacked by a shark."

The human next to him snorted a laugh. "Where did you hear that? There aren't any sharks in the Delaware."

"Police scanner. My husband's an officer."

Robin's brows rose. Sharks indeed. The humans wouldn't recognize the bite of an *each uisge*, but Robin would.

Hell. He'd thought they were far enough from the river to be safe from the *each uisge's* appetites. The *each uisge*, or water horse, was infamous for taking its prey to the water to devour it. It was not a taste Robin understood, nor did he ever wish to acquire it.

There was a reason some naturally gravitated toward the Black, and *each uisges* were a prime example.

However, there should have been very little left of the victim. Perhaps he'd been interrupted in his feeding, enough so that he'd left partially devoured remains to be found by the humans. It was rare mistake indeed, but not unheard of in younger fae with McNeil's...proclivities.

"I'm telling you, Robin Goodfellow is here somewhere!"

Robin did his best not to seem as if he was paying any attention to the hissed conversation going on off to his right somewhere. Neither of the voices was familiar, and he dared not look, but he caught the scent of fae and *each uisge*. It had to be Lord Wyght, the only male Black Court Sidhe, and McNeil.

Robin bent down and examined the dangling earrings of a particularly gifted craftswoman.

Michaela would look lovely in the gold and silver jewelry that was on display. He had a sudden, vivid image of her draped in nothing but silver, gold and her own dark hair.

He shivered. It was the first time he'd ever felt arousal while wearing the body of a woman, and he wasn't sure he cared for the sensation. It was familiar, yet alien, this throbbing need that had taken him over.

"What do we do? If Oberon sent the Hob, then they're more than likely on to us."

Oh? Robin smiled at the vendor and pointed to a particularly stunning necklace made of dripping stars. He'd see Michaela wearing it before the night was through. "How much?"

The vendor named a price, but Robin wasn't paying any particular attention. He dug into his purse for the required amount, his attention on the two men arguing not ten feet away.

"We stick to the plan. Those were Her orders, and I for one am going to obey."

"But what if—"

"No. Let the Raven Lord deal with the Hob, Wyght. We do our part, nothing less. Understood?"

The Sidhe lord grunted his displeasure. "Why I have to take orders from you I will never understand."

Robin paid for the necklace in cash, waiting patiently for the receipt. He was in no hurry to move. This was getting better and better.

"What about the redcap? Do you think he'll speak?" Wyght was nervous. Perhaps Robin would visit the redcap in the hospital. If he had information on Titania's plans, Robin would get them from him.

"One survived? Shit. Does the Fear Dearc know?"

"I have no idea. Lord Raven doesn't exactly come to my tea parties."

Robin picked up his bag and moved closer to the speakers. If they were aware of the surviving redcap, they might be aware of Michaela as well, and that would not do. McNeil would destroy her and leave nothing but bones behind.

"We need to tell him. Deal with it, McNeil."

"What was that, Wyght? Which one of us is in charge again?"

The silky threat in the water horse's voice was clear to Robin, but Wyght didn't appear to notice. "I'll be bringing that little fact up with Her soon. You'll be sent packing. Why you were even allowed out of that loch you were haunting, I'll never understand."

"Maybe because I'm more useful than some pansy fairy with his head in the clouds." McNeil laughed, the sound surprisingly sweet. "That doesn't work on a fae of the water, Wyght."

Robin tilted his head in surprise, but kept his gaze glued to the knitwear on the table he'd moved to. McNeil was resistant to a Sidhe's glamour? Intriguing. He'd been aware water fae had a slight resistance to mental manipulation, but to find one who laughed in a Sidhe's face? He was either older than Robin had assumed, and therefore careless with his kills, or he had some special resistance Robin was unaware of. He'd have to ask Duncan when next he saw the Sidhe Lord. Duncan, at just over five hundred years old, was a powerful Sidhe, one who could influence any but the strongest of minds.

"Be aware, any one of these seemingly innocent humans could be the Hob. From now on, we stay silent unless we're in the privacy of our rooms. No more panicking, Wyght. I mean it. You wouldn't want your Clan to be without a leader, would you?" There was a sweet-sounding chuckle, and the sound of footsteps. The scent of *each uisge* faded, leaving the sour stench of fear behind.

"One day, I'm going to cut him up and turn him into glue." Robin grinned and heartily concurred.

Chapter Eight

"Michaela?"

She turned, dazzled once more by Ringo's good looks and winsome smile, but something about his appearance bothered her. The diamond studs in his ears were hot, but... "Are you wearing lip gloss?"

Ringo put his hand to his mouth, wiped it, and showed her his palm. It was clean, the shine she'd imagined no longer present. "Why on earth would I wear lip gloss?"

She relaxed. She'd probably just imagined it. Ringo wouldn't make a date with her and then be with someone else. Would he? "At a fairy convention? You have to ask?"

Moira, who'd stuck with her most of the day, giggled. She'd made a hell of a companion, snarky and sweet at just the right moments. She'd turned some surprisingly dull workshops into something Michaela would remember for a long time to come.

"Believe me, my sweet. My interest is solely in the fairer sex."

She tilted her head, and forever after she'd say the devil made her do it. "You could be a transvestite, like Eddie Izzard."

Ringo blinked, his expression shocked. Maybe she shouldn't tease him.

Jaden, on the other hand, had the most impish grin on his face. "You know, there are a lot of movie titles that would be a lot more fun if the word transvestite were part of it. *Day of the Transvestite Triffids*, for instance."

Moira grinned. "*The Transvestite Son of the Mask.*"

"*Freddie the Transvestite Got Fingered.*" Michaela stumbled as Ringo came to a dead halt. "What?"

Ringo's dark brows quirked upward. "I thought that movie was made."

A tall, cool blond put his arms around Jaden and Moira, tugging them close. "There are a lot of movies that would have been better with a transvestite in them. Like *Showgirls*."

Jaden relaxed into the blond's embrace. "That *was* a movie about transvestites."

Michaela shot a look at Ringo, who winked. She turned back to the blond, who was watching her interaction with Ringo with some amusement. "Duncan, I presume?"

"And you must be Michaela." He held out his hand. "It's a pleasure to meet you. Moira enjoyed her morning with you. Thank you for that."

Michaela smiled. The affection on his face for both his partners was obvious. "We had fun, even if she did mock me in wing building class."

Moira laughed. "I don't think that instructor will ever recover. She was muttering something about whiskey when we left."

"Did you give her grief, *amoureaux?*"

Moira gave Duncan an innocent look so patently false Ringo was choking back yet another laugh. "Me?"

Michaela shook her head. "Who's up for pizza?"

Jaden rubbed his stomach. "Mm. With extra garlic." When his partners shot him an odd look, he shrugged. "What? I want pepperoni too."

Michaela jumped when Ringo took her hand and placed it on his arm. "Ignore them, and maybe they'll disappear." The trio shot him horrified looks, only relaxing when Ringo laughed. She didn't understand why; it wasn't like he could *really* make them disappear.

He escorted her through the hotel's doors and into the cool city streets. "What trouble did you and Moira get into in wing building class, hmm?"

The Hob

Michaela pouted up at him. She probably looked as convincing as Moira had not moments earlier. "She didn't like my color scheme."

Moira tsk'd. "I don't know why not. Joker green, limeade, and wake-the-fuck-up yellow are perfect colors for fairy wings, especially when you add confetti like it was rainbow sprinkles."

"I know, right? And then she tried to get me to do something more dainty and 'fairy-like'. Pfft. Like she'd know a real fairy if one landed on her small, pointy head."

For some reason, Jaden found that so amusing he had to stop and lean against the wall until he caught his breath.

Michaela led the way into the pizza place, eager to spend time with Ringo and his friends. But before she could get a table, Duncan's cell phone vibrated. He made a face as he looked at the caller ID. "Work."

"Damn." Moira and Jaden exchanged a look. "Ringo—"

"Go. Protect your husband. I'm certain Michaela and I can find something to do by ourselves."

The look he shot her was full of heat, and Michaela damn near melted on the spot, her question about why Duncan needed protection forgotten. His eyes... God, his eyes were gorgeous. They were the most beautiful shade of hazel she'd ever seen, more blue than brown. They had a strange glow that *had* to be some kind of freaky light reflection, there and gone again so fast that maybe she'd imagined it.

If she hadn't seen it before, back when those men had attacked her and Kael and Ringo tried to help her, she would have believed that too. Maybe she was crazy.

Or, and here was a truly crazy thought, maybe Ringo was as magical as he seemed.

"Thanks, Ringo." Moira patted Michaela's arm. "We'll get together later, okay? We have that workshop on Gaelic, so don't forget."

"Hmm?" Michaela blinked. Oh, crap. She'd forgotten all about Jaden, Duncan and Moira, so lost in Ringo's otherworldly gaze she'd been mesmerized. "Yeah. That sounds good."

Ringo's grin was anything but subtle. He was obviously pleased by her distraction.

Crap. She'd been too obvious in her attraction. Maybe she should tone it down, cancel the date and plan another one. She'd only met him yesterday, but already she was ready to drop her panties and beg for mercy.

"Michaela?"

She could see that too. Ringo over her, loving on her, leaving his mark on her inside and out.

"Michaela." Her name was breathed into her ear, sending shivers down her spine. "Our table is ready."

Ooh. Table-top sex. She'd always wanted to try that.

Sharp teeth nipped her ear. "I have no idea what is going through your mind, but save it, if you please, for when we are alone."

Michaela almost moaned. Ringo's voice sounded...different. More formal, the tone lighter, yet somehow deeper. Wilder, and full of power. She focused back on the real world to find him staring down at her, the blue in his eyes nearly overwhelming the brown.

He wanted her too.

Michaela licked her lips, her breath stuttering when his gaze zeroed in on her tongue. He looked like he could eat her up in one bite.

She might let him.

"Are you hungry?" She whimpered and he stepped closer. "Michaela?"

She licked her lips again. "Pizza."

He nodded and placed his hand on the small of her back. The heat of his palm was overwhelming. "They have a table for us, my dear."

"Mm-hmm." She allowed Ringo to guide her to a table, settling her in the booth before sliding into the seat right next to her. He snuggled as close as humanly possible, his arm draping across the booth behind her, cocooning her in his warmth. She was practically in his lap, but she couldn't really complain.

God, she was turning into a slut. Ringo tapped his finger on the table, ignoring the menu the waitress placed in front of him as they both asked her for cola. A Ringo-centric slut-puppy with a plastic checkerboard tablecloth fetish.

"You mentioned that you are a nurse."

Her focus switched to his face, away from those long, graceful fingers with their black fingernails. She frowned.

Black? Huh. Maybe Ringo *had* been wearing lip gloss. Either that or he'd painted them for his costume for the con.

"What kind of nurse?"

"Pediatric." And that was as far as she was going. When she told people what she did for a living, she got one of two reactions. Horrified grilling, or awe. Like she was some kind of fucking superhero. She was anything but. Those kids? They were the superheroes, not her.

She didn't want any of that from Ringo. Let him come to want her before she told him about her job.

"I also like to go snowboarding and race dirt bikes."

He smirked. "Indeed. Those ambulance drivers seemed thoroughly acquainted with your hobbies."

"I like the speed." Was that a note of jealousy she detected? "Those guys are my buddies. I know most of the people who work at the hospital, and they're two of the best. They have my back."

"And some don't?" His arm slid over the top of the booth and around her shoulders. That absolute, total focus on her would have creeped her out had it been anyone but Ringo, but for some strange reason his undivided attention didn't bother her at all.

She leaned in closer to him, basking in his warmth. "Some are total asshats whose only redeeming quality is that they'll die someday."

He chuckled silently. "I have a few coworkers like that myself."

"What do you do?"

"I'm in security." He grinned. "The waitress is on her way back."

"Pepperoni?"

"Is there any other kind of pizza?"

"Oh, my kind of guy."

He nipped her earlobe once more, his teeth remarkably sharp. "I certainly hope so."

Hell. She wanted to feel those teeth on her neck nibbling away so badly she could almost feel it. She smiled her thanks at the waitress as she handed over their sodas. Michaela picked up hers up and gulped it down in one long swallow.

Ringo placed their order, getting her another soda as well. He seemed amused by her.

Well. Perhaps it was time she seduced him back.

She picked up a piece of ice from her cup and ran it over her lips before sucking it into her mouth. Ringo's hand tightened on her shoulder before tangling in her hair.

"You're playing with fire, my dear."

She held up another piece and licked it. "Good thing I have ice."

Ringo surprised her by dipping his head and sucking the ice from her fingers. "What ice?"

"I don't sleep with someone on the first date."

Now where the hell did that come from? She was *dying* to break her golden rule, especially when the brown in his eyes almost completely disappeared, leaving them blue and clear as glass. She tilted her head, studying his face. Was that a hint of green hidden in the clear blue? She could study those changeable eyes of his forever.

"Good to know." He licked her fingers, sucking on the tips until she was ready to beg. "I might have to try harder for our second date, then."

She was going to die happy. She tried to distract herself from the feel of his warm tongue tracing her palm. "You work with Kael?"

He placed a kiss on her wrist before answering. "He's in training."

"Ah." She frowned, some of the bubble they'd wrapped themselves in bursting. "Shouldn't you be with him?"

His eyes were now completely blue, glowing in the crappy fluorescent lighting. "No."

Okay then. "I like your eyes."

Her cheeks began to burn. Apparently her brain-to-mouth filter was in the gutter along with the rest of her mind.

"Thank you." He looked ridiculously pleased.

She decided to run with it, since he seemed so happy. "I've never seen hazel eyes with more blue than brown in them. And yours are such a pale blue, they glow."

His lashes lowered, hiding his remarkable eyes. "Do they?"

He seemed less pleased. The day suddenly seemed less bright. "Did I say something wrong?"

He looked up at her, scowling when he saw her frown. There was more brown in his eyes too. Crap, she had said something wrong.

"No." He touched her cheek, tracing the delicate bone. "No, not at all."

One moment, he touched her like he was going to throw her over the table and mount her like a beast. The next, he treated her as if she were the rarest flower he'd ever seen, with a reverence she'd never before encountered. She could easily see herself becoming addicted to those soft touches, the wonder on his face, just as much as the feral predator.

Maybe more so.

After they ate, Ringo paid the bill, much to her chagrin. She'd planned on going Dutch for their first date, but he'd managed to distract her with some silly story about a friend of his named Ron, and the practical jokes they played on each other. "Meet me for dinner."

She pouted. "I wish I could, but I can't. I'm on night shift at the hospital for the next two weeks."

The blue flared in his eyes again, and this time it really did look like they were glowing before he lowered his eyes again. "Breakfast, then?"

She tilted her head. "I could do that." She'd have just enough time for a little sleep before she had to shower and put on her costume. Breakfast before the con sounded like heaven.

He escorted her out the door and back to the hotel. "Breakfast, then." He tilted her chin up, and Michaela held her breath. She knew what he was asking.

Michaela accepted the kiss eagerly. She couldn't wait for her first taste of him.

Instead of the soft, first-date kiss she'd expected, Ringo swept in and conquered her, taking her mouth the way she'd daydreamed he'd take her body. His tongue invaded her, sweeping inside as if he had the right, tasting everything she was and possibly might ever be.

Dear God, he tasted *good*. Better than anything. Better than ice cream, than falling snow. Better even than the tang of your lover's skin when you were having really incredible sex.

He tasted familiar, and that was the best part of all. Only her dreams of Robin had tasted like this.

Michaela kissed him back, giving him everything he demanded and more. Someday, probably sooner than she'd expected, they'd wind up in bed together. If he lived up to even a fraction of the promise in that kiss, she'd do everything in her power to keep him forever.

The kiss had barely ended, his lip still on hers, when he spoke again. "I look forward to breakfast."

She whimpered. She'd never met anyone who made the promise of pancakes sound so hot.

Robin watched as a dazed Michaela made her way back to the conference. The taste of her lingered on his tongue, confirming his worst fear and greatest hope. "Jaden."

The vampire, who had been leaning just inside the conference center's doors, bowed his head and followed.

Only the best would guard his truebond.

Chapter Nine

Robin, his blonde, female disguise once more firmly in place, made his way toward the back of the conference area. He'd caught sight of Raven MacSweeney, his dark head turning this way and that. The man appeared to be following someone, and Robin intended to find out whom. Of all the delegates, he was the one who had Robin's threat meter topping out.

He tried to convince himself that MacSweeney's interest in Michaela had nothing to do with it, but Robin was not in the habit of lying to himself. If MacSweeney tried to take Robin's woman, he'd discover just why Robin was Oberon's personal Blade. There would be nothing left of the Raven Lord, not even smoke and ashes.

MacSweeney darted down a corridor and Robin followed. It was less populated here as convention goers darted into rooms and took seats. MacSweeney paused, watching one doorway in particular. Robin faded from sight and drifted forward, looking into the room that had Raven's undivided attention.

Robin frowned. He recognized that pair of rotten pumpkin wings bouncing their way back out the door.

Damn. The Fear Dearc was rumored to have fearsome powers, and Robin did not wish to test them around so many humans. The ensuing fight could damage or destroy many lives, something Oberon would wish Robin to avoid if at all possible.

"Michaela."

Then again, there was always a first time for everything.

Michaela paused, smiling at MacSweeney like he was her long-lost brother. The only thing that kept Robin sane was the fact that the heat, so prevalent in her gaze when she looked at Ringo, was absent. "Raven! How's the art thing going?"

Art? What in blue blazes was she talking about? And since when was she on a first-name basis with the bastard?

"I'm not really an artist. Not professionally, anyway." MacSweeney leaned against the wall, effectively cutting Michaela from the herd.

"What do you do, then? Because I have to say, I think you could make a living off your art."

MacSweeney's shoulders moved in an almost-shrug. "I'm in security."

Michaela laughed. Robin moved so that his view wasn't blocked by MacSweeney's broad, soon-to-be-decomposing back. "I have a friend who told me earlier he's in the same business."

Shit. Well, Robin had already effectively broken his cover, but if MacSweeney confirmed Robin's interest in Michaela...

"Oh? Who?"

"Ringo." Her cheeks flushed.

MacSweeney's head tilted. "Ringo? Like the Beatle?"

Michaela wrinkled her nose and grinned. "Like the Japanese word for apple."

"You'll have to introduce me sometime."

When hell freezes over. Out of the corner of his eye, Robin noted Jaden's presence. So the vampire hadn't lost sight of his charge after all. To all but the most discerning eye, the vampire was invisible.

"I think you'd get along. Unless you're business rivals." She smiled sweetly. "Then, maybe not so much."

MacSweeney chuckled and reached out. He brushed his fingertips along Michaela's arm. "Have dinner with me?"

Michaela shook her head. "I can't. I have the night shift at the hospital tonight."

Damn it all. She seemed genuinely regretful. Now he'd have to kill MacSweeney just on principle.

"Which hospital do you work at?"

NO. She couldn't. Robin moved forward, ready to step in.

"Philadelphia Gen—"

"Michaela!" Robin sagged in relief as Moira Blackthorn practically jumped Michaela from behind. "The lecture's about to start."

"Sorry, I'll be right there." She turned back to MacSweeney with a grimace. "I have to run. It was nice talking to you again."

"You too." MacSweeney dared to put his hands on Robin's woman, bringing her hand to his lips for a soft, sweet kiss. "I'll see you around."

Robin wondered if Michaela heard the threat or not. From her relaxed posture, he was guessing not.

"I look forward to it."

Over his dead body.

Michaela allowed Moira to drag her off with a farewell wave to MacSweeney, sealing the dark fae's fate. MacSweeney watched the women until they were safely behind the closed door of the conference room, a strange expression on his face. Robin couldn't quite place it. Was it regret? Longing?

Loneliness?

Finally, the corridor was empty except for Jaden, Robin and MacSweeney.

"I know you're there, Hob. You too, Blackthorn. Come out, come out wherever you are."

Robin allowed his blue eyes to shift into view, leaving the rest of his body invisible even as Jaden stepped out of the shadows. "Raven MacSweeney."

MacSweeney smirked. "Robin Goodfellow. I'd say it's a pleasure to meet you, but even I'm not that big a liar."

Robin bit back a reluctant smile. "Indeed. I could say the same."

"Aren't you supposed to be not here? You should be in the conference room with the rest of the, ahem, delegates."

Robin had almost forgotten about Jaden, so focused had he become on the Fear Dearc.

"Lord Jaden Blackthorn, I presume? Your bondmate is quite sweet looking. Does she taste as good as she looks?"

Green fire flashed in Jaden's eyes. If the Fear Dearc threatened either Moira or Duncan, Jaden would attack to protect his lovers. Perhaps that was what the Fear Dearc hoped for. It would certainly open up the Gray Court to recrimination, as MacSweeney, a delegate, had diplomatic immunity for the conference.

But Jaden took a tack that surprised even Robin. He grinned, that mischievous one that had first drawn Robin to the vampire. "I wonder how sweet Michaela would react to you threatening her newfound friend?"

One of MacSweeney's dark brows rose. "Does she know you set Moira on her in order to spy on me?

Robin laughed. MacSweeney's ego was large, indeed, if he thought Moira was a spy.

MacSweeney's attention remained on Jaden. "No. You're using your bondmate to protect her. From me?" MacSweeney put his hand to his chest with melodramatic flair. His nails, like Robin's, were black. Whether it was an affectation or natural remained to be seen. "I'm flattered."

"What can I say? My wife has excellent taste. Case in point, I noticed she didn't like you."

Gods love Jaden Blackthorn. He could annoy a saint, and MacSweeney could never lay claim to that title. The smirk was gone from his face, replaced by irritation. "Don't interfere, Blackthorn. Whether you believe it or not, my intentions toward the human are honorable."

"As honorable as a Black Court fae can ever be, which means not."

MacSweeney's gaze narrowed. "Let it go, bloodsucker."

"I don't think so, birdbrain."

MacSweeney took a deep breath. "I give you my word, Michaela will come to no true harm while under my protection."

The ring of magic was in his words, a vow the Fear Dearc would have to enforce whether he wished it or not. If it were any woman but Michaela, Robin would have been intrigued.

"She's under *my* protection." No vow needed to be said for Robin to feel the magic settle around him. Robin flashed into view, changing his clothing to match his appearance. The tight leather pants, high boots, long jacket and silk shirt were far more his style than anything Ringo wore. Robin would not allow MacSweeney to lay any claim his bondmate, magical vows or no. He offered the Fear Dearc a mocking bow, his red hair sweeping around him like a cloak. "Let none say the Hobgoblin does not protect his own."

MacSweeney returned the bow. "Be aware, I have every intention of making her mine."

Robin smiled sweetly, aware his fangs were showing. "You may try."

"Raven? Is everything all right?"

Robin stilled. He had not seen the door behind MacSweeney swing open, but Michaela stood just behind it, her head peaking around the edge. Her eyes widened when she caught sight of Robin, her gaze sweeping him from head to toe. She bit her lip, and Robin damn near growled at the lust in her quickly guarded expression.

Hell. Now he had to be jealous of himself.

MacSweeney moved quickly for a soon-to-be dead man. "Everything is fine, sweetness. You go back to your class."

"It sounded like you were arguing." She smiled when she saw Jaden and waved. "Hi, Jaden. You looking for Moira?"

Jaden shook his head. "Nope. But I'm glad you're looking after her for me."

Michaela wrinkled her nose. "She called the instructor a 'flaming arse-shite moron with delusions of grandeur'. I don't think we'll be in here for much longer."

Robin laughed. He could picture the fiery Moira doing just that.

"Who are you?"

Robin continued to chuckle as he swept Michaela a low bow. "Robin Goodfellow, if it pleases you."

Her eyes went wide with delight. "And if it didn't?"

"Then I would have to sigh and lay claim to some other title. Puck, perhaps?"

Her grin turned damn near evil. "Peter Pan?"

"Please." He waved that name away with a disdainful sniff. "Credit me with some taste. I am hardly in the business of seducing children, thank you."

"I bet you'd look good in the tights."

Robin cocked one brow at her, delighted when she shivered in response. "My dear, I would *kill* in those tights."

Michaela's grin turned puzzled. "Why do I have the feeling we've met before?"

Robin preened, secretly pleased that she recognized him on some level despite the fact that he wasn't currently wearing his Ringo disguise. "I'm just that pretty."

She laughed, open and unaffected, charming him once more. "Yes, you are. But it's not that." She tapped her chin and studied his face intently. Robin had no fear she'd link him to Ringo. Ringo stood a good two inches taller than Robin. That alone should throw her off balance.

She nodded her head. "I know what it is. It's your eyes." She pointed to MacSweeney. "You two have the same eyes." Her gaze darted between the two, her expression turning sly. "Are you brothers?"

Robin blinked, and MacSweeney turned pale. The Fear Dearc laughed, but it was a shadow of its former glory. Indeed, he looked wan, almost sick. "I've never met him before in my life."

"Oh." Michaela looked almost disappointed, but was soon distracted by Moira marching out of the conference room.

Moira shook her fist through the door. "May the curse of Mary Malone and her nine blind, illegitimate children chase you so far over the Hills of Damnation that the Lord himself can't find you with a telescope!" She turned and started at the sight of Jaden, Robin, MacSweeney and Michaela. "Oh. Not you guys."

Jaden broke down, laughing so hard he couldn't breathe. MacSweeney shook his head, and Robin grinned.

Michaela, however, put it best. She patted Moira on the head. She was so tiny she had to reach up to do it. "Is it someone's Miller time?"

"She said I wasn't Irish enough. Me!" Moira flung her hands in the air. "And she said my Gaelic was all wrong." She stuck her head back in the door. "*Go n-ithe an cat thú is go n-ithe an diabhal an cat.*" She slammed the door shut, nodded firmly and dusted off her hands. "Take that."

MacSweeney proved he wasn't a blithering idiot by backing away from the enraged leprechaun. "I...think I need to go. Michaela, always a pleasure."

Michaela waved good-bye, but her attention was mostly on Moira. "What the hell did that mean?"

MacSweeney took off as if the hounds of hell were on his heels before Moira could respond.

Moira sniffed. "May the cat eat you, and may the devil eat the cat."

Michaela bit her lip, holding back her obvious laughter. "Um. Remind me not to piss you off."

Moira, muttering under her breath, stomped away, followed by a giggling Michaela. "Nice to meet you, Robin!"

"And I, you." Robin, grinning at Moira's antics, turned toward Jaden, only to find the vampire studying him with a speculative look in his eye.

"She's right, you know."

Robin cocked an eyebrow. "About?"

"You and the Fear Dearc. You *do* have the same eyes."

"Hmph." They did not. Raven's eyes were cold as ice, while Robin's were a warm, sunny blue that made his Michaela smile.

"We have another problem, by the way." Jaden gestured for Robin to follow him.

"Oh?"

"I overheard two humans talking. One of them had to leave the convention to deal with a body that was pulled out of the river this morning."

"And?" Not another one. The *each uisge* should not have had to feed again so quickly.

"It was partially eaten. There was mention of sharks."

"Damnation. That would be the second in two days." What was McNeil thinking? Every fae did their best to hide their presence from the humans, even Black Court fae. No one wanted to start a war with the mortals. The price would be far too high. "I'll have to investigate." Any possibility that a fae would crack their Seeming and alert the humans to their presence had high priority, on Oberon's orders. Not even Prince Evan's safe return was more important. No single fae was.

"I'll keep an eye on Michaela and have Duncan let me know if there are any problems with the delegates. So far their biggest complaint is MacSweeney is absent and the Black Court is refusing to start without him."

Robin nodded. "In that case, it's off to the river for me."

"Be careful, Robin. This whole thing stinks to high heaven. The Black Queen is up to something more than tweaking Gloriana's nose."

Robin tapped his chin thoughtfully. "Indeed. The question is, what?"

Robin strolled behind the assistant coroner completely unseen. It wouldn't be long before they reached the remains, and he'd be able to determine whether or not the *each uisge* truly was responsible for the death.

He was betting that the water horse was the culprit. After all, what were the odds that a shark was in the Delaware River during the early parts of spring?

"Take a look at this, Alvarez. She's chewed up pretty badly."

Robin hovered behind Alvarez as the man squatted beside the body. "Shit. Second female in two days."

Robin's brows rose. Two *women*? He hadn't known that. The urge to pull out his phone and contact Jaden to check on Michaela was strong, but he would be returning to the convention shortly. He would see for himself that she was safe.

"Have the cops done their CSI shit?"

"Yes, sir."

"Bag and tag her then." Alvarez shook his head. "The coroner's gonna have a fit with this one."

"Think they'll find the same thing they did last time?"

Alvarez shot the young man a look as they bagged the body. "I still think the lab needs to run the results again."

"We were lucky to get them back so quickly as it was. With the possibility that there might be a shark in the water the mayor has really put the pressure on."

"Yeah, but human saliva found in the wound?"

Damnation. McNeil had left evidence on the damn body?

The assistant shook his head. "We were lucky we got anything, what with her being in the river. Odds are good any hair or fiber is gone. They're going to try and run a DNA match, see if we have a potential serial killer on our hands."

A human disease, serial killers, and one Robin had not thought would touch the fae. It appeared he might have been wrong.

They zipped up the bag and moved the body onto a gurney. Alvarez tapped the edge of the body bag. "This woman wasn't out boating."

"What makes you say that?"

They lifted the body into the ambulance. "She's dressed in high heels and a miniskirt, with no jacket to ward off the chill in the air, and a Nightlife club stamp on her wrist."

The man working with Alvarez slammed the ambulance doors shut. "Shit. How the hell did she get here? That club's over on Market. I don't think she came to the waterfront because she had an urgent need to shop at IKEA, for fuck's sake."

How indeed. Robin turned his attention to what was in the area. The girl was killed near here, of that he was certain. The taint of death filled the air, and it wasn't the stench of the river itself. No, the girl's death was all over the place.

Across the street was the shopping center that held the aforementioned IKEA, along with several other stores. The scent of fast-food burgers mingled with the scent of the river. Several yards away sat the rusting hulk of the *SS United States*, imposing and sad at the same time. In one direction he could see one of Philadelphia's numerous bridges spanning the Delaware, and in the other, the skyscrapers of Center City. If it were not for the police and the ambulance, it would look like any other peaceful day in the city.

It was obvious to Robin that McNeil needed to be put down. The teeth marks alone were condemnation of the act. Leaving the body near a busy shopping center, unforgiveable. And to add the final nail to his coffin, there were no other *each uisges* in Philadelphia but the visiting McNeil. It was enough. Robin would get permission from Oberon to take out the trash as soon as he spoke to him.

But for now, he had a mate to return to.

Chapter Ten

Michaela put her purse in her locker and clipped on her badge. She was in so much trouble. Her car wouldn't start and had to be towed, and since she couldn't get a hold of any of her friends to help her she'd been forced to wait. Now she was two hours late, and even though she'd called in with plenty of time to spare, she just knew she was going to get chewed out over it. She had run across Jaden, who'd offered her a ride, but she didn't know him well enough yet to climb into a car with him.

While her instincts told her he wouldn't hurt her, there was a first time for everything.

She yawned. Man, she hated the night shift. As heartbreaking as her job could be sometimes, she preferred the daytime with its drama, its giggles, its happy sighs and quiet cries. There were some who thought Michaela put too much of herself into her kids, but as far as Michaela was concerned you couldn't put too much in. These kids were fighting for their lives, their tiny bodies wracked by a disease that felled grown men and women. They had more courage, more beauty in their little hearts than anyone Michaela had met, and they deserved to get everything she had to give.

Her devotion to her job had destroyed more than one relationship. She hoped Ringo would understand.

Gah. Ringo. Her nurse's shoes squeaked on the newly polished hospital floor. She felt so damn guilty for drooling over that redhead this afternoon, but what could she say? He'd been the embodiment of every fantasy she'd ever had, so close to her fantasy man she'd nearly pinched herself to see if she was dreaming. Hell, even his name appealed to her. The man calling himself Robin Goodfellow was a tall, slender man with the wiry build and the broad shoulders of a swimmer. He had waist-length red hair that danced around him in a fiery halo, and laughing blue eyes in a face that would have made Michelangelo weep. He'd been wearing, of all things, a long, double-breasted black coat with wide lapels that nipped in at his waist and ended just below his knees. Under that was a white silk, button-down shirt opened far enough to expose his throat, and just a hint of a blue silk waistcoat that matched his eyes. His tight black pants had been tucked into knee-high boots with the slightest heel.

He'd looked like a fairy-tale prince with a modern twist. Just looking at him had almost made her ask, *Ringo who?*

Almost.

There was a special place in hell for women who lusted after two men at the same time. It didn't help that Robin matched every fantasy she'd ever had of Robin Goodfellow. Ever since she was little girl, she dreamed about a red-haired rogue with laughing eyes that alternated between blue and green depending on his mood. That imaginary man had been her first love, and no one she'd ever dated had stood up to even the thought of him.

Until Ringo.

Michaela hissed in pain as she banged her sore wrist. She'd managed to keep the bandage hidden all day, but the short sleeves of her nurse's scrubs would make it obvious she'd been injured. Without a doubt, she'd wind up called in to see her supervisor, the biggest prick on the planet. Her last supervisor would have suggested she get her wrist looked at, maybe even X-rayed. Her new one would blame her for getting hurt and claim that her work would suffer because of it, thus making the children suffer. Michaela had done everything in her power to prove herself to Mr. Schnyderite, but he had a grudge against her.

Maybe it was because she'd told him he had a better chance of sucking Ed the ambulance driver's dong than getting in her pants, but her very married supervisor was a womanizing fucktard of the first order. More than one nurse had gone to HR to complain. Too bad he seemed to have an in with the head of the department. He always managed to get out of any trouble. In some cases, he'd come out even better and a valuable nurse would quit rather than be stuck under his thumb.

Some days she felt awful for hoping Mr. Schnyderite's insides were sucked out by a vacuum toilet, but not all days. Not by a long shot.

"Ms. Exton. In my office. Now."

Speaking of Dick McGrabbyhands. "Coming, sir." She entered her boss's office and closed the door. "You wanted to see me?"

He tapped his pencil on his desk in an annoying rhythm. "You were late today."

"My car broke down—"

"I don't want excuses. I want nurses who know their place and arrive on time."

Michaela gritted her teeth and smiled sweetly. "Yes, sir."

"You're lucky I haven't fired you."

Considering this was the first time she'd been late in over a year, he hardly had cause. "There's been no complaint about my work."

"Oh? What about the nurses who had to cover for you while you dawdled?"

Penny and Trish were the last people who would complain. They'd all covered for each other, and Penny had been far more sympathetic than Mr. Schnyderite when she'd called in. "They've assured me it was not a problem, sir. If they've complained, I'd like to hear it."

She wasn't surprised when he opened a file rather than answer her question. "Your performance has been below average." He made a mark on the piece of paper before she could protest. "Just so you know, there will be no promotion in your future, immediate or otherwise. However, I am calling for a peer review." He closed the folder without looking at her. "Dismissed."

"Yes, sir." Michaela marched out of the office and very carefully did *not* slam the door.

"Sorry, Mick." Trish shrugged at her from behind the nurses' station. "I tried to tell him, but you know how he is."

"Yeah." Michaela shook her head. "I just wish I could get him to lay off me." If he didn't she'd be forced to transfer to another hospital, and if she had to do that... She shuddered. She would be low man on the totem pole again. Odds were good she'd get the worst shifts, the worst hours and the absolute worst parents to deal with. She'd been at PGH for five years now. She didn't want to leave if she didn't have to, but if the situation with her boss didn't change she might not have a choice.

Michaela sighed. She had more important things to worry about, starting with the guy whose life she'd saved yesterday. "Listen, there was a guy who was brought in by emergency yesterday. He was hit by a car right in front of me and I worked on him. I want to check on him. Think you can cover for me?"

Trish glanced down the hallway. "Go. I'll tell McGrabby you're in the little nurse's room."

"Thanks." Michaela scuttled away, eager to get out from under her boss's evil eye. Ugh. Maybe she did need to change jobs. Not even the kids made that man worth it.

She got to the elevator without being seen and managed to make her way down to emergency. Ed and Will were there, filling out paperwork. "Hey, guys. That guy you brought in yesterday. Any idea where they've put him?"

Will grinned and waved his bottle of water at her in greeting. "Michaela. How's McGrabby?"

"My life would be so much better if he didn't have a penis."

Will bent over and clutched his manhood in protest. "Man. That's just wrong. Not even McGrabby deserves a Bobbitt." He shuddered, his hands still cupped protectively over his privates.

Ed laughed. "Your vic's in ICU with internal injuries. His name is Samuel something-or-other."

"Samuel Snodgrass." Will straightened up and shot his partner an astonished look. "Dude, how could you forget that? The man sounds like he belongs in Hogwarts." He picked up his bottle of water and took a drink, handing the bottle to his partner when Ed held his hand out.

Michaela bit back a laugh. "Seriously? His name is Sammy Snodgrass?"

Will snickered. "That's what I said."

"Sounds like a gangster name in a Bugs Bunny cartoon, doesn't it? Like he's BFFs with Rocky and Mugsy." Ed gave in and laughed. "His parents must have hated him."

"Poor guy. I'm going to go check on him, see how he is. You two stay out of trouble, okay?"

"You too." Will frowned, his expression turning serious. "Listen, if you ever need a reference, I know some docs over at Lincoln who would love to have you."

"Yeah. Give us the word and we'll have your resume on their desks so fast Dick's head will spin."

Michaela smiled. She had the best friends. "Thanks, guys."

"No problem."

"See ya later."

Michaela made her way to ICU and asked for Samuel Snodgrass. When she explained to the on-duty nurse why she was there, the older woman let her in. Since Candace used to work on Michaela's floor, they'd known each other for a while. She was another nurse who'd bailed when Dick had taken over, but she'd had enough seniority to get a transfer rather than having to leave. "Just don't wake him. He's been restless all day. Keeps muttering something about the press, but he sounds scared as hell." Candace grimaced. "That boy's been through something bad, I just know it."

Michaela nodded. Candace's instincts when it came to the abused were pretty good. If Candace was saying he'd been through something pretty bad, it was probably *really* bad. "Will do. You know me, Candace. I check on kids all night long. I'll be quiet."

"Yeah, but this guy's been restless. He woke up screaming. Twice. I've never heard anything like it. It was like he was being tortured."

"Could it be sleep paralysis?" The vivid, nightmarish hallucinations that accompany sleep paralysis could make a person believe they were being tortured. People who suffered from the disorder reported seeing demons perched on their chests, witches digging claws into them, even alien abductions. Because their bodies were locked by the natural paralysis that occurs during REM sleep, they felt helpless to defend themselves, adding to the trauma of the disorder.

"I don't think so. He wakes up and immediately begins thrashing, like he's fighting something. It could be a form of night terrors."

Or maybe he was reliving something that actually happened to him. Michaela hurried toward her patient's room. "I'll see if I can find out anything."

"Thanks, hon. If anyone can get him to open up, it would be you."

Michaela entered the room, surprised to find the man awake and staring at the door. "Hi, Mr. Snodgrass. Do you remember me?"

He nodded and licked his lips. "M-Michaela."

She gave him her best smile, the one that always made the kids smile back. "That's me. I wanted to check up on you, make sure you were okay."

"Hurts." He shuddered, his face wrinkling into a grimace. He was probably one of the least attractive men she'd ever met, with short dark hair and squashed features that spoke of more than one fight in his lifetime where faces were prime targets. Still, the way those dark brown eyes watched her every move as if she were the second coming was sort of endearing. And creepy.

Endearingly creepy. Two words she usually didn't usually think of together, but they worked for Sammy Snodgrass.

He struggled to lift his broken arm and reach for her. "Help. Me."

She stood by the side of his bed and took his hand, hoping to soothe him. "What do you need?"

He gripped her hand so tightly she could barely wiggle her fingers. "Loyalty and protection I give to thee. I am your man, and you my liege. By this oath I am bound to thee, by the law of three times three."

"What?" Okay, she had a crazy man on her hands. She tried to pull her hand out of his, but unless she was willing to hurt him she couldn't get free.

"Loyalty and protection I give to thee. I am your man, and you my liege. By this oath I am bound to thee, by the law of three times three."

"Um, Mr. Snodgrass, I don't think—"

"Loyalty and protection I give to thee. I am your man, and you my liege. By this oath I am bound to thee, by the law of three times three." He sank back against the pillow as if a great weight had been lifted off his shoulders, but his gaze never left her. The pained expression that had gripped his features dissipated. The tight hold he'd had on her hand loosened. "Beware, my lady. There are those that will harm you because of your association with Robin Goodfellow." He took a deep breath, the movement flexing massive shoulders. He gave her what she assumed was meant to be a reassuring smile but looked more like his dick was caught in a meat grinder. "I will be there soon to protect you, I swear."

Oh, boy. How the hell did she keep getting into situations like this? "Mr. Snodgrass—"

"Snod. My name is Snod." He smiled, and his homely face became almost human. "You saved my life, and I am yours."

She cocked one eyebrow in disbelief. "I don't think my apartment building will let me keep a person as a pet. Besides, what the hell am I supposed to feed you?"

He started to laugh, but it became a wracking cough. She soothed him back down, petting his arm and muttering nonsense until his eyelids began to flutter once more. "I will be there soon, my lady. Until then, trust no one." He frowned, trying to fight the sleep he needed to heal. "Promise me."

She patted his hand. "I promise I'll be careful."

His lips curved into a serene smile as he finally fell asleep. She blew out a breath and moved to the foot of his bed, reading his chart.

Busted ribs, bruised lungs, a broken arm and numerous contusions. All in all, it could have been much worse. As it was, the doctor had marked down his remarkable recovery rate. It seemed Snod had been in bad shape when he'd been brought in, but that all the tests showed he was healing much more quickly than expected. The doctor was planning on running extra tests.

Michaela tsk'd and put the chart back. Doctors loved unnecessary tests. If the man was healing, what was the problem? Did the doc think Snod was an alien or something?

Sheesh. Michaela closed the room's door and headed for the elevator, nodding thanks once more to Candace as she passed the nurse's station. Sometimes the doctors didn't know when to leave well enough alone.

Now all she had to do was sneak onto her floor, avoid Dick for the rest of the night, and meet Ringo for breakfast tomorrow.

I wonder if that dude dressed as Robin Goodfellow is available for lunch?

Michaela groaned and covered her face with her hands. God. What was she going to do?

Robin watched as the elevator doors closed on Michaela, then glided silently, invisibly, toward the redcap's room. He'd planned on killing the creature, but listening to its oath of fealty had startled him, made him wary. If he destroyed the creature, Michaela would more than likely attempt to find out who had done it and why it had been killed. She would wind up destroying herself in the process, and that Robin could not allow.

At least the Seeming prevented the creature from registering on human tests as anything but a mortal. That would have been an unholy mess, but the gods had ensured that the fae were protected, even from the rapid technological advances of the humans.

Still, how did the woman get into these situations? It amazed him, it truly did.

"The only reason you're still alive is the woman who left."

Robin paused at the doorway. He recognized that voice, and it left him cold.

"I am hers, and she is mine."

The hospital shook as Robin's eyes flared green. It should be him saying that, not some redcap lying broken in a hospital bed.

"I will protect her, even from you, Lord Raven." The redcap's deep, rumbling voice was filled with conviction. He would fight the Black Court fae to keep his new mistress safe.

Robin took a deep breath and tried to calm his rage. He hadn't lost control so much since he'd been very young. The last time someone had claimed something of his...

Well. They were still uncovering Pompeii.

"And that is why you will live, despite Lord Bres." Raven laughed, the sound dark and vaguely familiar. "Though if he were to lay hands on you there would be nothing left but dust."

The redcap growled. "I will protect her even from Lord Bres."

Robin's brows rose. That was, indeed, brave of the creature. The Fomorian was one of the oldest, and last, of his kind, and ruled the redcaps with an iron fist. He'd once been king of the Tuatha Dè and forced them to act as slaves to the Fomorian rulers. Somehow he'd wound up with the beauty of both his Fomorian father and his Tuatha Dè mother, making him one of the most exquisite-looking people to ever walk the earth. Very few could resist his charm when he chose to employ it. Even fewer wished to incur his wrath. He was vicious to those who crossed him in any way. He ruled the most brutal thugs in the fae world and relished the role.

All except this one, who'd pledged himself to Robin's truebond. *Ah, the irony.* When Bres discovered his lackey had grown a spine he would make the creature suffer pain unknown to mortal man.

Raven seemed almost curious. He watched the redcap with all the attention an entomologist would give a new species of bug. "Bres will not like this, and you know what he does to those he doesn't like."

"Lord Bres no longer has power over me."

"What?"

Indeed. What was the creature talking about?

"Lord Bres knew. Lord Bres tried to hurt me, but Michaela came and made the pain go away. I will protect my lady with my last breath." The creature sighed. "She makes the pain go away."

It was said with such childish wonder Robin was shocked to his core.

"I will protect her even from the Hob himself."

Now that, Robin could not allow. "Indeed?" He sauntered into the room, his boot heels clacking on the polished linoleum. He was pleased to note Raven had been unaware of his presence, as the Fear Dearc started most delightfully. "And how do you propose to do that, I wonder?"

Raven's eyes narrowed viciously. "Stay away from Michaela, Hob."

Robin tilted his head and laughed. "I think you have no say in the matter, Fear Dearc."

The redcap's gaze was bouncing back and forth between them like a Ping-Pong ball. "No one hurts Michaela."

Robin bowed slightly to the creature. It belonged to Michaela now and, perforce, to him. Robin Goodfellow took care of his own. "On that, we agree."

The Fear Dearc shot the redcap a sour look. "Indeed."

Robin took a deep breath. "We need to..."

What was that scent?

The Fear Dearc's head cocked to the side, a gesture so familiar Robin was shocked. "Need to what, Hobgoblin?"

Robin frowned. Where had he smelled that elusive fragrance before? He took a step closer to Raven, who took a step back.

There. That wild, feral scent that surrounded the Raven Lord. What in blazes was it?

"I don't think so." Darkness swirled around Raven, dark wisps that engulfed him until there was nothing left but the lingering scent of smoke...and Hob.

Robin took a deep breath, and the world swirled around him in a dizzying wave.

No. It was not possible. He refused to believe it.

The son of Robin Goodfellow could not be Black Court.

Chapter Eleven

Oberon forced himself not to sigh. Damn mortals and their ingenuity. He wanted to find the person who'd developed both the Internet and video calls and flay them alive. Lately it seemed every Tom, Dick and fairy wanted the great King Oberon to mediate their disputes.

Now Gloriana was calling him for "updates". There had been a time when he had been able to do his job in peace. Now he was acting as his own damn secretary. Perhaps Robin was right and he needed an assistant. But truly, who could he trust? "We have received no word yet, Gloriana. Be patient. It has only been a day."

The White Queen sniffed disdainfully, her bright, iridescent wings fluttering behind her. "I see no reason why my nephew is still in the hands of the bitch queen. Mark my words, Oberon, she's up to something."

Of course she was. Titannia didn't take a step unless it benefited her in some way. "Allow the delegates to at least attempt a negotiation, Gloriana."

She scowled, the expression taking her pert prettiness and turning it ugly. "Why did you send *him* as the arbiter? He's a traitor to the White, and biased."

Oberon bit back a growl. There were days when he wished he'd never met Titannia. If he had not, Gloriana would not have been elevated to the position she was in, but the word of the gods was inviolate. Gloriana's light was supposed to counteract Titannia's darkness, but more and more that light seemed more like inflexible ice, unyielding and due to shatter at any moment. "Lord Duncan Malmayne-Blackthorn did nothing to—"

"He bonded with a vampire. How much more proof do you need?"

Gloriana's inflexible attitude toward the turned fae was rooted in her last encounter with Titannia. Oberon understood her anger at the Black Queen, but she'd allowed her prejudice to spill over onto an entire race of beings, banning them from the White Court with all the venom of a woman scorned. Even those of pure heart, like Jaden Blackthorn, were denied entry. Indeed, Gloriana's policy was to kill them on sight if they even approached the White Palace. Not even his Blades were allowed inside if they were vampires. "Not all vampires belong to Titannia."

"Fool yourself if you must, but do not attempt to fool me."

Oberon quirked one brow, wishing she were in front of him. If she were, his power would put her on her flat ass. "You dare to call me a fool?"

Gloriana had enough common sense left to backpedal, but only so far. "I think you have blinders on where Robin Goodfellow is concerned. You always have. All know the vampire is one of his favorite pets."

"Robin is mine, Gloriana." The threat was clear. No more need be said. Robin had been and always would be Oberon's. His was the only loyalty that Oberon never questioned, never truly doubted. While Robin might give in to fits and starts of mischief, Oberon had only to say the word and Robin was at his side, ready and willing to do whatever Oberon wished of him. He never had to ask for more, for Robin was always willing to give him all.

Gloriana bowed her head. "As you say."

"Indeed. I do say." Oberon smiled and Gloriana shivered. Good. "The negotiators are in place, the mediator is present and ready to work. We still do not know where the boy is, but my Blades are searching." He ignored her grimace of distaste. Ever since Jaden had become the lord of Clan Blackthorn she'd become sour where his Blades were concerned.

Hell, even before then she'd started to sour toward them. Robin believed that, if not for her interference, the darkness could have been rooted out long before the Malmaynes gave their allegiance to the Black.

"I am no longer certain negotiation is necessary. They've had the boy long enough to have turned him. He's of no use to me."

Oberon blinked slowly. He'd worried Gloriana would turn her back on the boy, and now he had proof. "You would leave him to die?"

"He's more than likely already dead. You know how she is. This is a feint for her true objective, a means of distracting me."

On that, at least, they were agreed. "Then perhaps if we find the boy, we find the objective."

Gloriana smiled. "She is dark, but she is not dim. No, Evan will have no place in her grand scheme as anything more than a red herring. If the negotiations fail, leave him to his fate."

Oberon smiled back. "No."

He cut the connection before she could answer. He was not hers to order around. The boy, if he was untainted, would become his, as would the whole Yates family. He had no illusions that Gloriana would bother keeping her brother and his children around once Evan was retrieved alive. No, once a member of a family or clan was proven to be Black Court, they were all painted with the same dark brush, at least in Gloriana's eyes. He'd gotten more remnants of White Court families, devastated by losses their own queen imposed upon them in her purges, than he ever got of Black Court.

Oberon pulled up the genealogy charts for the royal family of the White Court and started sending out orders. Plans would need to be put in place for the refugees. Gloriana might have become the ice queen, but Oberon, whether anyone believed or not, still had at least half his heart.

The other half had died centuries ago, buried alongside his bond with Titania.

My one and only truebond. Oberon snorted. The universe, it seemed, had a twisted sense of humor if Titannia was its idea of Oberon's perfect match. He could no longer remember when it had started to go wrong, the lies, the cheating, the never-ending arguing and one-upmanship. Nor could he remember who had started it all. If he could pinpoint the moment when she gave in, gave herself to the demon, it might ease his mind. But he could not. Perhaps, someday he'd be able to look back at all he'd lost when she'd betrayed him and feel...something. Anything but the yawning empty nothing that had been left behind when the gods, to save his life, had severed his truebond.

Until then, Oberon would guard what was left of his heart and soul and pray nothing stole them from him. If they were lost, the world itself would be lost, in ways far worse than even Robin Goodfellow could comprehend.

Michaela flopped into bed, groaning. She glanced over at the clock. Four hours. She pulled the sheets over her head and moaned. She'd get four hours of sleep before she had to get up, shower, dress and meet Ringo for breakfast. Michaela yawned and made sure her alarm was set. She hadn't even bothered with a nightgown, falling into bed naked and with the evening's makeup still on.

Maybe she'd get lucky and see the faux Robin Goodfellow too.

She smiled, her eyes drifting shut. Both men were hotter than hell, entertaining, and looked at her like she was chocolate mousse and really good coffee, and they didn't know if they wanted a bite or a sip first. Most men viewed her as the "cute one" of her friends, but she bet if Amanda were right next to her they'd *still* only have eyes for Michaela.

Of course, pigs could fly out of her vagina singing "Hail to the Chief" too. Anything was possible.

"Who is Amanda, and what makes you think I could possibly want her more than you?"

All it took was a feather–light touch to her instep and Michaela was giggling like a child.

"You know you are the only one I want in my bed."

Michaela nodded and then shook her head.

"Do you doubt me?"

Michaela shrugged. It wasn't him she doubted. It was herself, her fickle, wavering heart that seemed to want two men, one of whom she'd barely met but looked like her deepest, darkest fantasies, and one who was a dream all on his own and treated her like she was worth more than gold. She'd loved Robin forever, but Ringo called to her in ways she'd only felt with her dream man.

"Shall I prove it to you?"

She opened her eyes to find Ringo hovering over her, those beautiful, changeable eyes of his burning into her. He touched her again, his palms sliding along her skin, leaving goose bumps in their wake.

"Please."

Ringo kissed her deeply, taking her mouth the way he had after lunch, claiming her with lips and tongue and teeth until she melted beneath him, pliable and wanting. He smiled and lifted the sheet away. "As you wish."

Ringo wasn't a man who did things by half measures. He immediately latched on to her nipples, suckling them into ripe, wet points of neediness. He stroked her body like it belonged to him, soothing her one moment and inflaming her the next. It wasn't long before she was writhing beneath his touch, demanding he give her what she craved.

God, she wanted him.

Ringo nipped her stomach, his tongue rimming her belly button before he reached between her thighs. He moaned his approval of her closely shaved pussy before diving in, taking her clit between his lips and sucking on it until she was drenched and shaking. She was so close to coming it tingled along her spine, made her thighs quiver.

She grabbed hold of his head, burying her fingers in his hair. She wasn't above begging if it got her what she wanted. "Ringo. Please. Make me come."

"I need to hear you say Robin."

She looked down, shocked to see bright red hair running through her fingers. Laughing blue eyes sparkled with lust, and something more. Something untamable.

"I am going to take you, pleasure you until you scream my name."

Before she could protest, Robin crawled up her body and slid into her, stretching her farther than any lover ever had before.

She gasped. It was the most perfect sensation in the world, one she never wanted to end. They'd never done *this* before, but dear God she hoped they had about a thousand repeats. "Robin."

"Indeed." Robin kissed her deeply. She could taste herself on his tongue. "Now, we dance."

Robin didn't begin to pound into her the way she'd expected. He set up a slow, hip-rolling rhythm that had her clutching his arms and shoulders, her fingernails digging into his skin. Little crescent marks appeared, blood red against pale flesh, and he smiled when he saw them.

Her own skin was slicked with sweat, her limbs shaking as he denied her over and over, bringing her close to the brink only to back away at the last minute.

If he kept this shit up she was going to kill him and take matters into her own hands.

He laughed as if he read the threat and was amused by it. "Do you want to come, my dear?"

She whimpered, incapable of speech.

"Then say you are mine."

"Robin..." How could he even ask that? She'd been his since she was a child.

"Say it, Michaela."

Ecstasy beckoned, blurring her vision. She licked her lips, wanting another taste of him. "Yours. I'm yours, Robin."

"Yes." The hissed word seemed to release something inside him. Now the pounding she'd expected earlier began as Robin thrust into her over and over. The sound of flesh slapping against flesh was so loud she was surprised it didn't wake the neighbors.

"Yours, all yours, fuck me, please, God." She was babbling, begging, so ready to explode she was near tears.

"Now, my dear. Fall. I will catch you, always."

Michaela lost breath, sight, all sensation but the one rocketing through her as Robin brought her to one of the most explosive orgasms she'd ever had in her life. His muttered curse, in a language she didn't recognize, barely registered.

"Robin."

She wanted to cradle him close, feel slick, wet skin against her own, breathe in the perfume of his hair. She'd waited so long for this moment, for him to come to her, claim her. Make her his in every way that counted.

She'd waited all her life for him, and he'd finally come.

What she got was an armful of pillow, and a body throbbing from a dream of an orgasm that destroyed any sensation she'd ever experienced while awake.

Fuck. If just the *dream* of Robin could do that...

Shit. She rubbed her thighs together, relishing the ache. No real man could live up to the dreams she had of Robin Goodfellow, not even the beautiful Ringo. The moment Ringo morphed into Robin, she should have realized what was really going on.

She giggled into the pillow she cradled it close. Still, that had been one *hell* of a ride, hadn't it?

Robin Goodfellow sat straight up in bed, his silk sheets soaked in sweat and come. He bent over, still painfully aroused by the perfect dream he'd had of Michaela. The urge to go to her, to claim what was so obviously his, nearly overwhelmed his common sense.

He slid out of bed and headed for the shower, too excited to sleep any further. In a matter of hours he would be with his truebond again. He ran his fingers over the crescent marks and grinned. He stared at his disheveled reflection in the mirror, his eyes flashing from blue and green. The red crescents of her nails still marked his skin, and Robin willed them not to heal. She'd marked him in her human way, and he relished it.

Let the Fear Dearc try to lay his false claim. Michaela had declared that she was his, and Robin was holding her to it.

Make no mistake. Michaela will be mine.

It couldn't be soon enough.

Chapter Twelve

"Mm. Pancakes." Michaela licked syrup off her fork and Robin suppressed a shudder. He wanted to feel that tongue on his flesh, tasting him as she did the sweet treat. "These are so good. I don't get to eat them often enough."

Robin titled his head. "Why not?"

"Too damn busy." She grinned. "The con is a semi-vacation for me. Between working at the hospital, volunteering at the soup kitchen, and my weekend hobbies, I don't have time to indulge in leisurely breakfasts."

Robin's brows rose practically into his hairline. "Soup kitchen?"

Her fork paused. "I didn't tell you about that?

"No. You did not." Yet another sign of his bondmate's generous spirit...and desire for an early grave. Did she not know how dangerous such places were?

"Oh." She shrugged as if it was nothing, but her tense posture gave her away. She was worried how he would react, and well she should be. "I volunteer at the soup kitchen twice a week."

He bit back his natural reaction, the one that said he should simply spirit her away, deposit her on Oberon's doorstep and leave her there until the Christian's second coming. The woman's disregard for her own safety was going to give him gray hairs. "Have there been any incidents there?" If so, Robin would send someone in her stead.

He admired her desire to help, he truly did. But there were other ways to handle it that wouldn't send him to an early grave.

"Not really." She giggled. "We did have one guy, though, that smelled kind of like Taco Bell and the city dump had an illegitimate child. Does that count?"

Robin smiled. Michaela had a certain way with words. "I've smelled worse."

"What could be worse than that?" Michaela rested her chin on her hand, gazing at him as if he held all the answers in the universe, and all of them were put there to amuse the two of them.

"You don't want to know."

"Aw, c'mon. That's not fair. You brought it up."

"Do you truly wish to know?"

"I asked, didn't I? So? Tell me."

Robin tsk'd. "Paris during high summer."

She pouted. "That's the best you can come up with?"

"Have you ever been to Paris when it's exceptionally hot? They *love* their dogs, take them everywhere. And those pretty poodles need to *go*, as it were. So they do. Everywhere." He shuddered in disgust. He'd tossed out more than one pair of boots thanks to Parisian dogs, unable to bring himself to clean the mess up. "I don't think there's a curb law in Paris. If there is, the Parisians ignore it."

She bit her lip.

"Then there is the overwhelming stench of body odor. Climb onto any train or bus, and you are certain to catch a good, strong whiff of *eau de Parisian*. Yet they make some of the best soaps in the world. It's like visiting a farmer who refuses to eat produce. And the public restrooms not only charge you for use but are rarely clean. Some are downright hazardous."

"But you always hear about how beautiful Paris is." Her moue of disappointment was adorable.

"It is one of the most glorious cities in the world, have no doubt of that. Someday I may take you there, show you the Eiffel Tower at night, glittering against the dark backdrop of the sky. Or the *Arc de Triomphe*, where you can look out and see the glittering *La Grande Arche de la Défense*. You would love the *Musée du Louvre*, with its rich history and fantastic sculpture."

"I've always wanted to see the Winged Victory of Samothrace."

She spoke so wistfully he would see to it that she got her wish. "And so you shall, some day."

"So, you speak French?"

He picked up her free hand and kissed her palm, his gaze never leaving her. The faint hint of maple syrup on her skin nearly overcame her intoxicating scent. "*Vous êtes ma belle dame.*"

She swallowed so hard it was visible. Her cheeks flushed beautifully. His truebond liked to hear him speak in French.

"*Je vais te poser tu sur un lit de pétales de roses et de faire l'amour avec tu toute la nuit.*"

She squeaked.

Dear gods, she really would be the death of him. Lust and affection were riding him hard, demanding he leave this house of pancakes and end both their misery in his bed. "Did you understand what I just said?"

"Not one single word. But it sounded wonderful." She sighed and batted her lashes at him, the little minx. "Tell me more about my eyes."

He laughed wickedly, delighted when she shivered. "*Ton regard a volé mon âme.*"

She licked her lips. "Bad, bad man. I knew it the moment I met you."

It wasn't her eyes he was interested in. "*Je voudrais avoir ta cœur, ma chère.*"

She wagged her finger at him. The expression of wanton delight had him gesturing for the waitress. "You're evil."

He cocked one brow. She had no idea.

She threw back her head and laughed. "I knew it! Be nice, Ringo."

That name jolted him. He wanted to hear Robin drip from her lips, to hear her moaning it, screaming it, as she had in their dream. Ringo was the lie. He wanted her to have the truth. All of it. And wasn't that a frightening thing to contemplate? The only ones who knew the whole truth of the Hob were Oberon, his father, brother, king and friend; and Ruby Dunne, who'd shown him that maybe he could show himself for who he truly was yet still be loved.

Anyone else who saw him in his true form died. He prayed to the gods that Michaela would be like Ruby, loving him despite what he was.

"Hey. Is everything all right?"

"Why do you ask?" He didn't think his expression had slipped.

"You spaced out on me, and your eyes went from brown to blue, but your expression was pretty sad."

He smiled, hiding his shock. When had his eyes slipped completely to blue? That was unacceptable. His disguise would keep them both alive. "I'm fine, my dear, but I fear our pancakes are not." He looked down at the soggy-sweet mess on his plate. "Alas, there is no resurrecting them from syrupy death."

She cupped her hands in front of her mouth and tooted "Taps". "Good-bye, pancakes. Your sacrifice will not be forgotten. At least your death was a delicious one."

When she saluted her plate he grinned, letting go of his fear. She would either accept him, or not. Either way, he would court her until he had her in his home, his bed. His life. "Indeed."

When it was time to return to the con for the day, Robin found himself strangely reluctant. He did not want to let Michaela out of his sight even for a moment. The thought of her wandering around a hotel filled with Black Court fae had his heart in his throat. "You will be careful."

The command came out before he could censor it, but he doubted he would have in any event. She needed to take better care for herself.

She shot him a look, but nodded. "Aye aye, captain." She saluted him the way she had the soggy pancakes, crisply but with an edge of laughter.

"Hmph." Robin took her precious face between his hands. She was so delicate, so fragile. What was he to do? Her life was measured in seconds compared to his. Would his immortality become hers when he claimed her?

Could he claim her? He was no Sidhe, nor dragon. Yet the bond worked even for vampires, fae created from humans, so perhaps there was a way he could—

"Earth to Ringo, come in, Ringo."

Yes. He could get Jaden to convert her. That would work. Then, if he couldn't bind her himself, her vampiric bond would work, making them one.

"Screw it. I'm just going to be late."

Soft, sweet lips touched his, licked the seams of his closed mouth, demanding entrance.

Robin took over the kiss, closing his eyes and savoring the sweetness of his bondmate mixed with maple syrup and early morning. He took his time, tasting her thoroughly, in no rush to release her into the convention without him at her side, keeping her safe.

He'd never met a woman he wanted to kiss for the rest of eternity. He'd happily keep their lips bound together. The world, the Court, not even Oberon meant a fraction to him of what Michaela did.

Her arms wrapped around his neck, holding him close, and Robin vowed to do everything in his power to keep her there.

"You summoned me, my lord?"

Oberon sipped his wine, refusing to turn from the window to greet her. More than once she'd managed to catch him off guard. How she snuck past his guards, his Blades and his Majordomo, Harold, he had no idea. The house sprite should have detected her presence immediately, but she'd scared Harold on more than one occasion by greeting the brownie from behind.

He would never tell the brownie this, but it was funny as hell.

"Indeed." Oberon placed the glass down on the table and turned to greet the only woman who still had the power to unnerve him.

The Seer.

She looked as fragile as she always did. Her Japanese heritage was all over her. With her almond-shaped eyes and small nose, she looked like an anime doll brought to life. She was barely five feet tall, and so dainty, a stiff breeze could knock her over. She shared the same full lips and golden skin as her daughter, but where Akane's unusual eyes held a golden star in the center of the left one, the Seer's eyes were a pale jade green, with a silver star in the center of each.

Those stars were the sign of a true Seer, marking both mother and daughter as having the Sight. But where Akane could only see events that were currently occurring, the Seer could peer into the past, present or future with impunity. And unlike Shane Dunne, her predictions always came true. They weren't possibilities.

They were definites.

Hence why, more than once, Oberon had offered her the protection of the Gray Court. Both Gloriana and Titannia would kill to have the Seer under their thumb, but the Seer avoided all of that by declaring herself completely neutral. She would dispense prophecy to all three Courts equally, without regard for good or evil.

It would, eventually, get her killed, but as she liked to tell him when he expressed his concern, "It will not be today."

Oberon had never seen the Seer when her Seeming was wrapped around her. Those glittering, gem–colored eyes were front and center, her dark haired, golden beauty framed by the white, hooded dress she always wore. Mystic topaz jewelry, set in silver, was the only other color on her.

"I need you to tell me if what Robin is hiding from me is a danger to either myself or the Court."

"Which Court, my liege?"

Oberon frowned. The silver stars had widened, a sign she was using her power. Did that mean Robin's secret could threaten one of the other Courts? "The Gray."

She took a deep breath, letting it out in a long, cleansing exhale. The silver stars nearly swallowed the green, leaving only a strange accent around them, like the center of a Christmas ornament. "Heart and soul return to thee when Oberon goes into the sea."

Oberon blinked. Maybe he should have called Shane Dunne. "I...see."

She bowed. "My liege."

"Wait. I understand you can't tell me exactly what that means, but—"

"Shane Dunne has some of the answers you seek. I am truly sorry, but the rest must be revealed in time. But know this..." The green disappeared completely, leaving behind pure metallic silver. "If you do not find the loop in the hole, and your destiny escapes your grasp, the Gray Court *will* fall." She smiled, and Oberon's eyes narrowed. It was never a good thing when the Seer smiled. "On a side note, Robin has found his truebond. And she is human."

Oberon shivered as fear filled him. If Robin had found his truebond, then not only would the mission be abandoned but the woman would be in danger. She would be seen as a weakness by every Black Court fae at the conference.

She would be eaten alive, and Robin, in his grief, would destroy the world.

The Seer bowed to him. "Pleasant dreams, my king."

Oberon barely nodded as the Seer left the room. He picked up the phone and dialed Harold. "Get me Shane Dunne. I want him in my office five minutes ago." *Wait.* "Pleasant dreams?" What was that supposed to mean?

"You rang?" Shane Dunne grunted as his mate elbowed him in the side. "Your Majesty?" He hauled his tiny bondmate close. "Was that supposed to hurt?"

Akane Russo rolled her eyes as her bondmate dragged her into the room. "Behave, Jethro."

Shane gave her the biggest, stupidest grin Oberon had ever seen. "Sure thang, Miz Akane."

Oberon sighed. It was going to be one of those days. "I need to talk to you about some things the Seer told me."

Both Akane and Shane sprang to attention, each in their own way. While Shane still lounged about, his mate close to his side, those blue eyes sharpened, became more focused. The star in Akane's eye twitched, and her shoulders straightened. Robin's Blade was ready for action.

"First things first. The Seer had some words for me that I need clarifying, and she told me you could do so."

"Hit me."

Oberon was tempted to do so. "Heart and soul return to thee when Oberon goes into the sea. Also, if I do not find the loop in the hole, and destiny escapes my grasp, the Gray Court will fall."

The two exchanged an enigmatic glance. "I'm not sure you want the answer."

"Why is that?"

The Hob

Shane gave him a look more direct than any had dared since Robin. "Tunguska."

"That is not an option." Never again would he trust a woman with his heart.

Shane shrugged. "Like I said. Next question."

Oberon took a deep, cleansing breath. "And if I ignore the warning?"

Shane whistled, and Harold wheeled in a cart. On top was something covered in dark velvet cloth. "Want to see?"

"Do you have both outcomes?"

Shane nodded. "Which one do you want to see first?"

"If I let destiny slip."

Shane pulled away one of the velvet cloths. There, done in nearly black glass, was Oberon's face. His *fanged* face. "*She* wins."

Shane nodded. No one needed to spell out who *she* was. Titannia would somehow get to Oberon, change him into a dark, loathsome creature who would destroy the world on her command. And Robin would follow where he led, or die trying to stop him.

"Show me the other." The outcome he wanted least of all, but might stop Titannia in her tracks.

"As you wish." Shane lifted the second cloth.

It was magnificent, but whereas the last sculpture sent shivers down his spine this one evoked a sense of loss and loneliness. A lone figure stood in shining silver, head bowed, shoulders bent. Flowing down its back, a long sweep of metal he presumed to be the figure's hair crossed over the figure until the tips blended into glass and metal waves. The "foam" of the broken waves brushed the feet of the figure, and how Shane had gotten that effect he had no idea. The figure's features were blurred, but even without them was obvious something dear had been lost, maybe never to be found again. One glistening

127

hand reached toward the waves, either tossing something away or summoning something back.

A female figure rose from the waves, her upper body the only part of her visible. She reached for Oberon, their fingertips barely touching, a look of such pure yearning on her face that even Oberon was moved. Something about that figure in the water pulled at him.

Worse, he recognized the ornate pearl ring on her outstretched hand.

It couldn't be.

"A siren." The missing princess, to be precise.

"Yes." Shane smiled, the expression sympathetic. "You're going to go through hell, and in the end, the decision will still be yours."

"It's not possible. A mate covenant has already been written for her by her family."

Akane shrugged. "Find the loop in the hole."

Find the—? "You want me to find a way to break the mate covenant."

"I don't know if that's what you're supposed to do, but my mother wouldn't have told you that without a reason."

"She's right. I don't know how all of this is supposed to play out, but she's yours and you're hers." Shane pointed toward the black-fanged face. "The alternative is not an option."

On that, they agreed. Damn it. "Is she the one Robin has stashed away in his home?"

"Yes, but she left this morning."

"Oh?"

Shane grinned. "She has her own problem to take care of before you meet."

"You told her to go."

"I did." Shane crossed his arms, practically daring Oberon to take objection.

"Jethro." Akane, at least, had the sense to look appalled.

The Hob

"No, Akane. He has the chance to have the world in his hand, but he'd rather court disaster than a woman."

"I don't want the world. I never have. That was Titannia's folly, not mine."

Shane had the common sense to look abashed. "You know what I mean." And he hammered home his point by once more embracing his bondmate.

Oberon decided to change the subject. He had much to think on, but the hybrid had made his case. Oberon, for all his bluster, would not allow the Gray Court to fall. He would seek out the siren and make her his, whether he liked it or not. "Speaking of women, Robin, it appears, has found his mate."

"Excellent."

Shane appeared truly delighted for Robin, something Oberon marked in the hybrid's favor. Robin was easy to love, once you got to know him, but few took the time to do so. It was a tragic side effect of being the Hob, one they'd both learned to live with. "And she's human."

Shane's gaze became instantly worried. "Not so excellent."

Akane looked up at her truebond. "She'll need to be protected."

Shane shared a look with her that was full of amused affection. "Are you going to go eat the bad guys?"

"I'm thinking about it."

"That might give the babies indigestion, *mo chroí*."

"They'll get over it." She shot him an irritated look. "Besides, they're your kids. I'm pretty sure they'll eat dirt and shit diamonds."

"You're just irritated that you haven't opened the puzzle box yet."

"I hate you *so* much right now."

"Children." Really. How did Robin put up with them? It was like refereeing between two toddlers. "Jaden is guarding Robin's mate."

Shane shuddered. "He won't be enough. Nothing will be enough to save her."

The two hybrids exchanged a look that sent shivers down Oberon's spine. "What have you seen, Shane Joloun Dunne?"

The power of the High King compelled Shane to answer. "Her death."

Chapter Thirteen

Kael tossed a grape up into the air and caught it in his mouth. "Robin and Michaela, sittin' in a tree. K-i-s-s-i-n— Ow." He rubbed the back of his head where Robin had just smacked him.

Robin leaned on the back of Kael's chair and bent over until they were nearly cheek to cheek. He smiled sweetly. "It would be but the work of a moment to end you."

Kael coughed and wisely let it drop. "So. McNeil has a hard-on for Lord Wyght, and not in the fun, bed-filled way. Lady Malmayne is disdainful of them both and refuses to speak to Blackthorn. In fact, she's called for a different mediator, claiming Duncan Malmayne-Blackthorn is biased against her."

Duncan should be, as her new mate was now the head of the Black Court Malmaynes. Henri had never been very bright, but he was clever, and it had served him well. When Constance was destroyed by dark magic, Henri, with Cecelia's endorsement, had been declared the new head of the Clan. Surprisingly few had objected. Those who had, joined the Gray, as no Malmayne was welcome in the White Court any longer. Those who had chosen to join the Gray were currently under the rule of a young lord named Tristan Malmayne, who was doing his best to integrate them into Gray Court life as seamlessly as possible.

Once a Clan went Black, no member, no matter what their intentions, was allowed in the White Palace. They would be killed on sight on suspicion of being spies. Gloriana took no chances where Titannia was concerned.

Indeed, there was a good chance that Prince Evan would be killed before he ever reached his aunt's palace. Robin would put nothing past Gloriana. The boy had been in Black Court hands for weeks now. She would feel she had no choice but to destroy not only a potential subversive, but an embarrassment to her house. Knowing her as he did, Robin would not put it past her to blame either the Black Court, claiming ambush, or the Gray, claiming the Blades had failed to protect her kin. The White Court, lovely lemmings that they tended to be, would follow where her opinion led them.

Bah. At times they were no better nor worse than the Black, for all their posturing and holier-than-thou attitude.

Robin would offer the boy sanctuary. If he took it, he should be safe from Gloriana's fanatical ways. If not, Robin would at least know he'd tried.

"Lord Raven has been suspiciously absent from the proceedings, which is causing the Black to try and delay until their errant leader can be found."

Robin blinked. He'd been bouncing between guarding Michaela and attending the convention, ears wide open, leaving Kael and Duncan to deal with the actual negotiations. If Raven had been absent from the arbitration also, that could only mean one of two things.

He was stalking Michaela, or he was dealing with the boy.

He draped his arms around Kael's neck and pondered, ignoring the wild fluttering of Kael's pulse. The boy would learn his fear was well-earned, or he would not, depending on Robin's choice. "What room does the Raven Lord currently occupy?"

Kael rattled off a room number and Robin memorized it. "It's one of their executive suites, with a king bed. Plenty of room for his minions to gather and plot and mua-ha-ha without disturbing anyone."

Robin sighed. He would have to assign the boy to Akane and Jaden for in-depth training. The three of them would get along like oil and fire. Gods help them all.

"They even refuse to state their demands until the Fear Dearc is present, which is causing some tension with both the White Court delegation and Blackthorn."

"Damn." Unless they clearly stated what they wanted, Robin's hands were tied. "What does Duncan say?"

"Blackthorn believes it's a delaying tactic and I agree." Kael spun in his seat, his expression earnest. "There's something more going on here than Evan's kidnapping. Lady Malmayne, for all her bluster, is nervous as hell. McNeil won't let either her or Wyght out of his sight, even to take a piss. And he's getting more and more upset over the fact that the Fear Dearc wasn't there yesterday or the day before."

"And there are only three more days left to the convention we're using as a cover." Three more days to find Prince Evan and uncover Titannia's plot.

"Yes. We need to move, and fast."

Robin tapped his black nail against the table. "We need to get you into Lord Raven's room."

Kael took a deep breath and blew it out, nodding his agreement despite his fears. "Now that Jaden and Duncan Blackthorn are here, you don't need me to listen in. I'll be of more use to you in his room."

"Be careful. If Raven discovers your presence, your life will be forfeit, and not at my hand."

"I'm aware of that."

"Do well, and I will discuss your recruitment into the Blades with Oberon."

Kael started, his eyes wide with astonishment. "Are you serious?"

Robin's brow rose arrogantly.

"You are." Kael fell back against his chair and ran his hands down his face. "I'd accept, especially if it kept Evan from going home."

This time both of Robin's brows rose. "Then Gloriana does mean to rid herself of the boy."

"And my uncle, and his brother, and his mother."

Robin scowled. "That goes too far."

"She's become unreasonable. If they got to 'the half-breed', they might have gotten to the entire family. Since she lost the Malmaynes she's been monitoring the other Court Sidhe like prisoners of war who might escape at any moment. Some have disappeared from their Clan homes, and haven't been seen in weeks." Kael shook his head. "She's always been tough, but she's never been this bad before."

Robin growled, the sound inhuman. "This needs to be brought to Oberon's attention immediately."

"I think she's insane."

Kael's whisper could easily be construed as treason if heard by the wrong ears. Robin had to act fast if he were to save Kael. Not even Robin knew the extent of Gloriana's powers when it came to those who owed her fealty.

Robin grabbed Kael by the collar and swept him to the Gray Palace. He marched him into Oberon's study, bowing before his king. "Swear fealty to the Gray, Kael. Now."

Kael, his face pale, got down on one knee immediately. "I hereby renounce all ties to the White Lady, Queen Gloriana, Queen of the White Court, Lady of the Seelie. I declare myself Oberon's man from this day forth, in honor and in faith, having no other oaths to forswear. By the gods I pledge my loyalty to the Gray Court, High King Oberon and his descendants. I declare myself the sworn servant of the Gray Lord, High King Oberon, King of the Gray Court, Lord over the Fae. I pledge my sword and my honor to uphold the laws of the Court. I and my house will abide by the laws handed down by the High King. I will faithfully perform all services required by Crown and Court. So swear I, Lord Kael Oren."

Oberon's expression was calm, but his gaze was pure, icy silver. "I, High King Oberon, the Gray Lord, Lord of the Fae, hereby hear your oaths and accept them in the name of Crown and Court. I declare you our loyal servant, sworn to our bidding. From this day forth my sword shall defend you, my magic protect you, and my wrath be mighty should you fail of your duty. All former oaths to the White are hereby null and void, by my power as High King. So swear I, Oberon, High King."

Kael quivered as the weight of Oberon's magic settled over him. He was now Gray Court, bound to Oberon.

"I wish to sponsor Kael into the Blades."

Oberon's calm facade cracked. "What is this about, my Hob?"

Robin nudged at Kael until the pooka stood. "Tell him."

So Kael did, outlining for Oberon Gloriana's attempts to halt any further incursions into her Court by the Black. When he was done, Robin took over. Oberon needed to know that Robin had not brought the boy here on a whim. Kael's life was in danger the moment the words had left his lips. Once Gloriana was declared queen, her powers had grown to match those of Titannia, keeping the queens perfectly balanced. It was entirely possible she could hear her name spoken on the lips of those sworn to her. If so...

This was the only way to save Kael from a charge of treason.

Oberon sighed and pinched the bridge of his nose. "I'm going to request that you join the Blackthorn Clan."

Robin laughed, delighted, even as Kael scowled. "Why, if I may be so bold as to ask?"

Oberon shot the pooka an amused glance. "Because something tells me you'll fit right in." The look he shot Robin was less amused. "I had an interesting discussion with the Seer and Shane Dunne today."

"Interesting how?" This was bad. If Oberon knew about Michaela, he could order Robin to bring her here.

Wait a moment. That was actually a *good* idea. If Oberon was aware that Michaela was Robin's truebond, he would protect her with his life.

"I know that the girl you had hidden in your library was the missing siren, Princess Cassandra Nerice."

"Oh?" This was not good. Why did Shane have to give away his secret? Shane was the one who'd sent Cassie to Robin in the first place. He should have known, better than anyone, that Cassie wished her presence to remain quiet.

"*Hobgoblin.*"

Merde. "Yes, my king?"

"'Heart and soul return to thee when Oberon goes into the sea.'"

Robin tilted his head. "What does that mean?" He had a bad feeling about this.

Oberon leaned forward, and Robin shivered at the expression on the High King's face. "It means that, according to the Seer, the woman I must mate in order to save the Gray Court was in your home."

Oh, hell. "Was?" Had Cassie left without notifying him? If so, why?

"Shane told her to go. Why, I have no idea. He refused to explain it to me."

That sounded like Shane. "If Shane told her to go, he had a very good reason for it."

"You trust him, then."

"I do." Strangely enough, Robin did. The entire family was home to him. He missed them far more than he'd thought possible. He wanted to take Michaela to meet them, almost as much as he wanted Oberon to approve of her. Ruby was going to love her. Moira, Jaden and Duncan already did. And Aileen would mother her just as she did Akane and Ruby.

Oberon reluctantly nodded his head and straightened up. "So be it, then."

"Just one thing, my king. If Shane tells you to do something or go somewhere, go." If Oberon ignored Shane's directive, the ending he was striving to avoid would come to pass, of that Robin had no doubt.

Oberon nodded again. "I will."

"Is that all, my liege?"

Oberon frowned. "No." He sighed and pushed his hair out of his face, the silver strands settling behind him, neat as a pin. The day Robin saw Oberon mussed and uncaring about it was the day the world as he knew it came to an end. "Shane saw something else as well."

"What?" He didn't like Oberon's tone. He'd gone formal and cold, something he rarely was when speaking with Robin. He caught Kael shivering out of the corner of his eye and realized the pooka was reacting to his king.

Oberon's eyes paled to almost white. "Jaden will not be enough to protect your mate."

Robin's claws and fangs descended. His eyes glowed. "Then I will protect her myself."

Oberon sighed. "Hobgoblin—"

Robin refused to hear more. He'd left his bondmate, his *truebond*, behind to bring Kael here, and while he did not regret his actions, he needed to get back. If Jaden was not enough, then let the world face the Hob.

He was ready for it.

He grabbed Kael and, in a swirl of darkness, left the High King's home.

"So? Still don't want to go to a fairy convention?"

Oberon sighed again and pinched the bridge of his nose. "I hate you so much."

"Aw, shucks." Shane Dunne stepped into the room with a grin. "And I was going to ask Ma to adopt you."

Oberon shuddered, and Shane laughed. Oberon found himself reluctantly returning the hybrid's smile. "Where is Akane?"

"Cleaning out your fridge."

"You realize this is the Gray Palace?" The odds of Akane eating the contents of his kitchen were miniscule.

Shane's brows rose. "She's a pregnant dragon."

Oberon blinked. "I'd better order takeout."

"You'd better head to Philadelphia." The grin fell off Shane's face. "Trust me, you *need* to be there."

Oberon nodded. "Robin warned me to follow your directions."

Shane winced. "Believe me, the consequences of ignoring my visions are worse than what happens if you obey them."

"How bad will following them be?"

Shane grimaced. "Bad."

Wonderful.

Chapter Fourteen

"Where to next?"

Michaela consulted the brochure. "Flower arranging?"

Moira snored.

"How to tell the magical properties of gemstones?"

Moira snored again.

"Fine." Michaela sniffed and turned the page. "Oh, how about a discussion on the fae in *A Midsummer Night's Dream*?"

Moira gagged.

"Hey, I like Puck in that."

Moira giggled. "I bet he'd *love* to hear that."

"Huh?" Michaela frowned at Moira, who'd gone pale. "Are you all right?"

"I'm fine." Moira's wan smile didn't fool Michaela for an instant.

"Are you sure? We could skip—"

"And what trouble are you two plotting, hmm?" The deep, purring voice of her fantasy man vibrated through Michaela, making her wish she could rub against him like a tabby cat.

Michaela turned to find the stunning redhead calling himself Robin Goodfellow standing just behind her, a wicked grin on his arresting face. She felt a blush stain her cheeks. "Hi."

Robin bowed and took her hand. "Michaela." He lifted his hand to her lips and kissed the tips of her fingers, his gaze never once leaving hers. "Always a pleasure."

The way he purred that last had her shivering with want. She swallowed, hoping to get some moisture into her suddenly dry mouth. "You too." Gah. She sounded like Minnie Mouse on helium. She cleared her throat and hoped the dogs in the neighborhood would forgive her someday for that assault on their ears, because she was pretty sure nothing human had heard her. "Ah, we were just discussing which workshop to sit in on."

There. That sounded totally normal.

"Well, then." Robin took her hand and placed it on his arm. "Why not consider—"

"Michaela. Fancy meeting you here. And in such…interesting company." Raven swept her a bow and took hold of her free hand. "Would you like to accompany me to an artist's panel?"

Michaela bit her lip. The chance to sit in on one of those was intriguing. She glanced at Moira to get her reaction. After all, she'd promised to spend the day with her.

Moira looked ready to pass out. She was so pale Michaela was ready to check her blood pressure. "What about *A Midsummer Night's Dream*?"

"What about it?" Raven shot Moira a glare before turning a charming smile on Michaela. "I could draw whatever character you wish for you."

She grinned. She knew just what character she'd love to hang on her apartment walls. "Can you draw Robin Goodfellow?"

Robin threw his head back and laughed. "Yes, MacSweeney, why don't you run off and draw Robin Goodfellow. In the meantime, I will escort Michaela and Moira to the talk on *A Midsummer Night's Dream*."

"Do you want me to show her the true face of the Hob?" Raven's voice was so full of soft menace Michaela was stunned. "Do you think she will still want you after the truth is revealed?"

What the hell were they talking about? The true face of the Hob? Who on earth was the Hob? The man beside her, calling himself Robin Goodfellow? And why was that supposed to frighten her off?

Something hinky was going on.

Robin's glare should have worried Michaela. The way his eyes went from brilliant blue to a startling green was even scarier, but she wasn't afraid the way she should have been.

Robin, like Ringo, would never harm her.

Robin tugged Michaela close and placed his arm around her shoulders. The warm scent of his skin filled her senses. *God, he even smells the same.* "Michaela is already mine."

"Then say you are mine."

The words her dream Robin had spoken came back to her. He'd used that same tone of voice then as well. He'd had no doubt what her answer would be, and had demanded it as his due.

Michaela blinked. She was acting as if everything in that dream had been real, but that was impossible. Right? She stared up at Robin, her heart pounding.

He looked *exactly* like her Robin. Right down to the teeny tiny beauty mark on his chin.

Right?

Moira grimaced, her gaze darting between the three of them. "Um. Aren't we meeting Ringo for lunch right after the next workshop?"

Ringo. Aw, crap. What the hell was she thinking? None of it was possible. Her Robin was just a dream. He couldn't be real.

Could he?

Michaela tried to tug herself free of Robin's grasp, but his grip firmed. He leaned down and whispered in her ear, sending more delightful shivers down her spine. "It will be all right, Michaela. Ringo will not object to you being with me."

She nearly choked on her own drool at a sudden vision of how she wanted to *be* with him. Oh boy, did she want to *be* with him.

"What a delightful imagination you have, my dear." Robin's breath tickled her ear and she shuddered. "We'll have to explore that later."

She was in such deep doo-doo. She looked up at Robin and smiled weakly. "I think Moira and I need to go." She needed to get her head examined. Why was she so attracted to two men? Why couldn't she be like normal people, and have one guy, one love?

Then she looked at Moira and wondered if maybe she was more like her newfound friend than she thought. The idea of being the meat in a Robin-Ringo sandwich was incredibly seductive. But then she thought about how high-maintenance such a relationship would be. Two guys to cook for, to clean for. To do laundry for. Two guys to argue over the remote with, to hog all the computer time, to pick up socks for.

Two guys who would make her every sexual desire come true. And hey, they could do the kitty litter, if she ever broke down and finally got a cat.

Ugh. Yup. It was time to find a nice, quiet loony bin and stare at some pretty white walls for a while.

"Then I will speak with you soon." And before she could react Robin swooped down, cradled her in his arms, and claimed her mouth, kissing her with a raw passion that turned her insides to jelly.

He tastes just like he did in the dream. Just...maple syrupy too.

She soon forgot about the sweet taste in Robin's mouth as the kiss stole her breath, her wits and her knees. She damn near collapsed, only held up by Robin's strong arm around her waist.

I'd better pack my bikini, 'cause I'm going to hell. Michaela returned Robin's kiss with fervor, burying her hands in his rich, fiery hair. It had a different texture from Ringo's, throwing her off, but his kiss...

Dear God, they kiss the same. Robin's kiss was nearly identical to Ringo's. So what the hell did that mean? Unless...

Nah. No way was Robin Goodfellow real. Things like that just didn't happen to a boring nurse from Philadelphia. No way, no how.

Robin broke the kiss and stroked her cheek, his expression full of the same longing she'd seen on Ringo's face not two hours before.

But oh, how she wished they did.

Robin watched Michaela and Moira head off, Michaela's steps wobbly and uncertain, Jaden barely visible in their wake. The vampire's powers were growing fast if he could pull such a trick off. Perhaps that was why fate had seen fit to give him two mates. Jaden would need to feed more than other vampires if he used his powers so often.

Raven was glaring at him, but Robin did not care. He'd staked his claim before the Fear Dearc, and now there was but one more thing more to take care of. "On the roof. Now."

Robin stepped into a doorway and disappeared, reappearing on the roof of the hotel.

The Raven Lord appeared soon after. He placed his hands on his hips, but he eyed Robin warily.

Good. The boy should fear him. He'd seen the way Raven tensed when he'd taken Michaela's mouth in front of him, how he'd held back a growl when Michaela, stunned, her lips swollen and her cheeks flushed, had stumbled in Moira's wake.

"Now what?"

Robin examined his nails. "Now you leave Michaela alone."

Raven snorted, amused. "No."

Robin glared at him through his lashes, allowing his eyes to glow so brightly they rivaled the noonday sun. "Yes." If Raven were the threat to his truebond, he would soon be a threat no more.

Something flashed through Raven's eyes, something startlingly familiar. He'd seen something similar recently, that flash of green that marked the children of the Hob. Raven's eyes had looked eerily similar to Jaden's. Robin tilted his head, studying Raven.

Now that he allowed himself to look at him, Raven had Robin's look about him. He, too, was slender, as was the Hob. His blue eyes were a close match to his, as well. His black nails tapped impatiently against his black leather belt, but his hair blew around him *against* the breeze.

The boy had sylph blood in him, then. That would explain his connection to ravens. Robin himself had a way with the creatures of the earth. Earth sprites were by turns drawn to him and terrified of him, something that had served him well. Even Moira, who cared for him, was wary of him.

Raven attacked first, as Robin had known he would. He disappeared in a swirl of dark smoke, only to reappear behind Robin. He took a swipe at Robin with his claws, but Robin was no longer there, disappearing in a similar swirl of dark mist.

The wind changed, and Robin scented it again, that elusive scent tantalizing him, taunting him with might-have-beens and deliberately forgotten dreams.

That earthy, feral aroma could not be Robin's. There was no way one of the worst of Titania's lackeys was his child.

"I will protect her, even from you." Raven disappeared again, but this time stayed gone. Robin stilled, stretching out with his senses, waiting for Raven to try again. He hated to admit it, but the boy had guts. Hobart had barely fought, choosing instead to beg for his life and that of his lover, Constance.

Robin had destroyed Hobart, leaving nothing behind but the thick, black sludge that ran through his veins, the same sludge that had poisoned and nearly killed Shane Dunne.

Robin wished things could have turned out differently. Hobart Klaussner, the man who'd tortured Shane and somehow brought the Child of Dunne prophecy to pass, had been his child, but had been nothing like the Raven Lord. He'd operated under the radar, born of a mother who'd once been a pooka but was changed into a vampire halfway through her pregnancy by Titannia. That was the only way the bitch queen could have laid her hands on one of his progeny, of that Robin had been certain.

He'd been a fluke, nothing more. He had to have been. If not...

Robin could not have lost another unknown child to that black-hearted bitch.

Raven popped into the air above him, nearly getting the drop on him. Robin dodged, impressed, and lashed out. He took a chunk of Raven's coat with him.

The boy might be his, but he certainly didn't have Robin's fashion sense. He dressed completely in black, like the raven he took his name from. Robin had yet to see him in any color.

Raven snarled at him. "Stay away from Michaela. She is *mine.*"

Robin laughed, evading the swipe Raven aimed at him with ease. "What care I for your words? Michaela has a mind of her own. She will decide which of us she wants, and there is not a damn thing you can do about it."

The Fear Dearc leapt into the air, his movements so swift Robin could barely follow them, avoiding Robin's return blow. He landed on the edge of the building and perched there in a pose that was so familiar Robin's heart broke. "You are no Sidhe, to Claim her against her will."

"Neither are you, it would seem." Robin straightened from his crouch. Hell and damnation. There was no longer any doubt in his mind.

This boy, this Black Court parasite, was one of Robin's get.

The arrogant smile on Raven's face turned bitter. Luminescent green fire danced in his eyes. "Finally figured it out, did you, Father?" He tilted his head, the gesture birdlike.

"How?" How had two of Robin's children wound up in Titannia's hands?

"The Dark Queen pays your women handsomely for your seed."

What? Robin froze in place, his attention fixed solely on the Fear Dearc, the Raven Lord. Baddest of the Black Court fae, save for Bres and the Black Queen herself.

But for all his reputation, Robin saw something in Raven's face, something quickly hidden, that made his heart stutter in his chest.

Longing. The same longing Robin felt each time he saw Michaela, or watched the Dunnes and their mates together. The same longing that had been in Aileen Dunne's eyes when her son had been missing, stolen by the Malmaynes in an attempt to get Leo Dunne's attention.

The boy wanted his father the way Robin wanted his children, but was too terrified to do anything about it.

"Indeed. She even allowed my mother the privilege of living. Be grateful to her. If she hadn't, I'd have been an even bigger bastard. She was the only gentleness I knew." Raven's smile softened, lost its bitter edge. "Michaela reminds me of her."

Raven was lying. He had to be. There could not be more of them out there, lost in the Black.

"Father?"

The mocking edge to Raven's voice was impossible to miss. The building beneath his feet trembled, nearly sending Raven over the edge. Without thought, Robin moved to save the boy.

His boy.

He grabbed Raven's arm, ignoring the claws that were suddenly embedded in his side, and pulled Raven off the edge. Dark poison pumped uselessly into his veins. No one had bothered to inform Raven that Robin was immune to it, an advantage Robin had been forced to use in his fight with Hobart. The vampiric pooka had been resistant to dying. Robin had been forced to make an example out of him. He'd prayed for the lost child he'd never known, his soul crying out for what had needlessly been lost forever.

If Titannia had, indeed, been taking his children, raising them in her image...

Raven stumbled against him, and that elusive scent, the one that had bothered Robin from the start, filled his senses. Under the stink of Titannia and sylph lay Robin's own feral tang. He could deny all he wished, but there was no longer any doubt.

Titannia had taken another one of his children from him.

Robin screeched in rage, the sound shattering the metal door behind them and cracking the tar and concrete of the roof.

Raven, his deep blue-green eyes filled with fear, tried to back away, but Robin would not allow it.

"How?"

Raven stilled, as a human would when facing a hungry tiger. "How what? That's a rather broad question."

"The Black Queen. How did she get to your mother?" Robin barely remembered the night he'd spent with the sylph, but her scent was all over their son, dark and swarming with fae magic. Combined with Titannia's, it had nearly obliterated Robin's. Only the tantalizing whiffs of Robin in his blood had saved Raven from death.

"You didn't know."

Robin frowned. That wasn't the answer he'd been expecting, nor was the strange wonder in Raven's voice.

The green fire in Raven's eyes died. He eyed Robin warily now, but his claws and fangs were sheathed. "Titannia always told us that you'd sold us."

Robin took a deep breath. Mandates of the gods or not, Titannia needed to die a slow, agonizing death. Robin knew just the Hob to deliver it to her. "No. I would never sell my children." He'd longed for a true family for centuries, and now his son stood before him, willing to hear him out.

Raven relaxed even further in Robin's grasp. "If that's so, then she's lied to us all."

Us all. Robin's worst fears were becoming realized. "How many of you are there?" Robin held on to his anger by a thin, easily broken thread. Too much more and he'd lose it, and the building would collapse beneath his feet.

He had to maintain his control. Michaela was in the building. There was nothing Robin would not do to ensure her safety.

"More than you'd hope, less than you fear."

He closed his eyes and prayed. "A number, if you please."

"Six—no, five, now that the highly annoying Hobart is dead. And not all of them are displeased to be there."

Robin's eyes popped open. "Were you?"

One of Raven's dark brows quirked upward. "Need you ask?"

Indeed. If Raven had been happy under Titannia he would now be sitting in the delegate's chair below, not confronting his lost father. "Then why did you not seek me out?"

Raven laughed, the sound bitter beyond words. "Seek out Robin Goodfellow, the Hobgoblin himself? Boogeymen frighten their children with tales of you."

Well. He had to admit, Raven had a point.

"It was drummed into us that even entertaining the thought of running to the Gray Court and begging for sanctuary would bring your wrath down upon our heads and the heads of what loved ones we dared to have. No. Coming to you was not an option any of us dared contemplate."

"I would have protected you. All of you." From Oberon himself, if need be.

"Even Hobart?" Raven grimaced. "There are those of us who enjoy the attentions of the Dark Queen."

That did not sound good. "What do you mean, attentions?"

Raven shuddered. "Each of us is forced to lie with her, to give her our seed so that she might bear a child with your power and her dark heart."

Robin, for the first time in centuries, felt nauseous. "She's *leannan Sidhe,* a vampire. She cannot bear children." Vampires were infertile, even the original. Titannia must have been desperate indeed to please her demon lord, if she tried to bear fruit in an empty womb.

"Her Majesty is not the most stable leg on the table." Raven grinned, the expression a pale imitation of his usual arrogant look. "Why aren't you still trying to kill me? Because I share your blood? Don't think that will stop me from claiming Michaela."

Robin growled. "Make no mistake. Michaela is mine." He shook his head, staring at the boy who looked nothing like him, but was more his son than any he'd faced before. "But so are you."

Raven, obviously stunned, laughed. "We'll see about that."

He moved to leap off the edge of the building, but Robin held out his hand, stopping him. "Wait. Your brothers and sisters. Is there a way to contact them?"

Raven scowled. "I am the youngest, and the least under Titannia's thumb. I would trust none of the others, were I you." He sighed, perhaps reading Robin's determination to save as many as he could. "Fine. I'll see what I can do. In the meantime, Father—" Raven's form blurred, "—prepare to fight for her."

Robin watched as his son launched himself from the rooftop with a raucous, mocking cry. "So be it."

Chapter Fifteen

Oberon swirled into being and stared at the strange humans in front of him. He could not believe some of the lengths they would go to in order to imitate the fae.

He shook his head and straightened his pearl-gray suit. His hair was bound in a tail at the nape of his neck by a titanium clasp with the symbol of his Court etched into it, the dark gray metal a foil for the symbol. A triple spiral triskelion, the bottom two spirals were white and black enamel, to represent the White and Black Courts. But the upper spiral, the one above them both, was done in pure, shining silver, the arms of the spiral reaching down to touch the white and the black, blending into them. It doubled as his crown when he was away from Court, and declared that the High King was present on official business. Silver glasses with gray lenses hid his eyes.

Some of the true fae attending the con saw him and quickly averted their eyes, aware that if the High King were present something must be wrong.

It was, and Oberon was uncertain how to deal with it. Shane had told him his presence was necessary in Philadelphia, but had refused to tell him why. Even pressing him with his power had not elicited a response, a fact that still stunned him. Shane had given in when pressed about Robin's truebond, but would not do so when asked why Oberon was needed in Philadelphia. All he'd done was wish him the same as the Seer.

"Pleasant dreams."

It was strange, and Oberon did not care for it one little bit, especially in light of the highly erotic dreams he'd been having lately. All of them revolved around a woman with huge turquoise eyes and long, pale limbs that glimmered in the light like they were dotted with tiny scales. Now he knew the name of the woman, and his heart hardened.

Princess Cassandra Nerice.

He might be forced into a matebond, but his half a heart would remain his own.

He walked up to the registration desk and requested the key to his room. Since there had been a slim chance that the delegation would require his direct intervention to reach an accord, he'd discreetly booked a room in the hotel. He refused to share space with Robin and Kael. City apartments were far too small for his taste, and he did not own one of the larger condos in Philadelphia. New York, Rome, Paris and Vienna, yes. Philadelphia, no. He'd been contemplating a home in Hong Kong, until he learned Titannia's Court was currently stationed in Beijing.

He'd be purchasing a home in Tokyo instead. And now that the dark queen was no longer in Russia, he might even consider a home in Moscow.

Oberon smiled at the girl behind the counter, amused when she blushed furiously. She was certainly cute, but not to his taste. There was no woman who could turn his head, despite what Shane had decreed. Oberon would never again be vulnerable to a woman's wiles. There was far too much at stake to allow his heart to become engaged.

"Sire?" Oberon turned, card key in hand, to find Duncan Malmayne-Blackthorn standing there, a frown on his face. "Should you be here?"

Oberon looked down at the key card in his hand. "According to your brother-in-law Shane, yes."

Duncan paled. "Ah. I see."

"I doubt that." When Duncan's brow rose, Oberon decided to explain. The man was, by truebond, mated to Robin's blood, and therefore family in a roundabout way. When Robin had given Jaden his blood it had changed him. Robin had inadvertently created a bond that was just as strong, just as familial, as that of a truebond, making Robin, in a round-about way, Jaden's sire. It was why Oberon had accepted Jaden as Robin's when his Hob had pointed it out to him. It had also allowed for the formation of Clan Blackthorn, a clan that accepted those of all the fae races and their human mates, giving not just Gray Court vampires, but hobgoblins, redcaps, Sidhe mated to vampires, even banshees, a clan to call their own. Robin's claim, and considerable influence, kept the rumblings in court to a minimum. It was the first time a vampire had ever been given lordship over a clan, and Oberon almost looked forward to what the Malmayne-Blackthorns would do with it. "There is an issue with Robin that needs my attention."

"Michaela." Duncan gestured and Oberon followed, content to let the other man lead him to a quiet spot in the hotel's bar. "It seems the Hob has found his truebond."

"Indeed, and I fear for both of them."

"Because of MacSweeney?" Duncan smiled sweetly at their waitress, earning himself a charming blush. "Coffee, please."

"Pinot grigio. Please." He waited until the waitress had left before answering. "I have no clue where the threat lies." He leaned forward, hoping Duncan would see the dilemma he found himself in. "Shane says nothing can stop this Michaela's death."

Duncan's skin flashed with silver sparkles before he got himself under control. "That would be bad."

"More like catastrophic, but yes. More, I need Robin focused on the negotiations. Gloriana is beginning to agitate, wondering when her errant nephew will be returned to her."

Duncan snorted. "I agree with Robin and Jaden. She'll kill the boy. He's been in Black Court hands too long."

Oberon nodded. "If he's untainted I will offer him sanctuary." It was one of many reasons he'd agreed to come to Philadelphia.

"What do we do about Michaela?"

The Hob

Put her under a glass jar until Robin could attend to her properly. Oberon had no illusions. Until the bond had been established, Robin would be unable to leave Michaela's side. No matter how he wished otherwise, his Hob's loyalties were now divided.

For that, Oberon could cheerfully throttle the human.

"We protect her as best we can. Move her to the Palace if need be. For now, keep her under watch and protected at all costs."

"Yes, sire. But first, allow me to contact Jaden to escort you to your room."

"No need." Oberon began to wave his hand in dismissal, but Duncan stopped him.

"There is more going on than the kidnapping of a prince, my liege. Please. I would never forgive myself if something happened to you."

He could not fault the Sidhe's sincerity. "Very well. Contact your bondmate, then."

The relief on Duncan's face would have been comical had he not caught sight of the woman standing next to Duncan's wife. Dark of hair and eye, she barely stood five feet tall. The most hideous orange and black butterfly wings graced her back. A pale green glow surrounded her, the mark of Robin obvious for any of Tuatha Dè blood to see.

The Hob had marked her as his, and may the gods help them all, Oberon would do his best to protect her.

Michaela darted past some pretty strange-looking fairies, praying none of them stepped on her gown. The dress had cost her a pretty penny, but it was so damn worth it. The moment she'd seen it, she'd fallen in love.

Hell, she wanted to be *married* in the thing.

Her A-line, princess-style gown was sleeveless, with intricate beading and crystals outlining the shirred waist and dotting the bust line. The skirt was also sprinkled with crystals and beads, making the mesh sparkle like raindrops on mist. When she'd described the color of the dress to Amanda, her friend had wrinkled her nose, wondering how lavender mesh over a pale mint green could work, but the effect was iridescent, and Michaela felt like she'd dressed in the ocean itself. The effect was beautiful and ethereal, and Michaela was in love. She felt like a modern-day Cinderella, down to her silver and crystal sandals and the tiara on her head. She had even found lavender- and mint-green wings that matched her dress perfectly and sprinkled them with silver glitter. She'd curled her long hair and swept it over one shoulder, keeping it loose and pretty. The only thing missing was jewelry, as she hadn't found anything she liked before it was too late to order it.

If the guys she snowboarded with knew how much she'd spent on an outfit she'd only get to wear once, and not for her wedding, they'd laugh their asses off.

"Michaela."

She shivered. She had no idea how to face him after that scorching kiss with Robin, but she had to. "Ringo." She looked over at him and laughed, hoping it didn't give away how nervous she was. "You look wonderful."

"Do I?" He preened, fluffing out his dark tail, touching his ears to make sure they were still in place. He'd dressed in black fox ears and a tail, a black button down shirt and slacks. The black nails were a nice touch.

"Although I have to admit, I'm surprised you don't have more than one tail." Kitsune, Japanese fox spirits like the one Ringo had dressed as, only had one tail if they were very young. A Kitsune could have up to nine tails, signifying great age and wisdom.

One dark brow quirked upward. Something about his expression reminded her of Robin. "How many do you think I should have had?"

"Nine." Odd. Her instincts told her that if Ringo really were a Kitsune, he'd be among the most powerful.

He smiled slowly. "Indeed." He took her hand and placed it on his arm, his thumb caressing the back. "Shall we dance?"

She tilted her head back and put on her best haughty face. "Yes, we shall."

He chuckled as he led her into the room.

"Oh, there's Duncan." She waved at Moira's husband, smiling when he waved back.

"Would you like to sit with them?"

"You don't mind?" She was already steering them that way, so she hoped not.

"No, not at all."

She didn't miss the slightly mocking edge to his tone, but she didn't necessarily want to be alone with Ringo right now. Not when she was so loaded down with guilt.

She'd sort of cheated with Ringo by kissing Robin. Except they'd only had two dates, and hadn't declared themselves exclusive. So it wasn't really cheating, but it felt like it. On the other hand, Robin had mentioned that Ringo wouldn't mind them being together. He spoke as if he knew Ringo very well, which meant she was breaking the number one dating rule: do not date the friend of the guy you're dating. Unless they shared women the way Jaden and Duncan apparently did, which meant it might work out. Or they didn't, which meant she was cheating, but she wasn't, because they weren't officially dating, and—

Gah. Now she was getting a headache. Maybe she should just hide in her room until the con was over and avoid them both. She snuck a peek at Ringo as he greeted Duncan, startled all over again at how she'd managed to attract the attention of someone so beautiful, both inside and out. Out of the corner of her eye she caught a glimpse of red hair, and her heart nearly stopped. She nearly gave herself whiplash checking to see if it was Robin, but it was just some lady in a bright red wig and black wings. Her heart stuttered back to life and pounded mercilessly.

She was *so* doomed.

Ringo shook hands with Duncan. The blond had dressed as, of all things, Prince Charming, complete with a bejeweled plastic sword. It looked oddly appropriate on him. "Where are Jaden and Moira?"

"On the dance floor." Duncan gestured, and Michaela laughed. Jaden was a demon on the dance floor, despite his green tights. He'd come as Peter Pan, complete with the red feather in his cap. But it was Moira who held everyone's gaze. Dressed in a skin-tight, sequined Tinkerbell costume, the redhead commanded everyone's attention as she gyrated around her tall, dark and handsome husband.

Duncan was shaking his head. "I told him he should have dressed as a Lost Boy, but Moira overrode me. She said if anyone was Peter Pan, it was Jaden." He shrugged. "What could I say? She's right."

"Peter Pan *is* the ultimate Lost Boy. Besides, his ass looks fabulous in those tights." Michaela blinked when she suddenly had the undivided attention of both men. "What?"

Duncan coughed, but it was obvious he was biting back a laugh. "Would you care to sit at our table?"

Michaela nodded before Ringo could respond.

"We'd be delighted." Ringo helped her into a chair, but his hand tightened on her own. He leaned down and whispered in her ear, making butterflies dance in her stomach. "I *will* find out what has you so on edge today, my dear."

She looked up at him, startled. He'd sounded exactly like Robin. Blazing blue eyes glared down at her before he turned away, answering some question of Duncan's she hadn't even heard.

What the *fuck* was going on? Maybe she was going crazy, because...

Because for just one second, he'd looked *exactly* like a dark-haired Robin Goodfellow.

"You need to be more careful." Duncan sipped his drink as they watched Moira and Michaela dance around each other. Michaela looked like a true faery queen, delicate, ethereal and regal all at the same time. Right up until she started doing squat thrusts.

Robin started to laugh as Michaela and Moira began to bump their asses together.

Jaden, who'd gone for his own drink, returned and watched the women with a puzzled expression. "Robin? Why is my mate bumping uglies with your mate?"

"Jaden," Duncan sighed.

"Is that supposed to be dancing? Or a new kind of martial art?"

Duncan grinned and put his arm around his mate. "Fae butt boxing?"

Jaden laughed and snuggled closer to Duncan, to the surprise of some of the party goers watching them. Robin had to admit, they made a striking couple, but they were stunning when Moira was with them. "My money's on Moira. Sorry, Robin, but your bondmate is teeny."

Robin shook his head. Michaela might be teeny, but she was mighty, as anyone who went up against her would discover.

"When will Robin make his appearance?"

Duncan might have looked nonchalant, but Robin could see the nerves building in the Sidhe as he watched the women. "Why do you ask?"

"McNeil is here, as is MacSweeney." Duncan risked shooting Robin a glance. "Oberon is as well."

157

"Bloody hell." Robin thrust his drink at Jaden. "Guard the king. I'll return anon."

Robin stomped off, aware that, on his orders, his Blade had gone from happily cuddling with his mate to deadly predator. Robin ducked into the men's room, relieved to find it empty. He stared in the mirror and allowed the change to flow over him. His scalp itched as his hair grew, turned bright red. His brown eyes went to sparkling blue. He pulled the ears and the tail off as his simple black outfit changed to his more traditional garb. The urge to show off for his mate was strong. Tight, white pants were tucked into blinding white leather boots with a black sole and heel. He added a matching white suit jacket over a black shirt, open at the neck, and a silver chain with the symbol of the Gray Court dangling from it. Robin allowed his eyes to go green and his black nails to grow to claws, knowing it would be both a warning and a threat to any who dared approach his truebond.

He left the tail and ears on the counter for any who wanted them. He would no longer need them. The charade of Ringo was, for the most part, done. If Oberon were here at the convention then, by damn, so officially was Robin Goodfellow.

Robin entered the ball and immediately scanned the area for Michaela. There she was, surrounded by three of the people he considered his, laughing and chatting as if she had not a care in the world.

He would see to it that she remained that carefree. He made his way to her side, slipping his arm around her waist. "Michaela, my dear."

She jumped, her gaze darting around the room like a startled bird. "Robin. Hi."

He almost laughed at the guilt in her expression. She didn't hide it nearly as well as she thought she did. She must be looking for Ringo in the crowd, wondering when her other suitor would arrive and, no doubt, fight Robin for her.

It was amusing to watch her try and figure out how to wiggle her way out of this one. While Robin had no intention of letting her suffer, the knowledge that she was torn between his two personas tickled him greatly.

"Robin, you look stunning, as always."

Robin bowed to Moira. "Why thank you. You look charming yourself."

"Who are you dressed as?"

Robin caressed Michaela's bare arm, careful of his claws. He had no desire to mar her soft flesh. "Why, Robin Goodfellow, of course."

Moira grinned. "Of course."

Jaden nudged him with his elbow, nearly dislodging Michaela from Robin's grasp. "Warning, dickhead at three o'clock."

Robin glared at Jaden before turning to see who Jaden was speaking of. "Raven." He tilted his head in greeting at his erstwhile son.

Raven glanced at Robin's arm around Michaela's waist and smiled. "Michaela, you look enchanting this evening." He picked up Michaela's hand and pressed a kiss against her soft skin. "May I have this dance?"

As they'd just started a slow song, one meant to snuggle into your partner to, Robin thought not. "My apologies, Raven. This dance is already promised to me." Robin swept Michaela onto the dance floor and pulled her close. The scent of her, the feel of her soft skin, the strength in her supple waist, filled his senses to damn near overflowing. He forgot all about McNeil, Raven, even Oberon, as the wonder of finally holding his truebond, acknowledging his claim to her in public, filled him with peace the likes of which he'd never known before.

"Um, Robin?"

"Yes, my dear?" Robin lifted the tiara from her curls and nuzzled his cheek against her hair, rubbing his scent on her like a cat.

"Hey, that's... Never mind. There's something I need to tell you."

"Hmm?" He pressed a kiss to the top of her head. He did not care for the way her voice shook.

"I... I'm here with someone else."

He pressed his face into her hair and smiled. He'd made the tiara disappear. His bondmate would wear true gems, not paste and glass. "Ringo won't mind, my sweet."

She looked up at him, and her expression was so full of sorrow he wanted to kick his own ass for making her feel even a moment's pain. "But I do. I feel like I'm cheating on him when I'm with you, and I feel like I'm doing the same when I'm with him."

"And this bothers you." When she nodded, he sighed. "If I give you my word that Ringo has no objection, will you take it?"

She shook her head. "I can't. Not until I speak with him."

He pulled her even closer. "You're an honorable woman, Michaela Exton." And far too good for the likes of him.

"I'm attracted to you both, and I don't know what to do about it."

He placed his finger under her chin and tilted her face up to his. Even without the tiara, she still looked like a queen. "May I make a suggestion?"

"Sure."

He chuckled. "No need to look as if you're facing the firing squad, my sweet. My suggestion is this. Meet with Ringo for breakfast tomorrow. Tell him, as you've told me, how you feel. I believe you'll find that your problems are solved if you do so." He pressed a soft kiss to her lips. "In fact, I know so."

"Okay."

"Robin. May I cut in?"

Robin hesitated at the sound of Oberon's voice. How had he missed his king's entrance to the ball? For all his talk that no one mattered more than Michaela, Oberon was his to protect as well.

Michaela winked up at him. "Sure, but which one of you is going to lead?"

Robin quirked a brow at her, but before he could respond Michaela was whisked from his arms by Raven. "Indeed. You two make a lovely couple. Don't you think so, Michaela?"

"Um…" Michaela's gaze bounced between Raven, Robin and Oberon. She shrugged. "They match."

Robin looked at his king's outfit and grinned. "Indeed, we do." Although as far as Robin was concerned, his outfit was much more chic than Oberon's. The High King's suit was pale gray, with a darker gray shirt and pale tie. He hadn't even bothered to try and mimic the fae the way the humans had. To the mortals present, he was just an extraordinary-looking man in a business suit.

To the fae present, he was the most powerful man in the room bar none. Not even Robin commanded the respect Oberon did. Gloriana and Titannia could posture and pose all they wished. Neither Queen could compare to Oberon, in looks, grace, strength or integrity.

Robin started as Raven whisked Michaela away into the crowd. This was not good. His attention was divided between his truebond and his king. He was torn, for the first time in his long history as Oberon's Blade. Not even in the golden years, when Oberon and Titannia had first wed and been blissfully happy, had Robin felt torn in his duty. Always, Oberon had been his first and last concern.

Now Michaela had taken that spot, and Robin was lost.

"Calm down, my Hob. From what I can see, she is safe."

He scowled as Raven twirled Robin's truebond. "Raven may not harm her, but he might seduce her."

Oberon chuckled. "I'm not certain she's willing to be seduced. At least, not by the Fear Dearc." Oberon's eyes narrowed. "Speaking of whom, did you know he was your son?"

Robin winced. "No, my liege. Not until just recently." He had much to tell Oberon, and not much time to do it in. Already the urge to rip Michaela from Raven's grasp was strong. Before long, he would be forced to go to her.

"She is unclaimed and vulnerable. That is why you chafe so, my Hob."

Robin bowed his head. "As you say."

"Speak with me. Tell me what is happening with the delegation. What have you learned? Has the boy been discovered?"

"No, unfortunately. Kael is in Raven's room, hoping to overhear something. Duncan has had little luck keeping the delegation on track."

"And why is that?"

Robin followed Oberon back to the Blackthorn table, but more than half his attention was on Michaela. "Cecelia Malmayne is refusing to deal with him, and the rest of the delegation is refusing to speak without their leader, Raven, present. Raven, however, has other things on his mind than the return of a prince." He made a disgusted noise in the back of his throat as Raven dipped a laughing Michaela. "Feh."

"Would you have me speak with him?"

Robin turned his attention back to Oberon at the lethal menace in his king's voice. It always startled him, the knowledge that Oberon would protect him, the Hob. Robin would lay down his life for his king, and not just because he was his ruler. Oberon was his best friend and, until the Dunnes, his only family.

Now he'd claimed Jaden as blood kin, and had a son and a bondmate to worry over. "No." He took a deep breath, praying Oberon understood. "I want to offer him a place in the Court."

Oberon's stunned expression lasted only a second. "I see."

"No, but you will." And when Robin told Oberon what was going on with Titannia and his children, Oberon would, indeed, see all too well.

"That was fun." Michaela giggled as Raven swept her in a circle.

"It was. We should dance more often."

Raven's expression was full of heat, but Michaela's fire was reserved for Ringo and Robin. Reluctantly, she pulled away, unwilling to hurt someone she was coming to think of as a friend. "I should get back to Robin."

"Why? He's still busy with Oberon."

Michaela snorted a laugh. "Oberon."

Raven's answering grin was wicked. "Yes, Oberon."

She snickered. "Good one. Next you'll tell me Titannia is here too."

"Gods, I hope not." Raven's easy-going expression morphed into one of concern. "I'd kill her myself before I let her near you."

Michaela blinked. "Murder's illegal, you know."

"So are a lot of other things, my sweet." Raven cupped her cheek. "If I had my way, they would never touch you."

"MacSweeney. So this is where you've been hiding."

Michaela felt Raven stiffen beside her. "McNeil."

"Introduce me, MacSweeney."

"Over my dead body, McNeil."

"That can be arranged." The dark-haired, dark-eyed monster turned his attention to her, and Michaela shook. She had no doubts that man standing before her was a killer. "Since my friend is being so reluctant to introduce us, allow me to introduce myself. Lawrence McNeil, at your service."

The faint hint of a playful Scots burr in his voice couldn't hide the evil lurking inside him. She could see it clear as day, like a dark miasma over his soul. When he went to take her hand, Michaela made sure both hers were curled around Raven's arm. "Charmed."

McNeil's brows rose but the smile didn't falter. "Perhaps you'll grace me with a dance."

When rainbow-farting monkeys flew out of her butt. "Perhaps."

His gaze darted to something behind her, and his grin took on an edge that had her wanting to dart behind Raven for protection. "I see you've met Robin Goodfellow and Oberon."

What was it with these guys? It wasn't as if the real Oberon...was...

She refused to look behind her. If she did, the snake might strike. "Yup."

The brief disgust on his face was banished by a smile that had probably made more than one woman cream her panties. It left Michaela utterly terrified. "I can see why you enjoy chasing her through the convention, MacSweeney. She's delightfully quiet. I like that in my women."

Raven pushed Michaela behind him and growled. She could feel his hair literally standing on end. "Go, McNeil, before I lose my temper."

"A human, MacSweeney? Really? Might as well fuck an ape." He laughed, and Michaela felt faint. "Although I must admit, she looks quite tasty."

Raven's arm moved so quickly it was a blur, but it left behind four bloody gashes on McNeil's cheek. "Stay away from her."

The cold, ruthless tone of Raven's voice should have frightened her, but it didn't. Raven was defending her, and she knew without a shadow of a doubt that he would kill McNeil before he could lay a hand on her.

McNeil wiped the blood away from his cheek and licked it from his fingers. "You're going to regret that."

She curled her fingers in the back of Raven's shirt. She wanted Robin, and she wanted this sick fuck to *go away*.

The Hob

Warm arms encircled her from behind. "Is there a problem, my sweet?"

Michaela relaxed in Robin's hold and let go of Raven's shirt. She turned in his arms and pressed her face into the side of his neck, whispering, "He's evil. I think he's going to hurt Raven."

"I saw." Robin pressed a kiss to the top of her head. "McNeil. Never a pleasure."

"I could say the same. The girl. Is she yours, or Raven's?" The laugh McNeil let loose had Michaela clutching at Robin and shaking in her shoes. "Not that it matters."

"It does." Michaela looked up to find Robin grinning at McNeil, fangs very much in evidence. She didn't remember seeing those before. "You know not the danger you court if you seek to harm her." Michaela gasped. Were those claws digging into her side? Before she could look, Robin pressed her head against his chest, holding her firmly to him. "I would think twice before acting on your hunger. The consequences would be...unfortunate."

The pleasant tone of Robin's voice didn't fool her for one moment. If McNeil so much as touched her, Robin would tear him apart. And from the growl Raven was letting loose, that was only if he didn't get to McNeil first.

"I see." McNeil sighed, but Michaela wasn't buying it. The dude was serial killer creepy, and she hoped she never saw him again. "Perhaps we'll meet again, Miss Exton. Until then, think of me."

"Not on my worst day." Michaela snuggled closer to Robin. He would keep her safe from the creepy guy. She waited until McNeil had moved away before she whimpered. "Robin?"

"Yes, my sweet?" He stroked her hair, attempting to soothe her, but it didn't work. Nothing could.

"How did creepy guy know my last name?"

"Fuck." Raven immediately moved in front of her, blocking her from McNeil's view. "Robin, I—"

"Calm yourself, Raven. I am aware it wasn't you."

"Then who?" That cold lethality was back in Raven's voice. Robin's hand continued to stroke her hair. "I have no idea."

Chapter Sixteen

He waited patiently by the door of his apartment, listening for Michaela's return. She'd called "Ringo" after the ball, arranging to meet him for breakfast immediately after her shift. Robin, anticipating her call, had readily agreed. After all, today he would claim his truebond, binding her to him for all eternity.

He hoped.

Hell and damnation, he had no idea if what he wished for was even possible. He was the only one of his kind. For all that he wanted her with every breath in his body, there was a chance that he would have but a scant handful of decades with her before the breath left her body. There was no one else to ask if what he sought to do was even within his power. But Robin would trust himself, and his bond with Michaela. He would know what to do when the time came.

He hoped.

Robin sighed. He was almost as nervous as he had been the first time he'd taken a step on new, shaky legs. In truth, his legs were almost that shaky again.

The elevator dinged, and Robin had the door open so fast he was surprised it was still on its hinges.

She grinned as soon as she saw him. "Ringo."

Robin fought to keep the smile on his face. Today, she would learn the truth of things, and Ringo would disappear into the ether. "How was work?" Robin asked, leaning casually against the doorjamb. He bit back a grin as he watched her limp down the hall and waited for the fireworks.

"Meh. It was all right. I've had worse."

Robin blinked in confusion as he compared what she'd said to what Jaden had told him. The vampire had followed her to and from work, keeping her safe while Robin consulted with Oberon. He'd called Robin, concerned over what had occurred. He'd feared McNeil was fucking with Robin's truebond.

Robin was already a heartbeat away from ending McNeil's life. If in truth he'd made Michaela miserable, then it would be a pure pleasure to act on his impulse, Oberon's orders notwithstanding. Oberon wanted him to wait until Prince Evan was secure before killing McNeil. Robin wanted the threat to his truebond eliminated immediately. And make no mistake, McNeil had threatened Michaela. Whether he hoped to score against Raven or Robin did not matter. He was planning on using Michaela against them, and that was something Robin would end him over.

The litany of misfortune Jaden had listed over the phone concerned even Robin. Michaela's car wouldn't start, despite having just been repaired, and had to be towed to the nearest garage. She'd gotten to work two hours late and been told by her boss that the Jell-O in the cafeteria stood a better chance of a promotion than she did. Someone put salt in the sugar bowl by the coffee machine and she'd been blamed for it. It had something to do with poisoning her boss, whom Jaden laughingly told him Michaela had nicknamed Dick McGrabbyhands.

Robin was not amused.

The cost for repairing her car was approximately a month's rent and not covered by her insurance, as she had only the basic necessary in order to drive, and the car was long out of warranty. Another thing Robin would address when she was his. His mate would not drive a beat-up orange Jeep.

To top it all off, the elevator had broken down and she'd twisted her ankle taking the stairs down to the first floor.

Then it started raining.

"Seriously. It's okay." She grinned at him. "I've had much worse shifts, believe me."

Robin was beginning to wonder what she considered a *bad* day.

Robin moved from the doorway and placed his arm around her waist, willing her to lean on him. He nearly sighed in relief when she put her arm over his shoulder with a quiet thank you.

There was no way he was taking her to a restaurant with both a sprained ankle and wrist. With a move too swift for her to protest, he swept her up in his arms and carried her into his apartment.

"I feel like a bride." Michaela wrapped both arms around his neck and giggled.

Robin smiled. If only she knew. He held back a laugh with some effort. "I like the scrubs."

She plucked at the dark pink, damp fabric. He would have to do something about that. He couldn't have her catching cold. "You like Hello Kitty?"

"It's...charming."

"In that case, you'll love the set I have in lavender."

He shuddered, delighted when she giggled. "My dear, we must really do something about your fashion sense." Then again, she could wear sackcloth and ashes and Robin would want her.

He would always want her. His prick was already throbbing behind the zipper of his slacks, eager to join with his bondmate.

"We need to get you in some dry clothes, my dear." Robin placed her in one of Kael's kitchen chairs, and then darted quickly into his bedroom. He called forth a comfortable terrycloth robe for her to wear, and fuzzy slippers to warm her feet.

If things went the way he hoped they would, she would need no other clothing for the rest of the day. Indeed, he planned on whisking her away to his home in Colorado before the day was through, to ensure neither McNeil nor Raven could lay a single claw on her.

"Here you are, my dear." He came out of the bedroom to find her hobbling around Kael's tiny living room. "What are you doing?"

"Exploring."

Robin shook his head and swept her into his arms again. "To the bathroom with you."

"How did you know I have to pee?"

He shook his head at her antics and deposited her just inside the door. "Change, if you please."

"Yes, sir." She smartly saluted him, laughing when he shut the door in her face.

Robin waited impatiently until the door opened again. He damn near groaned at the sight of her in the sapphire blue robe. She was naked under there, and he could not be happier about it.

He carried her into the dining area again and placed her in one of the chairs. He wanted her where he could see her as he cooked. She tended to get into trouble when he wasn't around. As good at it as she was, he wouldn't put it past her to somehow find trouble even within his temporary domicile. After all, she'd managed to attract not only Raven's attention, but that of McNeil as well.

He'd rather have Raven chasing after his woman than the water horse. While they weren't on the water front, it would take McNeil only minutes to have her by the river. If he got her there, nothing would be left of her, not even bones.

His hands clenched. Robin would kill McNeil before it came to that, Oberon be damned. He glanced at her and shook himself, reassured that, at least for the moment, she was safe and sound. He began to gather pots and ingredients. "Do pancakes sound good?"

She wrinkled her nose. "I don't know. Carbs. They go right to my hips."

He cocked eyebrow at her. Her expression was far too innocent. His mate wanted to play, and Robin was willing to indulge her. "Fruit or syrup?"

"I see how it's gonna be. I say jump, and you keep right on walking."

He began cracking eggs into the flour mixture. "Or flying. Maybe even swimming. I'm flexible that way. Again, I ask you. Fruit or syrup?"

Michaela chuckled and propped her chin on her good hand. "Butter and syrup. Please. You don't use buttermilk in your pancakes?"

"I prefer not to." He set aside a portion of the batter and added blueberries to it. "So. Tell me about the gentleman you met yesterday."

She started, looking guilty as hell. "Jaden told on me? Dirty little snitch." Her expression was disgruntled, but the wary look she shot him belied the playful tone. She was worried and did not want him to know it.

Robin thought she looked utterly adorable. "Yes, but he is supposed to be."

"Jaden works for you?"

"Indeed. And he is quite good at his job."

"So I was ratted out by a *professional* snitch. That makes it so much better."

Robin bit back a grin as he ladled batter into the hot pan. "I think I detect some sarcasm in your speech."

"I can see why you're so good at your job too."

Robin shot her a look, but she hardly seemed intimidated. No, his truebond was silently laughing at him, her eyes sparkling, the corners of that full mouth curving upward. He flipped the pancake and pointed the spatula at her. "You are changing the subject."

She crossed her arms and her pouted. "I met several people yesterday."

He shook his head. As much as he wished to press her on the matter, he did not have the right to do so. While he knew she was his truebond, no promises had yet been spoken. By human standards, she still had the right to see anyone else she wished.

By his standards, he would eviscerate anyone she so much as touched.

"Fine." She pushed her hair behind her ears and looked even guiltier than she had earlier. "I did meet someone."

Very carefully he took the finished pancake out of the pan and placed it on the plate. "Oh?" He ladled more batter into the pan. Soon she would understand, and there would be no more fear, no more guilt.

He would allow Michaela to come to no harm, even at his hand.

"I don't even know his real name, just the name he uses at the con." She bit her lip, looking more like a naughty little girl than a free-spirited woman.

"Oh? What name did he give you?" Robin pretended a nonchalance he wasn't feeling.

This was it. This was the moment when she'd say his name, and he'd end the lies once and for all.

She sighed. "Robin Goodfellow." She must've taken his silence for accusation, because she began to babble. "See, I've been fascinated by Robin Goodfellow ever since I was little girl. I would devour anything written about him, memorize anything I could find. I had this vision built up in my head of what he would look like, even what he would *smell* like. I've..." She gulped. "I've been dreaming about him since I was small, and I swear, that guy looks just like the man in my dreams."

Robin felt dizzy. He hadn't known that tidbit. No wonder she'd been as drawn to him as he had to her. The attraction would have been overwhelming when she saw him in his preferred form.

It had to be the fae blood in her, that she would dream of him like that, and from such an early age. But the only ones who created a dream link with their mates were... All but one of them had died out long ago. Was it even possible? His hands shook as he placed the spatula on the spoon rest. "And this man, he met your expectations?"

"Yes."

That last was said in such a small voice that Robin had no choice but to go to her. He moved the pan off the heat and turned off the stove, then pulled her from her seat and into his arms. He picked her up and carried her to the sofa, settling down there with her in his lap. One last question, then, before he revealed the truth. "Did you think he was the real Robin Goodfellow?"

She eyed him warily. "I'm not sure there's an acceptable answer to that. Also, you're taking this remarkably well."

"Tell me. I give you my word, I will not judge you any less for it." Robin was practically holding his breath, wondering what her answer would be.

"You'll think I'm crazy." The wariness was back, as well as fear.

"I will not, this I vow." Robin would put her fears to rest, of that he had no doubt. He leaned close, his lips brushing against hers. "Robin Goodfellow is as real as you are."

She whimpered, her lips puckering, begging for a kiss. "You're humoring me, but that's okay."

"You wanted him."

She pulled away, her eyes wide, tears gathering to fall down suddenly pale cheeks. "I—"

"Shh. I am not angry." Robin shook off the deeper tones he'd adopted as Ringo, allowing his true voice to shine through. His eyes turned from brown to blue instantly. "I wanted you, too, from the moment I saw you."

She gulped and licked her lips. "What's going on?"

Fear was beginning to replace wariness, another emotion that should never have hold of his bondmate. He smiled, his fangs showing, his eyes flashing iridescent green. "I think you know."

She made the most adorable sound, somewhere between a meep and an eek, that Robin had ever heard. She touched his fang with a trembling finger, whimpering when she realized they were real. "Who are you?"

Robin allowed the change to flow over him, adjusting her in his lap as he lost two inches and several pounds. Her weight did not disturb him, but now she was farther away from him than he liked. He pulled her closer, damn near moaning at the sight of his hair flowing over her arms and hands. This was the way it was meant to be, holding his bondmate as he truly was, not the illusion he'd shown to her before.

"Oh. My. God." She was shaking like a leaf, her hands fluttering over him as if dying to touch but afraid to do so.

He took hold of those butterfly hands and placed a kiss on each wrist, lingering as the scent of her skin burrowed into his psyche, forever a part of him. He looked at her through his lashes, grinning at her as she gaped at him in astonishment.

"Why, as you see, I am Robin Goodfellow. And you, my dear, are mine."

Chapter Seventeen

Oh, thank fuck, she wasn't insane. She cuddled in closer, burying her face in his neck. His warmth surrounded her as he hugged her tightly to him. "Jesus. It really *is* you. I thought I was losing my mind."

"Indeed, and I am sorry for that." He placed a soft kiss on top of her head in apology.

"I dreamed of you."

"I believe you."

She smacked him on the chest. "Where the hell have you been?"

He laughed. "Saving the world, of course."

"Hmph." She wanted to pinch herself, just to make sure she was awake. It was entirely possible she'd fallen asleep on the bus, and now she was nuzzling some poor schlub just trying to get to work.

"My apologies. I was unaware I was running that late."

She sniffed, hoping he didn't feel the way she was trembling against him. "Just don't make a habit of it."

He was chuckling and undoing her robe at the same time. "I promise, if only because I don't want to be one of the thousands who live in fear of your mighty fists of death."

"Aw, you remembered." It really *was* him, Robin fucking Goodfellow. "Wait. Why were you walking around as Ringo?"

He cupped her bare breast. "I told you. Work." He sounded completely distracted, and his gaze was fastened on the gap in her robe his hand had disappeared behind. With a flick of his wrist the material parted, exposing the breast he was toying with while leaving the other still covered.

She pinched him through his silky shirt as hard as she could.

"Ow!" Robin stared at her, shocked. "What did you do that for?"

"I just wanted your undivided attention."

One brow quirked upward. "You had it."

She pointed to her face. "Yes, but my eyes are up here."

He kept his gaze firmly on her eyes and cupped her breast again. "As I said, you have it."

She made a disgusted noise that had him laughing silently. "Men. All the same, no matter the species." Her eyes went wide as a sudden thought hit her. "Robin? How many different species are there, by the way?"

He closed his eyes, his shoulders shaking with laughter.

She hadn't asked the question she'd meant to, and if she wanted an answer she'd better ask it quick. "Robin?"

He smiled sweetly and ran his claw over her nipple. "What did you wish to know?"

Whether or not that monster digging into my hip is as big as it feels. It figured that someone nicknamed Puck would have a hockey stick in his pants. "What are you working on? And how are Jaden involved, and Raven, and creepy guy?"

"McNeil will not lay a hand on you."

"Ow, pinchy!" She slapped at his wrist until he loosened his grip. She rubbed at her breast and glared at him. "Fine. I'm awake."

He tilted his head. "You thought you were dreaming again?"

She shrugged. What did he expect her to say? "The thought had crossed my mind." She grabbed his hand and ran her fingers across his claws. And yes, the black nails he usually sported were normal length. These, however, were true claws, black and lethal and curving away from the tips of his fingers. "I like the manicure."

He shook his head. "You are stalling."

"Stalling?" She blinked up at him innocently.

"Dragging your feet."

She lifted her legs and wiggled her toes. "They are feeling a mite scuffed up."

"Michaela."

"What do you want me to say?" She lowered her legs. "My dream man is cuddling me in his lap and molesting my boobs after a so-so day." She snorted. "Why am I stalling again?"

"I have no idea."

"I want an explanation as to why Robin Goodfellow would be at a human fairy convention. I mean, other than the obvious."

"What would the obvious be?" He began stroking her breast again, but his gaze remained on her face.

"Fucking with the idiots pretending to be you."

"I gave up on that centuries ago. It got old after a while. There's only so much, ah, fucking one can do before one grows bored." He snickered at her horrified look. "Not that kind of fucking, my dear." He lay her down on the sofa, his body straddling hers. He parted her robe completely, exposing her bare flesh to his hungry gaze. She shivered as his eyes literally began to glow. "Shall I show you how not bored I am of other kinds of fucking?"

She opened her mouth to respond and gasped instead. Robin took her mouth like a conquering hero, with full knowledge that she belonged to him.

He was right. She did. If this wasn't a dream, if she really did have the chance to claim Robin as her own, she wasn't going to fight it.

She'd dreamt of him, and here he was, making love to her.

He reached between her thighs and stroked her delicately, his claws cold against her heated flesh. He parted the moist folds of her pussy and circled her clit.

She pinched him again.

"Ow!" He sat up, glaring at her with glowing green eyes.

"Claws." She pointed to her pussy. "Delicate bits." She shook her finger at him. "*So* not chocolate and peanut butter."

He closed his eyes, whether to keep from laughing or in exasperation she didn't really care. The claws, however, disappeared, making her one happy camper.

He draped himself over her once more, kissing her deeply. "Now. Where were we?"

Michaela arched up against his hand and whimpered into his mouth, eager for the pleasure she'd only felt in her dreams.

"Yes. Move for me." Robin nibbled her earlobe and kissed down the side of her neck until he reached her shoulder. "Dance for me, my sweet."

When he bit down and began to suck up a mark, Michaela danced. She writhed under his touch, his mouth, her breasts rubbing against the silky material of his shirt. The fact that he was still fully clothed while she lay exposed was more of a turn-on than she'd thought possible. The sharp edges of his fangs nearly broke her skin, adding a zing of danger.

He nipped his way to her breast, his tongue swirling around the edges of her nipple. His clever fingers began to stroke her harder, and Michaela trembled. She ran her hands over his shoulders, his muscles rippling under the silk shirt. His hair twined itself around her fingers as if it had a mind of its own.

She clenched his shoulders as he finally took her nipple into his mouth, sucking hard, bringing it to a throbbing, needy point. She planted her feet on the sofa and rocked her hips, demanding more. More fingers, more tongue, more Robin.

Pleasure and pain combined as Robin slipped a finger inside her, twisting so that his palm continued to rub against her clit. Pleasure began to build within her as she rubbed herself against his palm, demanding the orgasm his touch promised.

Robin switched to her other breast, scraping his fangs along the hard tip of her nipple before taking it into his mouth and sucking hard. Michaela bucked against him, crying out in pleasure as the orgasm washed through her.

"Robin? What's going on?"

Robin lifted his head and snarled at the sound of Kael's voice. In a swirl of dark smoke, Michaela found herself laid out on a huge, four-poster bed with a soft, dark purple down comforter. The robe was gone too, possibly left behind on Kael's sofa.

That was all she saw before Robin was hovering over her again, his expression feral. "No one sees you thus but me."

She had no real problem with that, so she nodded.

He blanketed her, the silk of his shirt cold against her breasts, his pants sliding against her as he rocked into her. His bright hair surrounded her, closing off the outside world. "Say it."

The pleasure he'd given her was still swarming her senses. She arched up against him, the feel of his pants rubbing against her core sending shivers down her spine. "Only you, Robin."

He kissed her and thrust against her, his tongue and hips synchronizing perfectly. She could imagine the feel of him inside her, hot and hard, stretching her just right. She grabbed hold of the back of his head, her fingers tangling in his hair, and held him to her, demanding more. Always more.

In response he kissed her thoroughly, leaving no part of her mouth unexplored. She wrapped her legs around his waist, wanting him inside more than her mouth.

Well, okay. She did want him in her mouth. She wanted to be in his mouth too. She took hold of his shoulders and, using her legs, twisted until he was on his back and she was on top of him.

One brow rose cockily. "You wanted something, my dear?"

She was going to wipe that smug expression off his face. "Yup!" She wriggled around until her pussy was over his face. She giggled at the sight of his slacks jerking as his cock tried to spring free. She undid his zipper, pulling him free.

Robin got the hint, tugging her hips until she was exactly where he wanted her. At the first thrust of his tongue into her pussy she nearly buckled.

"*Yes.*" She had to lock her arms before she collapsed on his thighs.

She grabbed hold of his cock and took it into her mouth, the taste of him filling her senses. She swirled her tongue around the head of his cock, lapping up the precome until he was squirming beneath her. He moaned beneath her touch, thrusting up into her mouth when she reached into his pants and cupped his balls.

Suddenly, Robin was naked beneath her, his cock proudly erect in a nest of bright red hair. She nuzzled his balls before taking his cock back into her mouth. Robin began thrusting up into her mouth. Michaela kept still and let him set the pace, wrapping a hand around the base so he wouldn't accidentally choke her.

He also began tonguing on her clit, making her moan in pleasure. She sucked hard and he stilled, letting her dictate his actions once more. She took him deep, as deep as she could without choking, and suckled him.

The reaction she got was not what she expected.

Robin moaned. His bondmate was going to drive him mad. She had him in her mouth, that hot, sweet mouth, trying to draw his essence from him before he was ready.

Robin had other plans.

He misted, coming to his knees behind her, much to her surprise. She squeaked when his hand landed on her pale ass, caressing the sting away. "Naughty, naughty."

She looked at him over her shoulder, her startled expression drawing a laugh out of him. She pointed to his cock. "I wasn't done with that yet."

He smirked and slapped his cock against her ass. "Neither was I."

"Oh."

He laughed at her meek tone, but the way she wiggled her ass at him left him in no doubt as to her true desire. Robin rubbed the head of his cock against her wetness. "Are you ready, my dear?"

In answer, she thrust back against him, trying to impale herself on him.

Robin stilled her with a touch. Gods, she was so beautiful, so fragile, his truebond, the woman who would be his heart and guard his soul. Robin slid inside her, watching as he disappeared into her wet warmth.

Michaela tried to get up on her knees, but some instinct within Robin had him pushing her back down. She was his, and she would not get away. He blanketed her body, his arms caging her, his cock pinning her, and rode her down until she lay flat beneath him. "Say you are mine."

"Robin." She thrust back against him, but he held fast. She would say what he needed to hear.

"Say it, Michaela." He needed to hear it said, and not in some dream.

"Yours." She looked up at him through her hair. "And you're mine."

Robin began to fuck her, rolling his hips against her ass, reveling in her flushed cheeks and dilated eyes. He closed his eyes and shuddered when an orgasm shivered through her, squeezing his cock. "Yes."

Robin opened his eyes, surprised to find he was glowing. Green light surrounded him, enveloped him and his lover, blanketing them in his power. He smiled, content, and let his power flow.

He would be able to claim his truebond after all.

"Robin?"

"Hush. You've consented to be mine, and I am making it so."

She rolled her eyes, an odd look when her face was half-turned away. "Not the green glow. Although we're adding it to the list to talk about later. I just..."

"Hmm?" He rolled his hips again, waiting for an answer.

She bent her knees and pushed back against him, driving him even deeper into her. "Fuck me stupid."

He shuddered. "As you wish."

Michaela gasped as Robin gave her exactly what she'd asked for. He lifted her hips, but she kept her shoulders down, giving in to that craving he seemed to have to cover her. His teeth clamped on to the side of her neck, his fangs not quite breaking the skin. His fingers gripped her hips, his claws scratching her. She didn't care, and he didn't seem to notice. The sting meant that Robin had finally lost control.

Robin began to pound into her, his hips snapping, the sound of their flesh slapping together echoing through the room. Michaela reached between her legs to stroke her clit, shocked when another orgasm rolled through her before she could touch herself. Her body clenched around Robin's cock, throbbing, robbing her of breath and sight.

That green glow intensified, seemed to feed off her orgasm. As it brightened, Michaela found herself spinning out of control, her body's responses no longer her own. Robin owned her, played her like a fiddle, wringing pleasure from her willing body in wave after wave.

Her fingers clenched in the pillow as he fucked her hard. Her nipples scraped against the comforter, tiny points of delight that only added to her ecstasy. It was as if every erogenous zone in her body was being simultaneously stroked, and Michaela loved it.

"Fuck." She gasped as she came again, the bright light overwhelming her, Robin riding her through the whole orgasm, keeping her on the edge.

He growled, and the sound wasn't human. Michaela didn't have it in her to care. Robin was bringing her to the heights of ecstasy, then showing her that there was more beyond even that. Michaela had not had more than two orgasms with any other lover, but with Robin?

She was in heaven.

His teeth pierced her skin and she shrieked as fiery pleasure raced from that spot, blinding her. "More."

He snarled, his hips snapping furiously, his hard cock pounding into her. His hair danced around her and she grabbed hold, pulling at it, tugging, trying to get him deeper, harder, faster, anything that would make her scream again.

Robin's claws dug into her hips, drawing blood, but she didn't care. She was coming again, screaming as he fucked her, already needing just a bit more.

"*Mine.*" Red-hot fire raced from where Robin's claws had pierced her skin, consuming her body, a fire only Robin could put out.

"*Robin.*" Gasping, breathless, ready to pass out from pleasure, Michaela felt herself poised at the edge of a cliff, ready to fall over, knowing he would be there to catch her when she did.

"Come."

Robin gritted it out between clenched teeth, his movements becoming less coordinated. Sweat dripped from his brow. His hair was tangled between her fingers and dark with sweat. The green glow was under his skin, under *her* skin, and she arched her back, eager to obey. She wanted to feel him in every fiber of her being, wanted him imprinted on her DNA. Every part of her body throbbed with the need to come.

Suddenly, Robin howled, his cock jerking inside her as he came, pouring himself into her. Whatever had held her back was gone, and Michaela was lost in a spiral of pleasure so great she didn't know where she ended and Robin began. Her vision went black as her body seized, coming so hard her whole body clenched. Her breath stolen, her body no longer hers, Michaela succumbed to Robin's order, and came.

Chapter Eighteen

Robin watched the sleeping face of his truebond, unwilling even for a second to take his gaze from her. He stroked her dark hair away from her face, careful not to disturb her.

Precious. She was infinitely so, and Robin thanked the gods that he'd been granted so sweet and loving a wife. Finally, the long loneliness of centuries was over.

She was his, and he, hers.

He bit back a snicker as she smiled in her sleep. She was going to stir up so much trouble wherever she went, gods help him. He could picture what was to come, how things within his home would change. Oberon would have a fit when Robin's mortal bride came to live near the Palace. She'd add color and sunshine again. Mayhap she'd even bring his king's heart back to life as well.

Michaela stirred beneath his touch and he stilled, loathe to wake her. The dark circles under her eyes were disturbing. His lover had not been getting enough rest, and it showed. He would have to see to it that once she was moved in with him she caught up on her sleep.

"Robin."

Robin held a finger to his lips, quieting Oberon, who'd opened the bedroom door. "Shh." He made sure Michaela was adequately covered before climbing from the bed. While his own nudity before his king did not disturb him, Michaela's did. He quickly donned a soft pair of cotton pants and shirt. He did not want his power to awaken her simply because he wanted to be clothed. The bonding had been intense, taking a great deal from both of them.

His Michaela was worn out by more than her work and a crazy convention schedule.

Robin padded barefoot from the room, Oberon hot on his heels. He led the way down the stairs, intending to take the king to his study, when a hand on his arm stopped him. "What happened?"

Robin glanced toward the upper landing and sighed. He had hoped Oberon would quell his impatience for just a few steps more. "I am bonded."

"So I gathered." When Robin raised a brow in query, Oberon grimaced. "I received a phone call from Kael."

"Damn." He'd forgotten about the pooka.

"He was frantic. Said he heard snarling, but when he searched found nothing but a lady's robe on his sofa."

"I'll contact him, let him know everything is all right."

"It is not all right, Hobgoblin. You left a fledgling Blade alone to claim your mate."

Robin winced. He sensed a lecture coming on.

"Not only that, but he had news to impart."

"Oh?" Robin's ears perked up.

"Hobgoblin."

He sighed. "Can we not put off the discussion of my numerous failures until after Prince Evan is safe and the bitch queen's plot revealed?"

Oberon studied him for a moment. When he began to speak Robin relaxed. "It seems Prince Evan is being held on a ship on the waterfront, the *SS United States*."

Robin started. That ship was near where the second body had been located. It made perfect sense now. McNeil was taking his victims to where he'd shackled Prince Evan.

"According to your pet gremlin, it's a gutted luxury passenger liner parked at Pier 84 in South Philadelphia. They've begun restoration efforts to remove things like asbestos, so it's possible whoever is holding him are posing as workers to keep the real construction crew from finding him. If they've got it cordoned off to remove toxic materials it would be simple to keep the boy away from the crew."

Robin tapped his nail against his lips, his mind racing furiously. If Red said that was where the data led, then Robin had no doubt the information was accurate. "I'd bet on McNeil being the motivator for location."

"Agreed. If so, your Blades know what they will be dealing with."

"Indeed. If the water horse gets the prince in the water, there will be no saving him."

"Worse, Kael claims he overheard Raven cursing about reports of bodies pulled from the river. Bodies with strange marks on them."

Damn. He should have kept a closer eye on McNeil. "He's right. Two bodies that I know of, with marks the humans believe to be made by sharks. Worse, he left behind saliva."

"And their testing would show it to be human."

He exchanged a glance with Oberon, already aware that the death sentence he'd been seeking was about to be handed down. "The teeth marks will not match with any known shark, either."

"Take him down, my Hob."

"As you wish, my king." Robin bowed. McNeil's fate was sealed.

"Can we count on the Raven Lord to remain neutral in this?"

Robin began to pace. "I do not know. I will speak with him, offer him a place here in the Gray Court, but his fear of the Black Queen may overshadow his need to escape her."

"Who do you trust for extraction? Someone must fetch the prince."

Robin grinned, aware his fangs were showing. "Why, myself, of course, and Jaden."

Oberon nodded. "And who will you set to guard your wife while you rescue Prince Evan?"

"Wife?"

Robin winced. His truebond could screech quite loudly, it seemed.

"You're married?"

Oh, now that would not do at all. The pain in her voice was unbearable. Robin rushed to where she'd tucked herself behind the bannister and pulled her into his arms. "Of course." She tried to struggle but he held fast. He kissed the top of her head, laughing when she snarled. "I claimed my bride last night."

She stilled, but her muscles remained tense. "I don't remember you asking me to marry you." She held up her left hand but kept her face buried against his chest. "There's no ring on this finger, mister."

He took her hand and kissed that all-important finger. "Then we shall see about placing one there."

She finally lifted her face from his chest and stared at him. "I still don't remember being asked."

As she did not look terribly displeased, Robin decided to play. He put on an offended expression, hoping she would see it for the mask it was. "I did ask."

She glared at him suspiciously. "When?"

He whispered in her ear, "I distinctly recall it. Remember? *'Say you are mine.'*" He nipped her earlobes

She shuddered, her cheeks flaming. "That's a demand, not a question."

He inhaled her scent, pleased when his own overlay hers, mingling together into a brand new whole. "We are more bound than any human paper can make us, more tied to one another than any human ceremony is capable of."

"But I'd still like the ceremony."

He sighed. "Michaela."

"Robin." Her serious tone caught at him. "This means something to me."

Then she would have it. He nodded. "Very well. Once my current mission is resolved, you shall have your ceremony."

She smiled, and he was glad he had acquiesced so easily.

"In fact, I know just the place to conduct it." He could not wait to introduce Michaela to the Dunne family.

"That's all well and good, my Hob, but your mission is not resolved."

Robin turned, tucking Michaela protectively under his arm. "Of course, sire."

Michaela gasped. "Holy schlamoly. You really are Oberon?"

Oberon's expression softened as he looked at Robin's wife. "Yes."

Michaela tugged on Robin's shirt. "Should I curtsey or something?"

"No, but you will need to take vows before the Court, swearing your allegiance to him as I have."

She opened her mouth, but quickly shut it again with a frown. He could practically see the wheels turning in her head. "If you're Oberon, where's Ti—"

Oberon's eyes had gone pale gray. Robin slapped his hand over Michaela's mouth before she could say the name. "That name is anathema here. And yes, I will explain, but later. For now, know that Oberon rules as High King over the Gray Court; the White Court is ruled by Gloriana. The Black Queen rules the Black Court."

Michaela nodded, and he removed his hand. "I assume *she* runs the Black, and that it's a bad, bad place?" When Robin nodded she shivered. "McNeil is Black, isn't he?"

"Yes, and you are to stay as far away from him as possible. He is an *each uisge*, a water horse, and feeds on human flesh."

She scowled, but her fear was obvious in her pale face and trembling hands. "I knew he was a murderer. He doesn't just feed, he enjoys it."

Oberon's brows rose. "How can you tell? You only met him briefly."

She burrowed closer against Robin's side. "There's a darkness in him, an evil. I can see it, plain as day. The man didn't just want to kill me; he wanted me to hurt first."

Oberon's expression blanked. "I see."

"She dreamed of me."

The pale silver of Oberon's eyes darkened to titanium. He glanced at Robin and nodded once. Robin was correct, then. Somewhere in Michaela's line a Tuatha Dè Danaan had dallied with her ancestor. "Perhaps it would be best if she remained here, then."

She tried to ease away from Robin, but Robin held fast. "Where is here, exactly?"

"Colorado, in the Rocky Mountains." Robin waved his hand. "This is my home."

Michaela pinched his side. "Really? You teleported me to Colorado?"

He waved his hand. "When we were..." He looked sideways at Oberon and grinned. "Enjoying each other."

Michaela blushed. "Oh."

"*Souhaite-tu visiter Paris au lieu?*"

She bit her lip. "I don't know what you just said, but say it again." She shot Oberon a shy glance. "When we're alone."

Robin laughed. "*Tu êtes un délice pour mon âme.*"

She shivered. "I have got to learn French."

"Robin, as charming as your bondmate is, we still have work to do." Oberon bowed his head to Michaela. "I am sorry, my dear, but I must steal him from you. But first things first." The aura around Oberon changed. His friend had donned the mantel of the High King.

"Whoa." Michaela was wide-eyed as she stared at the king.

Robin took hold of Michaela's hand. "Kneel, and I will whisper the words you need to say in your ear."

"What?"

"Trust me."

Michaela knelt without another word, stealing any last bit of Robin's heart he might have held on to. That unquestioning trust was his undoing, and he couldn't be happier.

Robin began to whisper, and Michaela repeated his words. "I declare myself Oberon's man from this day forth, in honor and in faith, having no other oaths to forswear. By the gods I pledge my loyalty to the Gray Court, High King Oberon and his descendants. I declare myself the sworn servant of the Gray Lord, High King Oberon, King of the Gray Court, Lord over the Fae. I pledge my sword and my honor to uphold the laws of the Court. I and my house will abide by the laws handed down by the High King. I will faithfully perform all services required by Crown and Court. So swear I, Michaela Exton—" she jumped when he pinched her and glared at him, "—Goodfellow."

Oberon smiled. Her disgruntled tone and rolled eyes had charmed the king. "I, High King Oberon, the Gray Lord, Lord of the Fae, hereby hear your oaths and accept them in the name of Crown and Court. I declare you our loyal servant, sworn to our bidding. From this day forth my sword shall defend you, my magic protect you, and my wrath be mighty should you fail of your duty. So swear I, Oberon, High King." He nodded to Robin as the magical bond of king and liegeman settled over Michaela, causing her to gasp.

Oberon's voice echoed eerily as he continued. "I acknowledge your bondmate, Lord Robin Goodfellow, and declare her Lady Michaela Goodfellow. Her voice is your voice in all matters pertaining to the Goodfellow house and line. They are hers to protect and defend, and she, theirs. May you find joy in one another."

Robin bowed his head. Oberon had just told the entire Gray Court that Robin was bound. No doubt word would spread like wildfire to the White and Black. "Thank you, my king."

Michaela mimicked him a scant second later.

Oberon relaxed. "Now, much as it pains me to do so, I must steal Robin from you."

Robin helped Michaela to her feet. "Back to Philadelphia, my liege?"

"Yes. Inform Kael that, if he wishes, he may accept training as a Blade. The boy has done well."

"Yes, sire."

Michaela tugged on his shirt. "Can I hop a ride back to my apartment?"

Robin's brow rose. He'd much prefer it if she remained safely in the confines of his home. "Why?"

She frowned. "One, I have to work tonight, just like you. Two, I promised Moira we'd sit in on that Irish fairytales workshop together."

"You want to go back to the convention?" Robin scowled. He did not like that thought one bit. "Where McNeil is?"

She sighed. "Tell me Moira isn't a fairy."

Robin snorted. "She's not a fairy."

"Oh."

His bondmate seemed disappointed. "She's a leprechaun."

She shook her head slowly. "Somehow, that makes perfect sense." Her nose wrinkled in that adorable way she had. "I'm going to need to brush up on my fairytale species, aren't I?"

"Yes. That should keep you occupied whilst I return to Philadelphia."

Robin turned to go, but stopped short. Her fist was clenched in his hair. "Not so fast. If you think you're leaving the little woman behind to bake you cookies, you've got another thing coming."

The Hob

Of course she was going to be difficult about this. "Michaela—"

"I *will* find a way off of this mountain, with or without you." She let go of his hair and moved to stand in front of him, a scowl on her face. "And if I have to do it alone, Mr. Goodfellow, the consequences will be ugly." She held up her fists.

Robin bit back a laugh. "The mighty fists of death?"

"Yup. Fear me, mister."

Robin shook his head. He hated to disappoint her, he truly did. "McNeil will not, my dear."

"Then we need to make sure he doesn't get a shot at me. But if he thinks he can scare me away...well. Okay. Normally, he'd be *so* right." She took his hand. "But not today."

He cupped her cheek. "And what is different about today?"

"If he scares me off, that just proves that I'm weak, and that can and will be used against you. If I don't take a stand right now, if I allow him to push me from my home, I give the Black Court carte blanche to bully me and, in effect, bully you." She kissed his palm. "You told me you were in security."

"I am the leader of the Knights of Oberon, also known as Oberon's Blades."

"Let me guess. They are fighters, cops...assassins?"

And much more, but she'd grasped the concept nicely. "Yes."

"Then you have to take me back with you. Set guards around me if you like, but if you hide me away I become a liability, and you know it."

She was right, but oh, so wrong as well. If anything happened to her, his oaths to protect and defend wouldn't matter any longer. Nothing would.

"I think you should remain here as well, Michaela." Oberon stared at Robin. "I think you should know that Shane Dunne has foreseen her death."

For just a split second he lost control of his form, but he pulled it back before Michaela could see too much. She wasn't ready for that part of him. She might never be. He turned to her, aware he looked less than human, with his fangs, claws and glowing green eyes. "You stay here."

She glared at him for a moment before turning to Oberon. "Did this Shane guy say how I was supposed to die?" Oberon shook his head. "There, you see? For all you know, leaving me behind could be the decision that ends me."

"Bringing you along is more likely."

She smiled sadly. "Did you ever notice that most of Greek mythology is based around trying to *avoid* fate?"

Robin growled. "Do you want to die?" He wasn't arguing with her about this. "Do you have any idea what will happen if I lose you now?"

"Of course I don't want to die! I just got my dream man, damn it." Her shoulders slumped. "I'm scared."

He pulled her into his arms. "Then stay here. Stay safe."

She hugged him back. "That's the problem. Where will be safer, staying here alone, or going with you? What if it's a fate that can't be avoided no matter which decision we make?" She looked up at him, and he could see the raw determination in her gaze. "Call Shane. Find out if he can give you more details than what you've got now. If he tells you I should stay put, I'll stay. I promise. And if he says I should go with you—"

He closed his eyes and gritted out through clenched teeth, "You go." He sighed roughly when she kissed his chin. "Damn you."

"Damn you too." The affection in her tone belied her words.

Chapter Nineteen

Michaela slipped through the front door of the hospital and tried to hide her smirk.

"You will be careful."

She rolled her eyes. For someone who was supposed to be invisible Robin was being awfully chatty. "Yes, dear." She turned her head and smiled at a patient, making sure the Bluetooth headset was visible. The last thing she needed were rumors that she talked to herself getting back to Dick McGrabbyhands. He'd have her off the floor in a nanosecond if he could, and that would give him all the ammunition he needed.

Not that it mattered for much longer. Robin had made it more than clear that he expected her to move to Colorado, to his home. She couldn't blame him. While she loved her life in Philadelphia, she was now the spouse of one of the most powerful fae in the world. And hadn't that been a long, intriguing conversation? Who knew there were brownies, sylphs, leprechauns and Sidhe running around, living normal, everyday lives?

Her family was going to love this. *If* she got to explain it. She wasn't certain how Robin, let alone Oberon, would handle the Extons when they descended on Colorado.

And she was mortal, which she knew was making Robin's protective instincts go into overdrive. There were things in this world she couldn't fight back against, McNeil being one of them. If one of those Black Court fae got their hands on her, they'd use her against Robin. No, it was safer for her to move to him, where he had safeguards in place, than to force him to move to her.

She would miss her friends and being so close to her family, but Robin was worth anything.

"Where is the mortuary?"

Michaela punched the button on the elevator and waited quietly. She couldn't answer him with all the people around. It might be early evening, but the hospital still had staff, patients and visitors ready to leave for the day. But she couldn't hide the smile threatening to overtake her. His disgusted, put-upon voice was just too cute.

He'd called Shane, who'd told him that Michaela had to go back with him to Philadelphia. In fact, he'd gone one better. He'd convinced Robin to allow Michaela to be the one to get into the hospital records and check out the names of the chewed-on bodies brought in from the Delaware River. Once she had the data they needed, she was to send everything she had over to someone named Big Red, who would dig further than Michaela's limited access would allow.

Without Michaela's assistance, the search Big Red would have to conduct would be far too widespread and take too long to do a lick of good. The river could have carried them beyond the *SS United States*; if so, they might not even be in her hospital's records, but it would give Red a starting point. Red had even told them that he could use that entry point in the hospital's computers to jump from coroner's office to coroner's office. Michaela was glad to help, even if what she was doing was illegal. No human cop could deal with a monster like McNeil. Robin and his Blades were the only ones who could, and this was the first step in establishing McNeil's hunting grounds.

McNeil needed to be stopped *now,* and Michaela was going to help do so. She was totally willing to do her part. McNeil was a man-eating, creepy-ass monster, and she hoped she never came face-to-face with him again.

The elevator arrived and Michaela stepped in, followed by her invisible lover. "Remember, do nothing foolish."

She kept the smile on her face even though it was becoming increasingly difficult. The mini lectures had started the moment her scrubs went on and hadn't let up once. Hell, he hadn't even made fun of her lavender Hello Kitty scrubs.

If he didn't knock it off, he was going to learn all about her mighty fists of death, damn it.

"Hell and damnation."

"What?" Michaela glanced around as she stepped off the elevator and onto her floor. Her best bet at getting to a terminal would be here.

"I think I saw McNeil."

"Crap." Why was he there? He had no business being around sick children. "Robin, you need to get him gone."

The snarl she received in reply was inhuman, full of rage.

"Robin, the kids. Please."

She felt a brush of wind, Robin's anger and fear manifesting as he sped away. The familiar sense of his presence was gone, leaving her alone and vulnerable.

Michaela mentally shook herself. Alone, maybe, but far from vulnerable. She'd taken care of herself long before Robin entered her life. She could do so again.

She hoped.

Maybe.

Hell, who was she kidding? There was some scary-ass shit out there, and if Robin didn't get back to her as soon as possible she really *was* going to freak the hell out and give McGrabby something to fire her over.

She made her way to one of the nurse's terminals, exchanging quick greetings with the nurse on duty, and began typing. She just hoped it wasn't obvious how badly her hands were shaking.

"Michaela, I didn't know you were on duty today."

Crap. "I'm not. I'm just checking up on a patient."

"Who?"

Michaela had an answer ready. "You remember that guy Will and Ed brought into emergency a couple of days ago?"

"The guy who wanted to be called Snod?"

"That's the one."

"Hasn't he been discharged?"

Michaela paused, her fingers still on the keys. "Really? He was pretty injured."

"I don't know, but that's what I heard."

"I'm going to check anyway. If he's still here I'm going to go visit him."

"Just don't let Dick see you. You know how he is. He catches you on the computer during off hours, he won't just fire you. He'll try and have your license revoked." The nurse grimaced. "Of course, he'll offer you an out, if you'll just go quietly to his office and lock the door."

Michaela shuddered, glad Robin hadn't heard that. She might hate Dick, but she didn't want him dead, and she got the impression Robin wouldn't tolerate Dick's grabby ways. "I bet if we all got together and complained to the higher-ups they'd have to do something about him. It's sexual harassment, damn it."

"What is?"

Michaela glanced up, startled to find herself almost nose to nose with Raven MacSweeney. "Um. Raven. Hi."

He smirked. "Hi. I missed you today. You never showed up at the convention."

Her one concession to Robin's fears, and her own. Damn it, she'd really wanted to go, too. "I was busy."

"Indeed?" He leaned against the counter, smiling at her like she was his whole world. "With whom?"

"Not now, Raven. Please." She began typing again. She didn't have much time, and odds were good Robin would be back any minute. She couldn't be found looking up records she wasn't supposed to. As it was, if anyone checked, they'd be able to see she'd logged in and what records she'd accessed.

Hell, she was going to quit anyway. As protective as Robin was she didn't see herself continuing as a nurse, even in Colorado, unless they had fae-only hospitals.

Besides, if she stayed here and McGrabby made another pass at her, Robin would probably hand him his ass on a silver platter. Literally.

"Aren't you going to introduce me?" The nurse batted her lashes at Raven, but Raven barely noticed her.

"Raven, Lynn. Lynn, Raven."

"Hi, Raven." Michaela almost gagged when the on-duty nurse, Lynn, cranked out an overly sweet tone. Raven was a looker, but there was no need to fall all over him like that.

"Pleased to meet you." From Raven's tone he was a liar. He sounded far from pleased.

Michaela quickly followed the instructions Big Red had sent to Robin. While the files transferred, she jotted down her own list of names and dates. It couldn't hurt to have a physical backup, just in case.

She got as much information to Red as she dared before shutting down the search and looking up Snod's charts. "Huh. You're right. He *was* discharged." With a clean bill of health, no less. How had he...?

Oh. He must be one of the fae. Unless werewolves were real too. All the romance novels said they healed super fast.

"Told you."

"Oh, well. I hope he does okay out there." She hadn't pressed charges, so the cops wouldn't be after him. But after that odd pledge, she had to wonder if he was like Robin, one of the fae. She was willing to bet that he was, and that she hadn't seen the last of him.

Robin would be thrilled. Not. He was far more possessive than anyone she'd ever been with.

Michaela moved out from behind the counter, pleased that she'd managed to avoid Dick's attention. "I'll see you later, Lynn, and thanks."

"You too, Michaela."

Raven grabbed hold of her arm. "Come with me."

"What—?"

"*Now.*"

Michaela tugged on her arm, but he had it in an iron grip. Raven pulled her to a deserted hallway. "What the hell are you doing?"

"I don't know what you're talking about." Crap. Was Raven fae, and if so, was he working with McNeil? But he couldn't be. He'd protected her from McNeil, and she still had the sense that Raven wouldn't truly hurt her.

Michaela gasped as Raven, eyes glowing a familiar, vicious green, slammed her into the wall. "You know *nothing* of the affairs you have meddled with. Do you understand the danger you have placed yourself in?" He reached into her scrubs pocket and pulled out the list of names. "McNeil will make a meal of you without a second thought."

"I can take care of myself." She scowled up at the big brute and ripped the paper back out of his hands. Really, what was it with these guys and ordering her around? She was getting tired of it.

"Can you?" Raven loomed over her, his hands on the wall just above her head, closing her in. One of his knees was bent, pinning her in place. "Can you truly?"

Michaela nodded and pressed a single-serving box of Cheerios into his groin. She always carried them with her to tempt the appetites of the kids who were allowed solid food but whose appetite was off due to medication. "My Taser to your balls says I can."

Raven, eyes wide, jumped back, freeing her.

"Made you look!" And Michaela took off like the hounds of hell were on her heels.

Considering everything else she'd learned that day, maybe they were.

"Damn it." She heard the pounding of his footfalls, knew he was after her. She rounded the corner at speed, her nurse's shoes squeaking on the linoleum. "Michaela!" She darted for the elevator, gasping in surprise when he appeared in front of her in a swirl of black smoke. "Stop running, damn it."

"Stop trying to scare me, asshole."

He snarled. "You think McNeil gives you even two seconds to be scared? He'll eviscerate you and feed on your entrails." Raven began to stalk forward, but Michaela stood her ground. "He'll strip the skin from your bones. He will make you suffer, if only because it will hurt Robin and me. There will be *nothing* you can do about it, because you're frail."

"I am *not* frail."

"You are mortal. To us, you are like an easily broken pane of glass." He cupped her cheek. "It would kill me if something happened to you."

She took a deep breath. "I'm with Robin."

He closed his eyes, the pain in his expression gone almost before it appeared. "I know." He kissed the tip of her nose. "But it would still kill me."

She debated whether or not to tell him about Shane Dunne's warning, but before she could decide warm arms wrapped around her from behind. "What would kill you, hmm?"

Raven stepped back as Robin staked his claim on Michaela. "You should have been guarding her more closely. Do you know what she was doing? What the consequences could be?"

Robin nodded. "Yes, and I voiced my objections. However, she's knocked hours, if not days, off of my gremlin's research time."

Raven grunted. "Your initial purpose in being here was to save Prince Evan. Why not concentrate on that?"

"We both know *she* is up to something more than the kidnapping of a White Court prince, Raven."

"Who is *she?*"

Raven looked uncomfortable. "No one you will ever meet, if I have my say." His gaze returned to Robin, his expression resolute. "She is, but I'm not sure what." He glared at the arm around Michaela's waist. "McNeil is here for some reason unknown to me. It's possible it has to do with *her* orders, or it could be something else entirely. Either way, you should take Michaela to safety."

"An excellent idea."

Michaela found herself once more wrapped up in dark smoke. Only this time they landed in Kael's living room.

Kael jumped with a startled shout, clutching his chest when he realized who was there. "Damn it, Robin. You almost gave me a heart attack."

Robin laughed. "I think you will live."

Kael stood and bowed extravagantly to Michaela, much to her amusement. "Nice to see you again, Lady Goodfellow."

She snickered. "It's the lavender Hello Kitty scrubs, isn't it?"

Kael's eyes twinkled. "What can I say? They're very lady-like." He flopped back down on the sofa with a grin.

"Wait. How did you know Robin and I had...?" She looked up at Robin. "What did you call it again?"

"Bonded, my dear. You are my truebond."

She ignored Kael's hissed-in breath. "So how *did* you know?"

"When Oberon welcomed you and declared you Lady Goodfellow, all the Gray Court felt it."

"Oh."

"Kael, we'll be moving on Prince Evan soon. Also, the High King has declared McNeil's life forfeit."

Kael grimaced and shot Michaela a quick glance. "Um, Robin—"

"She knows at least part of it."

Kael relaxed.

"I know you're here to rescue a prince, and that McNeil is a cannibal. Anything else, feel free to explain it." She flopped down next to Kael and went boneless. "I'm bushed."

"Poor sweetie. Bondings can take a lot out of you, especially when you're human. Or so I've heard." Kael patted her arm sympathetically, ignoring Robin's annoyed hiss.

Michaela laid her head on Kael's shoulder. "I hope to God there is a *Fae for Dummies* book."

Robin rolled his eyes as Kael shot him a smug look. "You'll be fine."

"Indeed, Ruby was out for days after Leo bound her." Robin joined them on the sofa and pulled Michaela into his arms. She switched to Robin's much more comfy shoulder.

The affection in Robin's tone had her ears perking up. "Who is Ruby?"

"Someone dear to me." Robin pressed a kiss to her forehead, instantly reassuring her. "She is family to me, much as Duncan, Moira and Jaden are."

"And she is mortal, just like you. Only now, because she bonded with a Sidhe, she shares in his lifespan. She'll live as long as her truebond, Leo Dunne, does." Kael grinned. "It was a huge scandal in the White Court for a while. Everyone thought he'd be bonded to a Malmayne."

"I don't understand."

Robin snuggled her like an overgrown, half-asleep puppy. He was a cuddler, it seemed, though from the shocked look on Kael's face that wasn't always true.

She could live with that.

"An arranged marriage was set up between the Jolouns and the Malmaynes, one that would have benefited both sides had it come to fruition. It was arranged by Armand Joloun, the father of Aileen Joloun-Dunne, making it near impossible for the Jolouns to back away from the deal without losing face with the Court." Robin ran his hand down her arm with a contented purr. "Which is part of why, when Aileen Joloun met her truebond, Sean Dunne, everything became, as they say, screwed up."

"Like I said. Totally scandalous. A high court Sidhe female, promised to another, ran off with some low-born Irish leprechaun. It was the talk of the Court for years. Totally eclipsed my aunt's marriage to the queen's brother."

"Did it?" Michaela's head was starting to hurt. She had a lot to learn, it seemed.

"Oh yeah. Uncle Edmond was the talk of the court for almost a century. Then Aileen Joloun defied her parent's wishes to marry some low-born fae without a drop of noble blood. At least Aunt Trisha had *some* noble blood, even if she was a pooka." Kael made a face. "And they still treat them both like dirt at court functions."

"Things will be better for them once they join the Gray."

Kael nodded at Robin's words, but he didn't look convinced.

Robin began toying with the ends of Michaela's hair. "At first, Aileen had no real objection. After all, Duncan Malmayne is a fairly attractive man, wealthy and powerful."

Michaela twisted in Robin's arms until she was staring up at him. "Wait, *the* Duncan? Our Duncan?" Robin nodded, looking pleased for some reason. "The blond who's mated to Moira and Jaden?" Now she was definitely getting confused.

"Yes. Duncan is five hundred years old, and at the time of the contract was well under his father's rule. He was not a clan lord, merely the heir, and thus subject to the whims of his lord." Robin settled her back down, stroking her back.

"Oh."

The Hob

Apparently she looked as confused as she felt, because Kael muffled a laugh. "When Aileen broke the contract and ran off with her leprechaun, the Malmaynes were furious. Duncan didn't care one way or the other; in fact, I hear he wished them well."

"But a contract was in place, and had to be honored." Robin gave an elegant shrug. "So it was the children of Aileen and Sean Dunne who would eventually be forced to fulfill it, whether they wished it so or not."

"Which they did, as Duncan and Moira are also truebonded. Now that ceremony, I hear, was quite the sight."

"What about Jaden?"

"He is truebonded to both, and as he was the first to bond the three of them together, they took his name, Blackthorn." Robin grinned. "And their Sidhe bonding ceremony was, indeed, a sight to behold."

"So Duncan and Moira married into Jaden's family. Got it." She didn't, not really, but she figured she could get more out of Moira later.

"However, before all that happened, the Malmaynes demanded that Leo be the one to bond with one of their females and fulfill the marriage contract. Leo refused, because by then he'd already met Ruby, and knew she was his truebond." Kael sighed. "The women of the Court were shocked when he refused to enter a tribond and fulfill the contract. 'After all, my dears, his mate is *human*.'" Kael sniffed disdainfully. She had the feeling he was mimicking someone specific, someone he had little respect for.

"So Aileen called in a favor I owed her. She demanded my help in rescuing her son, and that is how I met the Dunnes." Robin's smile was full of affection. "I did as they asked, and in return, they accepted me as none other ever had. To me, they are family, though we do not share blood."

Kael made a buzzing noise. "Wrong. I hear you share blood with Jaden, which really does make them family. Isn't that how the vampire became a clan lord?"

Robin froze. "True enough, but not something I discuss willingly."

Kael shrugged. "Anyway, Ruby is a human who truebonded with a Sidhe. She'll be able to tell you all about being a mortal married to a fae, and how to deal with the dangers that are sometimes attached to that."

"But will she understand the dangers of being married to Robin Goodfellow?"

Robin pressed his chin to the top of her head and breathed deep. She felt him relax, and wondered if perhaps her scent calmed him somehow. "Considering all that she has been through, she may have an idea, as will the rest of her family. The fae world has not been kind to the Dunnes."

"Some of it has." Michaela snuggled into her new husband.

She felt his smile against her hair. "Indeed. Some of it has."

Chapter Twenty

"You don't give me the small jobs, do you, Robin?"

"I require the best, and you are the best."

"Too true."

Robin grinned. The gremlin was very good at the work he did for Robin and was loyal to a fault, both things that Robin valued highly. "Besides, you love every moment of it."

"Also true." Red cracked his knuckles with an evil grin. "Sit back and watch, my friend, while I work my magic."

Robin leaned against Red's desk and hoped his truebond was sleeping peacefully. He'd left Michaela at Kael's home after extracting a promise from her to stay put. Last he'd seen, she'd been curled up on Kael's guest bed, half-asleep and looking oh so tempting. He'd left Kael strict orders to watch over her, much to her amused disgust. "Work away."

"Congratulations on your bondmate, by the way." Red's fingers began to fly over the keyboard. Data flew across the screen at a speed that would give any but another gremlin a massive headache. "She's an eleven."

That she was. "She has a good and fierce heart, as well."

"The best kind of woman." Red grinned, but his fingers never stopped flying. "She got a sister?"

Robin shook his head, amused. "I'm not certain. I could ask, if you wish." It hadn't come up, but Robin would find out soon enough. Red was a pretty man under all that hair, but scruffy. Even if Michaela had a sister, the gremlin would need a fashion intervention before Robin would allow him out to meet her.

Red pushed his unruly, dark brown hair out of his face with an impatient grunt. The light of the computer screen shone off his red-framed glasses. "McNeil has been a very naughty boy." The love of the hunt was in Red's voice as he chased the threads Michaela had given him. "He's been looking for snacks in all the wrong places."

"What have you found?" Robin leaned over Red's chair, staring at the incomprehensible flow of data.

"Bodies have been appearing near the *SS United States* since the first day McNeil arrived in Philadelphia." Red glanced at a different screen off to his right before turning his attention back to the one Robin considered his main one. "Which was the same day Prince Evan went missing."

"Damnation." That could mean more than fourteen women dead, as the prince had been missing for over two weeks.

Red glanced at yet another screen, this one above him and to his left. "By the way, Gloriana didn't ask the Gray Court for help until a week after the boy disappeared. Her brother and his family were asking for help from her the moment they realized he was gone. Going by their private emails, they're furious and heading for the Gray Court as we speak." He tsk'd. "Seems they liked the fact that Oberon jumped to help where their own relative didn't. Cold bitch, Gloriana."

Robin took a deep breath. "Did they have trouble leaving the White Court?"

"Yes, but I smoothed their way. They'll get to the Gray Palace safely, don't you worry." Red's grin was pure evil. "Man, she is *pissed*. She's talking about—oh shit."

"What?"

"She's putting a hit out on them." Red scowled. "They won't be safe until they give Oberon their oaths, and even then they might not be."

"I will deal with it." He'd assign them a Blade or two until the crisis passed. Gloriana was taking things too far with this stunt. What was she thinking? Prince Edmond was her *brother*.

Red nodded once in acknowledgement, already moving on now that the information had been passed along. "Take a look at this." Red pointed to the lower, left-hand screen.

The data froze, and Robin found himself staring at several tabbed coroner's reports. It was more than he'd feared, if the number of tabs spoke truly. "How many has he killed?"

"More than Philadelphia authorities want to let out, that's for sure. They've got this info locked down tighter than Trump's hair."

Robin counted the reports. "Six so far."

"Six they've *found*. I've got some missing persons' reports that match the MO." More tabs appeared, making twenty in all. Robin cursed under his breath. "Small problem, by the way. All the victims looked remarkably alike." Pictures flashed into existence over the tabbed reports. "Dark-haired, young, pretty girls, out hitting the clubs. They go missing, the families call frantic, and boom! The police are all, 'Holy shit, serial killer!' except the so-called shark bitten bodies are throwing them off. Now they don't know what to think."

"I do."

Red nodded. He leaned back in his chair and stared up at Robin, his formerly dark eyes—pupil, iris and whites—blood red. Glowing green text scrolled across them as Red continued to monitor the data on his screens.

Truly, the gremlins were strange fae, their powers over human technology rivaling no other species. Young, barely a hundred and fifty years old, they'd evolved from brownies, sprites drawn to assisting others but not averse to playing pranks on those they felt deserved it. They were the first new species of fae in a very long time, longer than Robin cared to count. Unlike most other fae, their Seeming came from all the different races of humanity, from Africa to Japan to the odd combinations North America had to offer. Irish fae, like Moira and her parents, tended to look like they came from Ireland; the

Sidhe looked like very well-bred Brits. Kitsune always looked Japanese, and Djinn always looked Middle Eastern.

But not the gremlins. They were true children of the "melting pot" that was the United States. Red's Seeming was a Korean American with perpetually windblown hair and laughing brown eyes. He was only fifty years old, dressed like a hobo, and was one of the richest men in the world.

Red's brow rose. "Orders?"

Robin tapped his chin as he considered whom he could place with the Orens. "Keep the Orens safe. I'm going to have Tristan Malmayne meet with them, bring them to the court. I'm certain dealing with another fae who fled the White successfully will ease some of their concerns." Robin ignored Red's grunt of amusement. "Make sure that Gloriana cannot find them before they reach the safety of the Court. Once there, one of the other Blades will take over."

"And McNeil?"

Robin grinned, his teeth nice and pointy. "I'll deal with McNeil personally."

"All righty then. That's not freaky or anything." Robin chuckled darkly as Red turned back to his machines. "Oh, and I'm setting up surveillance on Lady Goodfellow."

Robin's claws dug into the leather of Red's chair. "Oh?"

Red snickered. "Down, boy. I'm not gonna poach your girl. I'm just watching your back, as always."

Robin grunted.

"You have it bad. The great Robin Goodfellow, felled by a mortal." Red shook his head sadly. "The nymphs are gonna eat her alive."

"The nymphs may try. My wife is stronger than she seems."

"She'd better be. She looks like a Chihuahua could take her in a cage match." Red held up his hands when Robin growled. "I'm just saying."

"You need to get out more."

Red snorted. "Yup. Because the women are just lining up around the block for a shot at me."

"If you didn't resemble one of those nerds you idolize so much..."

"Hey, now that's just mean. Besides, I've been told I clean up nice."

Robin studied Red. He smiled sweetly. "Perhaps I'll take you under my wing, then."

Red's fingers stilled on the keyboard. "Uh...thanks?"

"You are most welcome," Robin purred.

"Shit." Red's fingers started to fly again as Robin chuckled. Dealing with Red was always such a pleasure. "Just try not to make me look like a monkey's ass, okay?"

"Monkey's ass, indeed. You could benefit from my fashion sense." Robin huffed, straightening the cuffs of his azure silk shirt.

"I don't think—" Red sat up straight, his attention suddenly glued to the monitors. "Take a look at this."

He did something that Robin couldn't see, the strange magic of the gremlins working through one of the most powerful of their kind. The screens snapped together, the images blending until Robin could see McNeil hovering over a young, blond man with eyes eerily similar to Kael's but full of terror. McNeil was dragging the boy through what looked to be the eviscerated, rusty husk of a ship. "Well, well. Prince Evan."

Red sat back with a satisfied grin. "Gotcha, you son of a bitch. Gotta love paranoid humans and their trusty surveillance cameras."

Robin stood, his movements fluid, ready to hunt. "Contact Jaden. Continue to monitor the prince, but make sure he shows up on none of the final footage the humans will see. I'll get the prince free."

"Aye aye." Those eerie, data-filled eyes looked up at him again. "Robin." Robin's head tilted, curious at the serious expression on the gremlin's normally jovial face. "You're one of the few people in this world I give a damn about, and that son of a bitch is sneaky as well as vicious. Be careful."

Robin bowed and disappeared, reappearing perched on the lip of one of the smoke stacks of the *SS United States*. He listened carefully for the sound of McNeil moving below, but could discern nothing. He leapt from the edge, landing lightly on the decking far below.

It was time to hunt.

Robin ghosted through the ship, invisible to all eyes, even those of an *each uisge*. He avoided the areas where the workers were. McNeil would stick to the shadows, avoid the possibility of being caught by so many humans. Unlike Robin, McNeil could not cloak his presence, let alone that of the prince. All Evan would have to do would be to cry out for help, and McNeil would be forced to fight. A slaughter on such a scale would bring more than Oberon's wrath down upon him, Robin was certain. Not even Titannia viewed the wholesale slaughter of humans with anything but disgust, if only because it brought attention to them. Even she abided by the laws set down by the gods regarding the Seeming.

The *each uisge* would be difficult to kill, especially on board the ship. The creature would draw strength from being so close to its element, while Robin, away from his own, would grow marginally weaker.

That wouldn't stop Robin from gutting McNeil and whisking Prince Evan to Oberon.

"Be still, brat."

Robin froze, the soft, hissed words with the slight Scottish burr bringing him up short. McNeil was closer than he'd surmised.

"My aunt will send someone for me."

The surprisingly deep voice of the prince was muted, slurred. McNeil must have drugged the boy. Robin caught no scent of other fae, though the fading scent of Lord Wyght was not difficult to discern. Surprisingly, he detected no hint of Lady Malmayne.

Raven's scent was stronger, meaning he'd visited the boy recently. Robin was going to have to do something about that.

McNeil laughed, the sound sinister. "I very much doubt so, boy. You've been with us far too long for your loving aunt to ever trust you again."

"You bas—"

The sound of flesh against flesh echoed eerily. "Be quiet, and I might let you continue living."

"Someone will come for me."

McNeil laughed. The sound was eerily pleasant. "Who do you think they'll send?"

"My aunt has men who work for her in covert ops."

Covert ops? Robin nearly laughed. Really, the boy watched far too many Bond movies. Gloriana was not M, for Pan's sake. Robin moved closer to where the voices were coming from, but the strange echoes of the ship were throwing him off.

"You think they'll send some White Court fop I'll eat for breakfast?"

Evan grunted in pain.

"Stop struggling or there will be nothing left for your family to find." McNeil chuckled. "Of course, if Robin arrives, I won't have to worry about that, will I?"

Evan whimpered. "W–which Robin?"

"Goodfellow, of course."

"Oh shit." Evan barely breathed the words.

Robin rolled his eyes. Really. What did the boy think Robin would do to him?

"Perhaps you should have accepted her majesty's kind invitation after all."

"I will *never* turn to the Black."

"Foolish boy." Robin turned the corner and found McNeil, his hand raised, Prince Evan glaring at him defiantly. For all the prince was wobbly on his feet, his conviction was strong.

Robin moved quickly, placing himself between McNeil and the boy. He popped into view before McNeil could swing and threw a straight arm punch, knocking McNeil back. "Hello again, McNeil."

"Goodfellow." McNeil wiped the blood from his chin. "Here for the boy, I gather."

Robin smiled. "By the order of King Oberon, I have been sent to mete out justice to you."

"For kidnapping? Going to throw me in jail?" McNeil smirked.

Oh, how Robin was going to love wiping that look away. "For murdering humans and endangering the fae race, you have been sentenced to death."

McNeil's expression turned dark. "I have to eat, you know."

Robin's brows rose. "No. I don't."

Robin was not surprised when McNeil attempted to rush him. Robin met him with a well-placed kick, sending McNeil flying into a bulkhead.

McNeil rallied quicker than Robin expected, tossing his own kick at Robin's head. Robin dodged easily. He'd fought far greater opponents than McNeil could ever hope to be. Unfortunately, when he dodged, it allowed McNeil to slip past him and farther into the ship.

"Damn." Robin turned to the young prince, who looked ready to pass out. "Stay put. I'll deal with McNeil and be back for you." Robin took off, ignoring the horrified look on the prince's face.

Robin snorted in disgust. Blades weren't just assassins, they were protectors. What were they teaching young fae these days?

Robin flew through the ship, chasing the salt-water scent of the *each uisge*. He grew wary as it grew stronger, turning a corner with caution. The son of a bitch was around here somewhere—

Robin barely dodged the punch that flew at him through a dark, opened doorway. He blocked the next, scowling at how close the *each uisge* had gotten to landing a blow.

"Feeding makes me stronger." McNeil landed a kick to Robin's thigh that staggered him. "Needless to say, I made sure I was well fed."

Robin growled and the walls shook. "And for that, you will die."

Robin threw his own punch, startled when McNeil blocked him. McNeil managed to land a punch on Robin that knocked his head back.

When Robin went to retaliate, McNeil wasn't there. The sound of pounding footfalls led him to a stairwell, the lingering scent of salt water a telltale sign that McNeil had gone up.

Robin ghosted through the floor, unwilling to give McNeil the advantage. He found himself on the upper deck, the blue sky blinding after the darkness of the interior of the ship.

A door slammed open and McNeil raced out as if the hounds of hell were on his tail. Robin raced after him, still ghosted but able to move much faster than a vampire in a similar state. He was a gust of wind, a breath of quick air, and ahead of McNeil before the water horse could react.

McNeil flew down another set of stairs to the lower deck, unaware that Robin was already waiting for him. Robin hit him with a flying sidekick that sent him reeling into the stairs. He extended his claws, ready to deliver the lethal blow.

McNeil blocked, knocking Robin's poisonous claws away from his flesh. "Not today."

"Yes, today." Robin cold-cocked the bastard. "At least you aren't monologuing. I hate that."

McNeil shook off the blow, using the railing of the stairway to propel himself upward. He swung himself around in a move worthy of a Kung Fu movie, surprising Robin with a blow to his shoulder.

Robin blinked. "That stung." Interesting. He might actually have to work up a sweat.

McNeil didn't wait around. He took off toward the edge of the ship.

Shit. If McNeil hit the water, Robin would be unable to follow him. He misted in front of McNeil, crouched, and did his own Kung Fu move. He swung his leg around in an arc, taking McNeil's legs out from under him.

McNeil hit the deck hard. Robin crouched over him, his claws ready to strike the killing blow.

"Hey! Who the fuck are you?"

Robin turned, startled, at the sound of a strange male voice. One of the construction workers was running toward them, a cell phone in his hand.

Hell and damnation. Was he taking pictures?

McNeil took advantage of Robin's momentary distraction to throw him off. He staggered to his feet and stumbled to the edge of the ship, diving off as Robin's claws scraped his back.

Robin took a deep breath. McNeil had gotten away.

Robin wanted to growl at the human who had interrupted his rightful kill. Instead, he smiled, adjusting the cuffs of his shirt. "Why did you interfere with a federal officer?"

The man blinked. "Whu?"

Robin pulled out his fake credentials, ones that had gotten him out of trouble on more than one occasion. "Special Agent Robin Goodman, at your service. The man you just stopped me from apprehending was a wanted kidnapper."

"What? Oh shit." The man's eyes went wide. "So those noises we heard weren't ghosts?"

Robin sighed. Where did the humans come up with this shit? "No, it's a scared young man who has been held here against his will."

"Should I call for an ambulance?"

Now wouldn't that be amusing? Perhaps Michaela's friends would show up to deal with the prince. "The young man is still in the hold, but safe for now. I will fetch him and return him to his family."

"Don't you need to, like, secure the crime scene or something?"

"That's what I'm here for."

Robin looked behind the worker to find Jaden, his eyes covered in dark glasses, smiling at the worker. "Agent James Black. Pleased to meet you." Jaden shook hands with the worker. "If you'll follow me, we'll let Robin deal with the victim while I secure the area."

Robin sighed in relief. The vampiric ability to scrub minds would ensure that the worker remembered nothing of what happened this day. Jaden's newfound ability to tolerate sunlight was coming in handy.

Once Jaden and the worker were out of sight Robin misted to the location where he'd last seen Evan. There, the prince huddled against the wall, his head pillowed on his knees. He lifted his head and stared at Robin when he appeared, then climbed to his feet. He squared his shoulders. "Am I going to die?"

"Do you wish to?"

Evan visibly swallowed. "What I wish doesn't matter. Are you here to kill me?"

"That depends entirely upon you." Robin studied his claws. "I overheard you rejecting the Black, but are you truly untainted?"

"I...I believe so."

"You *believe* so." Robin scented none of the Black on the boy save McNeil's scent, and that was fading. "Then *I* believe I have no reason to. Your aunt, on the other hand…"

Prince Evan hid his wince well. "She will tolerate no hint of the Black." He took a deep breath and let it out slowly. "Please. I only ask one thing. Protect my family. She'll hurt them, thinking them tainted as well."

Well. Color Robin impressed. The boy's last thought was to protect his family.

He leaned in close and confirmed his suspicions. The boy's scent was clean, far cleaner than any Robin had dealt with before. "You're a good boy." Evan barely flinched as Robin took hold of his arm. "I have one last question for you."

"Yes?"

"Have you ever spoken an oath of fealty?" And Robin whisked the prince to Oberon, content in the knowledge that Jaden would take care of any witnesses.

Chapter Twenty-One

Michaela shot a look at Kael and decided to take her chances. "I need to run back to my apartment for something."

Michaela wasn't certain what Robin was going to do when he returned, but she was willing to bet it involved whisking her away back to Colorado. He'd still been pretty snarly about leaving her with Kael when he left for his appointment with Big Red. She wanted to grab a few important things, like her nursing license and a few irreplaceable photos in case Robin grabbed her and hightailed it back to the mountains.

Besides, she wanted some clean panties, damn it.

Kael eyed her warily before replying. "No."

Michaela rolled her eyes. "It's not like I'm running to the convention." No matter how badly she wanted to. "I'm just going up two floors."

"Then let me rephrase it. *Hayl* no."

"Kael." Michaela gave him her best puppy-dog eyes.

From the look on his face he wasn't buying it. "What is so important that you have to leave the safety of the apartment, and thus put my life on the line?"

Michaela decided to have some fun with him. She decided to go with the one thing that had always squicked out her brothers. "I need tampons."

He crossed his arms over his chest. "Sit on a towel."

"Kael!" She smirked. "Fine. Here's some cash." She dug in her purse and handed him a twenty. "The kind I like to use are—"

Kael stuck his fingers in his ears. "*Lalalalalala.*"

This was just too easy. God, the look of utter horror on his face was priceless. "Make sure you get the multipack, since I might be here a few days. Oh, and some extra Ultra Absorbency ones would be good too." She sighed. "It's like a red Niagara Falls some days." She bit her lip. "Do you think you can pick up some Midol too? I'm starting to get cramps. Oh, and ice cream and chocolate covered pretzels, so I don't kill someone. You, most likely."

He whimpered. "Shit." He stood up with a scowl. "Fine. We'll go. But if he kills me and eats me, my ghost is haunting your ass."

"Won't he eat that too?" Michaela opened the front door and headed for the elevator.

"I hate you *so* much right now."

Michaela giggled and stepped onto the elevator. "C'mon. I'm in, I grab what I need, and I'm out. We'll be gone ten minutes, tops."

"That's nine minutes and fifty-nine seconds too long." Kael banged his head against the elevator. "I'm so dead." He glared at her as she bounced off the elevator a few seconds later. "You don't really have...female issues right now, do you?"

"Nope, but I do need some stuff from my apartment."

"It couldn't wait until Robin got back?" He followed her in, taking in her tiny studio in a single glance. "Hell, I thought *my* place was small."

"It's not exactly Robin's mansion, but it's mine." She made her way to the dresser and began pulling things off of it. The pictures of her parents, both deceased, and her brothers and sister, living in Cherry Hill, New Jersey. Her parents had a thing for "M" names, with Matthew being the oldest, followed by Martin, then Michaela and finally Melissa. Mel had just graduated from college and was looking for work. Maybe she could convince Robin to give her a hand?

God. How am I going to explain my move to them? I met my dream man a few days ago and I'm moving to Colorado with him? That would go over well. Matt was almost as protective as Robin. If he thought for one second Michaela was in trouble he'd be in her apartment with a rifle, ready to take on the world. She'd have to make sure she called them and let them know she hadn't completely lost her mind. She picked up the picture, unable to hold back her smile. They were going to love Robin, and Robin...

He'd get used to them. Eventually.

"Is that it? Just some pictures?"

"Family pictures." She held up the one of the four siblings. "See?"

"Huh. What else do you need?" Kael was twitchy, his eyes darting around the room.

"Are you okay?" Michaela took a step toward Kael, but before she could reach him a hand latched on to her arm. She shrieked as she was whisked away.

"God damn it! Stop scaring me like that!" She turned to smack Robin, only to find herself face to face with Raven. "Oh. It's you."

Raven sighed. "Yes, let's make it absolutely clear where I stand, shall we?"

"Raven." She put her hands on her hips and tapped her toes.

"No, please. Unman me." He glared at her. "Got any more Cheerios? Those worked nicely."

She shook her head. "What the hell are you up to?"

He flung his arms wide, his expression mocking. "The roof. What else?"

She blinked and looked around. "Huh. So we are." She sighed. The view of the city was stunning from up here, but she didn't have time to admire it. "What's going on? Why did you bring me up here? I know you're not going to hurt me, so don't even try to frighten me."

He took hold of her hands, turning them in his. He seemed to be studying them. "Such delicate fingers you have."

"Uh, Raven?"

The longing in his blue eyes was intense. "Do I have a chance?"

She wanted to cry at the loneliness in his gaze, but she couldn't give him the answer he wanted. "No."

He took a deep breath and released her hands. "I thought not." He tilted his head, the gesture reminiscent of Robin, and suddenly she missed her lover fiercely. "Do you love him?"

She smiled. "Now that I know he's real, I'm willing to admit that I can't remember a time when I haven't." Her friends were going to shit a brick when she introduced Robin to them.

His eyes closed briefly, but whatever he was feeling was hidden from her. "I see." He took a deep breath and opened his eyes. "Then there are some things you should be aware of."

"Like?"

"Robin is my father."

Michaela froze. "Um. What, now?"

He laughed, the sound hollow. "Robin Goodfellow is my father."

"Did he—"

"Know? No, not until a couple of days ago."

She needed to sit down. "I'm a mommy?"

He burst out laughing, but the sound was hollow. "*Please* don't call yourself that. I have a mother, thank you."

"Who?" She could barely breathe. While she was certain Raven's mother was in Robin's past, it was still a shock. It brought home how much older than her Robin was.

How old *was* he?

"Erin MacSweeney. She was a Gray Court sylph, but when she got pregnant with me the Black Queen captured her and kept her prisoner. She's still there, being held against her will, as a guarantee that I won't fail in my—" He eyed her warily.

"Your mission." She blew out a breath. "You're supposed to do something to Robin."

"And she will kill my mother if I don't."

"Catch twenty-two. Kill your father, or kill your mother."

"Exactly." His smile was weary. "You understand. I knew you would."

"You can't do it."

He scowled. "What choice have I?"

She took his hands in her own. "The right one." When he opened his mouth to argue, she stopped him. "Tell Robin. Get his help in saving your mother. You think he'll let her rot away?"

He flinched. "You don't know that he won't."

"I do. You're his *son*, and if there's one thing I know, Robin Goodfellow takes care of his own. That means you too."

"He just met me. He didn't even know I existed! How can I be certain he'll help?" Raven threw her hands off and began to pace. "You don't understand. She...she was the only light in the darkness." He whirled around and glared at her. "Until you."

Michaela winced.

"So how can you ask me to trust him?"

"Because of who he is." Michaela watched him pace. There was a restlessness in Raven that was absent in Robin. "If you can't trust him, then trust me."

"And if he's too late? If he can't save her?"

He looked so damn lonely, staring out over the edge of the building at the city below. His hair was blowing against the breeze, whipping around his face, and she wondered if that was his mother's sylph blood in him responding to his emotions. "Then he'll avenge her."

He snorted in disbelief. "It's not that simple."

"Yes, it is."

She'd know that voice anywhere. *Robin.* Warm arms encircled her from behind, his hair brushing against her. "Hello, Robin."

"Hello, Michaela."

"You're late." She snuggled back against him.

"Terribly sorry. My dinner date got cancelled at the last minute." The sharp look Raven shot Robin should have worried her, but she didn't have time to examine it. "Be right back, Raven. Please don't leave this spot. I'd hate to have to hunt for you."

Michaela sighed as dark mist whirled around her. They reappeared in Kael's living room. "Great. I finally got out of here and you put me back."

He turned her around and kissed the tip of her nose. "Stay *put* this time, my dear, or we will have words."

She saluted him smartly. "Aye aye, sir!"

Robin sighed and disappeared.

Michaela flopped down on Kael's sofa and called Kael's cell. She didn't even say hello when he answered. "I'm back in your apartment."

"Thank fuck."

"Robin brought me."

"Aw, shit."

His pained groan made her laugh. "He's mad at me, not you."

"That's what you think." He paused for a second. "How much is a plane ticket to Abu Dhabi?"

Michaela rolled her eyes and hung up her phone.

"Kidnapping. Very nasty business, that." Robin shot Raven a displeased look.

Raven rolled his eyes. "You whisked her away quickly enough, didn't you?"

"Why did you take her up here in the first place?"

Robin watched as Raven stiffened. Raven turned his gaze away, once more studying the city laid out below them. "None of your business."

His hair was blowing against the wind again. "I've Claimed her, bonded her to me. She is mine."

"So she informed me."

Robin waited, but that seemed to be all Raven was willing to say on the matter. "Tell me about your mother." The nearly imperceptible flinch told Robin all he needed to know. "I will help you, if you will allow it."

Raven glanced at Robin over his shoulder. "The plan was simple. Distract the great Hobgoblin, kill him if at all possible. Allow *her* agents to do what they'd planned all along. Recruit the prince, kill him if that wasn't feasible."

Robin nodded. "I had surmised as much. What is the bitch queen's plan?"

Raven shrugged and turned back to the city. "I don't know. It wasn't my job, and if captured I could rightfully claim ignorance." He took a deep breath. "You saved the prince."

"Yes, I did."

Raven's head drooped. "Then it was for naught. She's dead, and it's my fault."

"You don't know that for certain."

Raven shook his head. "You don't know *her*. She does not take kindly to failure. You are alive, and the boy is free. Therefore, my mother is dead. Anything else is irrelevant. Even if her main objective succeeds, I failed."

"I do know her. She was my king's bride for centuries." Robin moved until he stood shoulder to shoulder with his son. The boy was taller and broader than he, but not so much that Robin felt dwarfed. "If you are sure—"

"I am."

Robin nodded. "Then is it vengeance you wish to seek?"

"Against *her*?" Raven's lips twisted in a mocking parody of a smile. "I want to watch as her pet demon feasts on her entrails."

"So. Vengeance it is." One that Robin would be more than happy to mete out.

They were silent for a few moments before Raven quietly spoke. "Take care of her, or I will take her from you."

Robin smiled. The boy was stubborn. He reminded Robin of someone. "You will try, but you will fail."

Raven's twisted smile eased a fraction. "You wish."

"I know."

Raven's shoulder brushed against his. "The Black Queen will call us back soon."

"And the punishment?"

"Has more than likely already fallen upon me."

Robin clenched his hands. He very much doubted that was the only punishment Titannia would hand down. Raven would pay in more ways than one. "Stay."

Raven smirked. "And watch you make love to the only other woman I've ever given a damn about?"

Robin arched his brow. "I didn't ask you into my bedchamber, dear boy. Just into my life."

"Same difference." Raven brushed his shoulder once more against Robin's. "You'd trust me near your precious king?"

Robin took a deep breath, scenting the air around his son. Titannia's stench was fading, leaving behind only the scent of clean, fresh air and the Hob himself. His aroma was not the purest Robin had ever taken in, but the boy had no real ties to the Black beyond that of his forced coupling with Titannia. "Yes."

"You're joking."

The shock in Raven's voice shouldn't have surprised him. What else had the boy learned but mistrust firmly planted upon betrayal? "Do you truly think a dedicated agent of the Black could fool the Hob?" Robin turned and tapped his dark nail against his son's cheek, drawing blood. He licked the droplet off the edge of his claw.

Robin nearly sagged in relief. The boy was clean. There was no taint in his blood, no foulness to mar the salty taste. "It would take a greater one than you to fool me, Raven. You are no true agent of the Black the way your brother was."

"Hobart was *not* my brother."

Robin begged to differ, but he understood the sentiment. "As you say."

"Do you love her?"

Robin blinked. "Love who?"

Raven shook his head. "When I asked her, she didn't even hesitate." He glared at Robin. "Are you worthy of her?"

Robin tilted his head. What was the boy talking about? "I assume you mean Michaela."

Raven nodded once, sharply.

"She is mine, and I hers." His private thoughts and feelings were his own, and as such not up for debate. Not even with his child. Only with Michaela would he share his innermost feelings.

Raven turned back to the skyline. "She loves you." He snorted in disgust even as Robin's heart leapt for joy. "Why, I don't know." He brushed his hair back from his face. "She seemed to like the artistic type at first."

Robin didn't miss the sideways glance, nor the teasing tone. It was weak, but there. Raven was hurt by Michaela's confession, but cared enough for her to abide by her decision. "I—"

The mirror in his pocket quivered. Robin stepped back from his child and pulled it from his pocket. Oberon's face immediately appeared.

"I think you need to get down to Kael's apartment."

"Michaela?" Robin was ready to mist away, mirror or no mirror, if his bondmate were threatened.

Oberon's gaze darted to the side. "We have a visitor."

Robin exchanged a quick glance with Raven, and, of one accord, the two men disappeared, both intent on protecting the woman they loved.

Chapter Twenty-Two

"Really. It's okay. I know this guy." Michaela tried to move past the immovable brick wall High King Oberon was turning out to be.

"You're acquainted with a redcap?"

A what? "He's Snod." She wiggled her fingers in hello around Oberon's back. "Hi, Snod."

Snod bowed to her, his massive shoulders filling the doorway. "My lady."

"How did you find me?" Did she have her address stamped on her aura or something? Sort of a psychic *Eat at Joe's*?

"The oath bound me to you. My life for yours." Oberon started at Snod's words. Michaela hadn't thought anything could surprise the stoic king. "Loyalty and protection I give to thee. I am your man, and you my liege. By this oath I am bound to thee, by the law of three times three."

"I...see." Oberon stepped aside and waved elegantly. "Then by all means, enter."

Kael gulped. "I'm sorry I called you, sire, but I couldn't get hold of Robin and I didn't know what else to do."

"You did exactly right, young Kael." Oberon gave Kael a small, reassuring smile. "And when we get back to the Court I will be glad to have you as one of my Blades. You kept your head and dealt with a situation that could have proven volatile and, ultimately, deadly, with poise."

"Not all battles are won with fists." Robin materialized right next to Michaela, Raven just in front of them, blocking Snod from her view once more.

"Really, people. He won't hurt me."

"How do you know for certain?" Oberon was eyeing her with all the interest one would show a new species of lizard.

She shrugged. "I sense it, just like I knew from the beginning Raven would never hurt me."

"Your trust in strangers and your power to 'sense' if they mean you harm is long due for a discussion, my dear." Robin pulled her into his arms and cocked a brow. "Miss me?"

"You weren't even gone long enough for me to pee."

Raven choked on a laugh.

"You are bonded." Michaela turned to find Snod smiling at them. It was horrifying, yet cute at the same time. "This is good. Now I don't have to try and hurt the Hob. He will help protect my lady."

"Yes, I will." Robin addressed Snod firmly. He studied Snod through slightly narrowed eyes, a flash of green running through the merry blue until they glowed. "McNeil may be after your lady."

Snod straightened to his full height. "I will make sure he does not harm her."

"I know you will." Robin turned to Oberon. "He's hers, and therefore mine."

Oberon shook his head. "You have the strangest family, my Hob."

Robin grinned. There was a joy in him that hadn't been there before. "As you should know, my king."

"Speaking of which, introduce me to your son."

The command was unmistakable. Robin released Michaela and bowed before his king. "My liege, allow me to introduce Lord Raven MacSweeney, soon to be late of the Black Court."

Raven was pale, but he bowed to Oberon. "My king."

Oberon blinked. "I've been expecting you."

Raven winced. "Yes, about that…"

Oberon laughed lightly. "Your father vouches for you." He glanced at Robin. "At least, I assume he does."

"He does. His heart is clean. He is my son, by blood and soul."

Michaela bit her lip. She had no fucking clue what was going on, but she'd be able to grill Robin like a cheeseburger later. For now, she'd sit back, watch and enjoy the show.

Raven inhaled sharply at his father's words. "I— Do you smell that?" He scowled, turning in place and lifting his face. He inhaled deeply again. "Something smells wrong."

Robin looked at his face and sniffed, reminded Michaela of a bloodhound. "I don't smell anything unusual."

Raven scowled. "No. There's something wrong. I smell sea water." He grabbed hold of Robin's arm. "You have to believe me. Get the king and Michaela out of he—"

The last thing Michaela heard was a sound like a gunshot.

Robin shook shattered glass out of his hair. The impact of the blast had knocked him off his feet, but had done no real damage. He feared, however, that his bondmate had not fared so well. He couldn't feel her in his heart any longer. "Michaela?"

Raven, his back to the damaged wall, groaned and rolled to his feet.

Robin took in the remnants of Kael's apartment, barely acknowledging the damage the bomb had done. Kael's apartment was...shattered. The furniture looked as if it had been shredded. The mirror lay broken beside Raven. The windows had blown out, the curtains now billowing both inside and outside the room. The walls were covered in black soot, tiny embers glowing here and there.

He didn't care about any of it. He had to find his truebond, his love. "Michaela!"

"Here. She's here."

Robin turned. Oberon was kneeling on the floor, a broken and bleeding body in his arms. Robin shook his head, unable to believe the evidence of his eyes.

"No."

Robin didn't realize he'd spoken until he saw the sympathy, the pity, in his king's eyes. "I was too late. I moved too slowly. I am sorry, my Hob."

"No!" He knelt by Oberon, his hands touching, lingering in her dark, blood soaked hair. Her body was riddled with cuts, but the wound that had broken her, killed her, was the piece of bomb that had somehow landed in her throat.

Where was that odd sound coming from? That odd, rushing silence that...

That...

Oh. Oh gods. The void in his heart, the one she'd filled. That sound was the loss of his soul. How was he supposed to survive when his heart lay broken in the arms of his king?

"Robin." He tore his gaze away from the sluggishly bleeding wound in her precious neck and looked into the pale eyes of his king. It was bad, he knew it was, that it wasn't bleeding worse.

It shouldn't be, but it was.

Her brown eyes were open, staring. He touched her silken hair, that rushing silence growing still within him.

He hadn't told her he loved her yet.

"Robin, listen to me." Something touched him, something cold, but Oberon hissed and flinched. Now he, too, was bleeding, and Robin didn't know why. "I need you to stop."

Listen. Yes. He should have. This was his fault, and he would pay for it for eternity.

Had he listened to his son, he would have had Michaela out of there before the bomb went off.

He would have...

Her empty eyes stared up at nothing, all the warmth, all the laughter, gone.

He would...

Her lips were parted, blood trickling down bruised cheeks.

The Hob

Had she tried to call for him? Had she known that he'd failed her?

Robin threw his head back and screamed. Every ounce of what some would call humanity that had lived in him was gone, snuffed out with her life.

They would pay for taking his truebond. They would all *pay*.

Robin let loose the creature within him, his true self, the one he'd locked away when Oberon first found him, writhing and formless and full of rage. Only the glowing, hate-filled green eyes within showed that there was any thought behind the pure malice he had become.

"Hobgoblin!"

No. Not even that beloved voice could stop him. Robin would find the one who had taken love from him, taken laughter from him, and inflict pain upon them for all of eternity.

"Damn it, Hobgoblin. Listen to me."

The king's power rolled over him, but the madness riding him would not allow it to take hold. Robin swirled toward the broken window, forgetting everything but the need to make the killer hurt.

"I'll go with you." Raven, his eyes the same flaming green as his own, stood by his side. The air swirled around him, growing in intensity as he watched, his sylph heritage coming to the fore in his grief and rage. Robin allowed the boy to come with him, knowing he could not stop him without grievous harm. He would not kill his child to get to his enemy. There was enough left of Robin's sanity for that, at least.

Together, they moved to the open window and flew out it, invisible to all but fae eyes. Robin Goodfellow, aka the Hob, left behind the woman who had once stolen his soul.

He would grieve someday. He would eventually die without her. But before he did, he would find her murderer and shred him.

"It was McNeil. I know it. It had his brackish scent all over it."

Robin's voice was tinny. "Is that so?" McNeil would die slowly, screaming, breathing out his last as Robin watched.

"I want a piece of him, Father. I want to inflict my own pain."

If he could have Robin would have nodded. Raven had loved her too, and this last gift he would grant his son. "Yes."

Raven nodded and began flying toward the waterfront. "The water. He'll be hiding there."

"Near the ship." Robin's voice had become a hissing whisper, a remembrance of what it had once been. Already he could feel himself slipping into complete formlessness, but he had to hold on.

Once McNeil was dead, he would gather his love's body, and together they would slip into the abyss.

"There." A disturbance on the surface of the river, but Robin held back. "It's bait."

"I gathered. McNeil wouldn't be so obvious." Raven looked around and pointed toward the ship. "There. I'd bet anything he's on board."

"That's not—"

"The *SS United States*, I know." The luxury yacht docked so incongruously near the industrial section of the waterfront raised Robin's eyebrows as well. "It's getting ready to set sail."

Indeed, Robin could hear the sound of the engines firing up. "Then by all means, let's make it a ghost ship."

Raven grinned, the lust for blood obviously riding him hard. Together they dove for the yacht, using their powers to keep the humans from seeing them. The yacht was pulling away from the dock, rapidly heading out into the middle of the Delaware River.

The Hob

Good. Robin would follow it out past the mouth of the river and into the sea. There, he would shred McNeil's heart and unravel his soul, as he'd done to Robin.

"Can you smell him?"

Robin nodded. He no longer had a face to lift to the wind, but the stench of the *each uisge*'s evil was strong, flowing behind the yacht like a tattered black banner.

"When?"

Robin saw the way Raven's claws flexed. Claws had also ripped through the fronts of his boots. He looked like the Raven Lord in truth as he called his pets to him.

"At sea."

Raven nodded, gliding silent and invisible in the midst of his black birds. Whatever Robin and Raven left behind on that boat, the birds would feast on, leaving nothing behind but a mystery for the humans to talk about.

They waited a good ten minutes once the yacht had left the mouth of the river before descending on it silently, ready to execute McNeil. Raven landed first, quickly killing the pilot with a slash of his claws across the man's throat.

Robin waited. McNeil would make for the water once he realized he'd been boarded. When he did, Robin would be waiting for him.

Raven proceeded to move about the yacht like the wrath of god, destroying anyone who got in his way. He was swift and merciless, sparing none.

Robin was reluctantly impressed.

There. McNeil, at the back of the ship, moving toward the deck and freedom. Robin dove for him just as McNeil jumped, catching the *each uisge* inside the formless, death-dealing mist that made up his body.

McNeil screamed as the jagged edges of Robin's grief dug into his flesh and Robin's rage scored his skin. The gray smoke that made up his body turned red with McNeil's blood. Robin

235

slowly lowered himself to the deck, inflicting wounds every time he so much as twitched, and waited for Raven to join him. He could feel McNeil within him trying to break free, but Robin held fast.

"There you are."

The silky-smooth tones Raven used to address the *each uisge* were so similar to Robin's own that he nearly lost control. Had Michaela loved his voice as much as he'd loved hers?

McNeil shrieked as Robin swirled around him.

Raven whistled low. "Damn, Father. It's like you placed him inside a giant, swirling cheese grater." He tsk'd. "That's gotta hurt, McNeil."

"Let me go." McNeil's body twisted, transformed into his rarely seen true form: the torso of a human, the teeth of a lion, and the head and legs of a horse. His hands sported five lion's claws instead of morphing into hooves. The sharp hooves at the end of his legs kicked out, meeting resistance from Robin. Robin held fast, refusing to allow the *each uisge* to free itself.

McNeil would finally face justice.

McNeil squirmed in Robin's grasp, causing more slashes and cuts to appear on its dark skin. "Release me!"

"I will drag you into the abyss." Robin's voice had become a whispered hiss, barely audible over the sound of the sea.

Raven looked into Robin's eyes and smiled. Robin nearly wept at the anguish he could see growing in his son's gaze. He knew. Somehow, Raven understood that once McNeil was dead, Robin would begin to fade, to join his love in the beyond. And the knowledge was killing his child.

Raven nodded once and then turned his attention back to McNeil. He thrust his hand into Robin's sharp mist and ripped one of McNeil's fingers off his hand. He made it seem easy, like ripping a breadstick in half. "No."

McNeil shrieked with rage, but neither man cared.

Michaela would be avenged.

"Hell and damnation." Oberon sighed as he stared at the shattered window. "Robin. Damn it. If you'd only waited." He slowly stood, holding the battered form of Robin's mate in his arms.

The scent from her blood was...familiar. Intriguing.

Fae.

Yes. The nearly insane thought running through his head made him smile. It was possible. It could be done. It would save both Robin and Michaela, but would cost Oberon.

He could do this. For Robin, who'd always given him everything, Oberon could do this one thing and save them all.

Robin would have to find them on his own, though. Oberon could not do what needed to be done here. He'd take the girl back to the Gray Palace and there, he would save his best friend's wife.

"My king?" Kael, looking bruised and full of grief, keened at the sight of Michaela's limp body, but he stepped forward, his bow off-kilter. He had not remained undamaged. A gash over his forehead was bleeding profusely, staining the pale blond locks red. Bruises were visible on his jaw and his arms, along with numerous shallow cuts. One arm was held at an odd angle. Oberon was willing to bet it was broken. And from the way his pupils were unevenly dilated, he had a concussion on top of all of that. "Allow me to protect you until Robin returns or a true Blade arrives."

Oberon smiled. The boy would do nicely. Even injured, he reacted in a way that would make Robin proud. "A true Blade is already here. We just need to make it official."

Kael's face went white. "Oh. Cool." He then leaned over and proceeded to puke all over the scorched carpet.

Oberon sighed. He'd have to get the boy healing. He waited until the retching stopped. "Take hold of my arm." Kael's grip was shaky but firm.

"Snod will go too."

Oberon had completely forgotten the redcap. "I think not." He turned to face the creature, only to be stunned.

The redcap was crying, silent tears running down its cheeks as it looked at the woman in Oberon's arms. Snod wiped his cheeks with the back of his hand like a child. "I will go, and protect my lady."

Snod was just as blood-soaked as the rest of them, just as damaged, but he stood straight and tall even as tears continued to roll down his cheeks. The sorrow in his beady little eyes had Oberon sighing in defeat. "Very well. Grab hold, then."

Oberon silently teleported the four of them to the Gray Palace. "Harold!"

"Sire?"

Oberon strode for his personal chambers. There, hidden in the center of the palace, he would perform the rite that would bring Michaela back. "Kael is an apprentice Blade. He's been injured. Send for the healer to see to him. Also, the redcap is Lady Goodfellow's personal guard." If possible, Snod stood even straighter. "See to it that his injuries are tended as well." He turned to the redcap. "I'll be taking your oath when your lady is well again."

Snod bowed. "Yes, Sire."

"Sire? Lady Goodfellow?" Harold's voice was full of concern. The brownie had a soft spot for Robin and his antics. The knowledge that he'd truebonded had caused the brownie much joy.

He spared his butler a quick glance. "I will tend to her myself."

"I can heal him."

The quiet, melodic voice caught his attention like nothing else ever had. Oberon turned and found himself staring at...

Hell and damnation. It's her.

She was a tall, thin, rather gangly woman with a face that was too long to be called pretty, too interesting to be called plain. *Arresting* was the word that came to mind. Her full, bow-shaped lips were curved downward in a worried frown. Her nose was slightly crooked, as if she'd broken it at some point and it hadn't quite healed right.

Her eyes were absolutely huge even in her human Seeming, a turquoise so bright Oberon wondered if they were even brighter in her merform, for he had no doubt one of the sea folk stood before him. Intelligent and brilliant, they were her best feature.

Her forehead was really a five head, further elongating her face. She'd made an attempt to hide it with bangs, but it didn't work. Her hair in her human Seeming was chocolaty brown, but Oberon was certain it would be sea green in her true form. She currently had it pulled back in a ruthlessly tight ponytail, her sharply cut bangs hitting her eyebrows.

She had a sharp, pointed chin and quirked, full eyebrows he just knew would be firm when she argued, soft when she smiled. She wore tight jeans, low-heeled brown ankle boots and a snow-white crochet sweater that hit her mid–thigh.

On her finger was a distinctive pearl ring Oberon recognized immediately.

This was the missing Princess Cassandra Nerice of the Court of Atlantis, and Oberon's future bondmate.

For the first time since Titannia's betrayal, Oberon's body reacted to the sight of a woman. His cock swelled painfully, almost tenting his slacks. He'd had dreams of this woman that rivaled the most ribald actions he'd ever taken, both before and during his time with his faithless ex-wife.

And he wanted to act out each and every one of them on her, to see if she was as limber as she looked, as daring as she seemed.

He could not allow her to see his reaction. No woman would ever have that kind of power over him again. "I have a Blade who needs your skill, your Highness." She winced, whether at his cool tone or her title, he knew not, nor did he care.

He could not afford to care.

"I might be able to help with her, as well." Her hands were shoved deep in her pockets, so she pointed with her chin toward Michaela.

"Is this why you returned, your Highness?" Harold's guilty gaze darted toward Oberon. "My liege, I—"

Oberon's brows rose. "You knew the princess was hiding at Lord Goodfellow's?"

"The Child of Dunne, he..." Harold's ruler-straight shoulders slumped. "He said it was for the good of the Court, sire."

Oberon shook his head. "And you didn't think to inform me of what was going on?"

"Do we really have time for this?" Princess Cassandra waved her hand toward Michaela. "The longer you delay, the more likely it is you won't be able to bring her back. Her soul will be beyond even your grasp."

"You are aware of what I'm going to attempt?" How was that possible?

She shrugged. "You're going to do *something* or you wouldn't be carrying her the way you are."

"And how is that?"

She looked at him out of those huge, intelligent eyes. "Like she's precious."

Oberon nodded once. "Indeed. Now, if you would, take care of my Blade. I have much work to do if my plan is to succeed." He didn't, but the less she knew the better. What he would do was simplicity itself. It would strengthen Michaela, make her one of them, and bleed Oberon damn near dry.

It would render him vulnerable, and for that reason more than any other he had to keep the princess away from him.

"Yes, sire." Princess Cassandra bowed perfectly, turned on her heel, and took Kael's arm. "Follow me, please."

Oberon couldn't help it. He watched the princess lead his Blade away. The urge to follow was so strong he actually took a step in their direction, ready to follow her like a puppy. He shook his head, hoping to clear her from his thoughts, and looked at the body in his arms.

Princess Cassandra was right on one point. He did not have much time.

Where was she?

Where the fuck was she?

He tore through the Gray Palace, a mist of pure vengeance. Someone had taken his truebond.

Someone had stolen her from him.

"Hobgoblin."

There. That voice. He recognized it. That was the one who had stolen his truebond, who'd taken away his chance to carry her to the abyss with him.

With a roar he charged the silver-haired man, ready to rip and tear and destroy.

"Calm yourself, Hobgoblin."

That voice was able to reach him, the part that had once been civilized. He remembered that, along with laughing brown eyes and an earth-shattering trust.

"Robin."

Robin. Yes. That had been his name.

"You need to stop, Robin."

He shuddered. That *voice*. How could he be hearing that voice? That voice was dead, gone, oh, so precious.

"Please, for me?"

He turned his attention to the small female standing by the silver–haired man's side. She should not be there. She should be by *his* side.

She smiled at him, the love and trust in her gaze so easy for him to see. She stepped forward, ignoring the unvoiced protest of the silver-haired man. "I missed you, Robin."

"No!"

The female held up her hand, stopping someone from coming closer to them. Robin had been aware of the person's presence, but he had the female's aura around him like a protective cloak. He belonged to her, but not in the way that Robin did. He was a protector, doing his job, nothing more.

Robin shivered as the female approached. There was something different about her, but he hardly cared, because that sweet, enchanting scent surrounded him, pulled at him. He needed to be different, for her. He needed to be...

"Come back to me, Robin." She held out her hands and stepped into him, became one with him.

"Gods above," someone breathed, but Robin barely heard it. She was with him, inside him. One with him, and totally unafraid. He smoothed the jagged edges of his grief, lest they harm her. He tamed the raging anger, unwilling to shed her blood. He cradled her close, encased her in his warmth, his sheer joy of having her with him again.

"I need you, no matter what form you take." She stared right into his glowing eyes, her own filled with...love.

Love.

He remembered.

Michaela.

Robin's form swirled around her, coalesced until he knelt before her, his arms around her waist, his face buried in her abdomen.

Her hands stroked his head, pushed his wild, tangled red mane from his face. "Welcome back, love.

Robin Goodfellow, Knight of Oberon and the most dangerous being on earth save one, sobbed like a broken child.

Chapter Twenty-Three

He couldn't get her naked fast enough. The urge to taste her flesh, see if she was any different now that Oberon had done what he had, was consuming him.

He'd whisked her away with nary a word of thanks, unable to speak, only able to feel. He needed his truebond, had to reestablish his claim on her before he went mad.

He never wanted to go through losing her again.

"Robin."

The way she gasped his name as he suckled her nipple through her loose cotton shirt was music to his ears. It was music he'd believed he'd never hear again, so was doubly precious.

He'd make her sing again, and again, and again.

He realized he'd begun to glow when she looked up at him, her dark eyes reflecting his light back at him. He shredded her clothes from her body, his razor-sharp claws making short work of the thin cotton material Oberon had given her. She wore no bra underneath, nor panties.

His lord knew him well.

He sucked up a mark on her bare breast, needing some visible sign that she was alive, that she belonged to him. She tangled her hands in his hair as he kissed and sucked his way down her body. He was leaving behind visible proof of his possession of her, love bites that would slowly fade, only to be replaced as he made love to her again.

Never again would he let her far from his side. Never again would he place her in danger.

The Hob

Robin finally reached the apex of her thighs. He nuzzled the dark curls before clasping her thighs and spreading her legs wide.

"Robin."

Her whispered plea would be granted. Robin sucked her clit into his mouth, his tongue working the nub of flesh until she was squirming greedily beneath him. Her hands clenched around his head as she thrust against him, chasing the ecstasy just out of her reach.

She quivered and let out a low moan, coming apart beneath his mouth, her thighs clamping around his head as the orgasm bowled through her.

It wasn't enough. He needed more, needed to wring more pleasure from her.

He got off the bed and pulled her to the edge, the tattered remains of her outfit falling away from her. He stilled when he took a moment to look at her, debauched and lying wide open to his gaze.

Her hair, once a lush, very human brown, had turned to pure silver. The tanned skin had become pale and sparkling. Her eyes, languid with pleasure, were the color of molten gold.

She was even more beautiful than he'd thought possible.

He bent and took one golden nipple into his mouth. Her taste, her texture, it hadn't truly changed, just...brightened, sharpened to that of a true fae.

His urgency was abated somewhat by this sign that his wife was truly immortal now, that very little could cause her body to fail her as it had before. She was a true child of the fae now, her latent blood brought to the surface by the power of Oberon.

She was Tuatha Dè Danaan.

This time, when he kissed her sex, he made sure to love on her. He took his time, licking and stroking slowly, stoking her fires, enjoying the way she squirmed. He watched her pluck at her nipples, made note of the way she soothed the small hurt.

He stroked her skin, memorizing once more the smooth feel of it beneath his palms, the way she warmed at his touch.

When her orgasm rolled through her this time it took him by surprise. Her face exquisite in its glory, highlighted by the shining silver tangle of her hair.

She laughed when it was over, her voice husky with pleasure. "Do that again."

So he did, basking in her joy, reveling in her touch as she reached for him, finally, and pulled him to her. He'd long since done away with his own clothes, a mere thought making them disappear, so he slid into her without any obstruction.

She was smooth, hot, wet and wonderful around him, stretching to take him inside. Take him home.

He bottomed out inside her, his balls grazing her ass, and groaned. This, this was what he'd needed, to be inside her, a part of her. Robin grabbed hold of her hips and held her still as he ground against her, rotating his own hips in an attempt to feel all of her.

"Robin."

He hadn't realized he'd closed his eyes until he opened them at her soft cry. Her heels were on the edge of the mattress, her thighs spread wide to accommodate him. She'd taken hold of the edge of the bed, her knuckles white from the force of her grip. His hair was like a living flame against the paleness of her flesh, brushing against her knees as he began to fuck her.

Her choked, whimpering cry was yet another note in the song she sang for him.

Her thighs quivered as he fucked her, her body quaking, trying to hold the position. But Robin's satin sheets were too slick. She slid, almost dislodging him from her body.

"Hold." Robin gently pulled her leg toward him, kissed the ankle, and placed it on his shoulder. He repeated the action with her other leg, then wrapped his hands around her thighs. He quirked an eyebrow at her. "Now. Let's try that again."

The Hob

She giggled, and the sun shone down on him once more.

"Wait."

Robin paused just as he was about to begin fucking her once more.

She scooted back, sliding off his cock. This time, it was his turn to whimper.

She giggled again and crooked her finger at him. "C'mere, big guy."

Robin crawled up the bed toward her. For once he didn't care about appearance; he merely wanted to be inside her once more. On his hands and knees he crawled until he hovered over her, stealing a kiss.

She reached up and stroked his cheek. "Hi."

He shuddered under her touch, the hunger to claim her and the sheer, unadulterated relief that she was alive, whole, clashed inside him. "Hi."

"Make love to me."

"Always."

She wrapped her legs around his waist and Robin slid home. He couldn't seem to pull far away from her tempting mouth, demanding kiss after kiss as he stroked into her. This time, unlike their first frantic coupling when his power had nearly shattered them both, it was a gentle balm, covering them in a glowing blanket.

Michaela's eyes shimmered, sparkled with a matching golden light. He could feel that gentle, warm light touch him deep inside, waiting, asking for entry.

The base of his spine tingled, his cock swelling inside her. He was close, so close from a gentle lovemaking he'd never known the likes of before.

Michaela licked her lips, her breath coming in pants. "Now?"

He stole one last, wet kiss before staring into her eyes. "Now."

Michaela's eyes went wide as her back arched off the bed. Her legs clamped around him like a vise, her pussy clenching around him, nearly strangling him.

And her eyes, those glowing, golden eyes, became the center of his world.

Robin came with a shattered cry, pouring himself into his truebond everything that he was, taking in everything she offered as she claimed him as only a Tuatha Dè could.

They were one.

Michaela stood shivering outside the quaint farmhouse. It was an old Victorian, with white gingerbread accents and a wide front porch. It was a soothing pale blue color, the trim a blinding white. A huge wrap-around porch with a real porch swing gave the old Victorian a homey feel. The landscape around the house was filled with blooming flowers.

The screen door squeaked open, and out stepped a walking jeans commercial. The dark-haired man sauntered onto the front porch and leaned against the post, shooting a roguish smile at Robin. "Well, well. What have we here?"

Robin chuckled quietly beside her. He took her hand and led her up to the blue-eyed hottie. "Sean Dunne, I'd like you to meet my truebond, Michaela." Michaela noticed the startled delight on the man's face. "Michaela, this is Moira's father, Sean Dunne."

"Pleased to—" *Father?* This hunka-hunka was Moira's *dad?*

A soft giggle had her looking to the man's right. "I had the same reaction." A short woman with dark reddish hair was coming around the corner of the porch, a huge grin on her face. "Robin!"

"Ruby."

The Hob

The woman ran down the steps and flung herself into Robin's arms. "It's so good to see you again." She hugged Robin tight before turning to Michaela. "Is she...?"

"My truebond, Michaela. My dear, this is my very good friend, Ruby Dunne."

Michaela relaxed. She hadn't even realized she'd tensed up until she heard the difference in the way Robin spoke to Ruby versus the way he spoke to Michaela. With Ruby, there was affection, and an obvious history. But Michaela was tucked under his arm, his possessiveness obvious. There was a softness when he spoke to her, a pure and utter joy that was absent when he spoke to Ruby. "Pleased to meet you."

"You too." Michaela found herself enveloped much the way Robin had been. "I've been praying Robin would find his truebond."

"We all have." Sean Dunne came down the steps and gave her his own hug, pulling her gently from Robin's hold. Robin let her go without a word of protest. "Welcome to the family."

"We have much to discuss, if it pleases you." Robin walked up the front steps as if he belonged here, and from the way the Dunnes were reacting, he did.

Sean tucked Michaela under one arm and Ruby under the other and followed after Robin. "I gather it's good news for once?"

"Ruby? Where did you go?" A tall man who looked remarkably like Sean but with sparkling green eyes the color of grass came out of the house. He smiled when he saw Ruby. "There you are. I should have known you'd home in on Robin."

Ruby giggled and slipped away from Sean, crossing to the green-eyed man's side. The way she curled herself into him told Michaela all she needed to know.

He nodded respectfully to Robin. "Robin."

"Leo. I've brought my truebond to meet you all. Michaela, this is Leo Dunne, the middle Dunne child."

She blinked. This was Moira's brother? Geez, did anyone in this family get touched with the ugly stick? Was it even waved in their direction?

The delight on Leo's face was open, easy. He, like everyone else in the Dunne clan, seemed to hold Robin in great affection. "Really? Congratulations!" He held out his hand and shook Michaela's. "Welcome to the Dunne farm."

"Thank you."

"Sean? Leo?" The screen door opened once more, and there stood the most amazingly attractive woman she'd ever seen. She wasn't much taller or older than Michaela. The woman's hair fell to her waist, a straight, shining curtain of glowing red-gold. Slightly tilted green eyes the color of emeralds peeked out from under the longest, most lush lashes Michaela had ever seen. Her chin was delicately pointed, her nose fine and aristocratic, her lips full and pink. She could have graced many a magazine cover.

Michaela looked over at Leo and shook her head. "Let me guess. Your mother."

Leo laughed. "Yup."

"Oh, yeah. You and I are going to get along fine." Ruby winked as Sean left her to go to the petite beauty. The way Sean looked at her left no doubt in her mind that Sean and Aileen Dunne were just as truebonded as she was to Robin.

"You too?" Michaela tried to hide her grin.

Ruby nodded. "Yup. I had pretty much the same reaction when I first saw my in-laws. I felt like a potato in a flower garden. You know, like 'What the hell am I doing here?'"

Leo kissed the top of Ruby's head. "You're a rose in a field of wildflowers."

Ruby blushed and buried her face in Leo's chest, much to his obvious satisfaction.

Robin walked over to Aileen and lifted her hand to his lips. "You are looking particularly fine this morning, Aileen."

Sean reached over and removed his wife's hand from Robin's grasp. "Why don't you introduce your truebond, Robin?"

Robin, a wicked grin on his face, waved Michaela over. "This is she. Michaela, my dear, I'd like you to meet Lady Aileen Dunne, the matriarch of the Dunne clan and a lady far more fearsome than I."

"I should hope so. You're so not a lady." Michaela grinned up at Robin.

He chuckled, but before he could say anything two more people joined them on the porch. One was a tall, red-headed man with dark blue eyes and an easy smile. The other was a small Asian woman with the most unusual eyes Michaela had ever seen. One eye was dark brown with a startling light hazel star in the center. The other eye was a pure light hazel. There was a slight roundness to her stomach that meant she was pregnant, probably four months along.

The red-headed man smiled slowly at Michaela. "There you are."

Robin bowed. "Shane Joloun Dunne, meet Michaela, my truebond."

"Michaela. A pleasure to finally meet you." Shane shook her hand. "I was wondering how they'd get you to not be dead."

She blinked. "Um. Yeah. I'm glad they figured it out."

"Me too."

The woman at his side rolled her eyes. "Akane Russo Dunne." She held out her hand and Michaela shook it. "I'm Jethro's bondmate."

Jethro?

Shane immediately rocked back on his heels, the intelligence on his face fading into an expression that could only be described as Gomer Pyle. "Well, Miz Akane, y'all sure are lookin' pretty today. Shame you're gonna ruin those shoes helpin' me milk cows and all. What kind did you say they were? Ferragari?"

Akane rolled her eyes. "Ignore him. He just likes to see steam come out of my ears." Her expression wasn't warm, the way everyone else's was. It was more wary, contained. "You're Lady Goodfellow, hmm? I was expecting someone taller."

Michaela ignored the way Robin growled at her side.

Akane did no such thing. She immediately bowed her head, baring her neck. "I meant no disrespect, sir. I was merely playing."

Robin reached out and caressed the nape of Akane's neck, his claws extended. Akane winced. "So long as there is no malice behind the playing."

"Yes, sir." Akane stood, but not before Michaela saw a drop of blood on the back of her neck.

Michaela stared at the woman who was barely taller than she was. "You're a Blade, aren't you?"

Akane nodded. "Yes." She rubbed her tummy. "Except when I'm an incubator."

Shane took Akane into his arms and snuggled her. "But you're such a pretty incubator. Much cuter than the one in the hen house."

Akane elbowed him in the stomach, but she was the one with the pained expression afterward. Shane just laughed.

This family was weird.

Robin "I'd also like to introduce you to Snod, Michaela's oath-bound bodyguard."

Snod nodded his head and waved hello genially, but he watched the Dunnes like a hawk. He was very overprotective and far sweeter than Michaela had expected. He was a gentle giant, and Michaela would face-plant anyone who gave him grief.

Akane was the first to pick her jaw up off the floor. Now that Michaela knew that redcaps were typically Black Court, she understood the reaction a bit better. Still, Snod should be judged on his own merits, not those of his people. "Hello, Snod. Jaden's gonna love you."

Snod just smiled, and continued to watch them, his expression pleasant but his posture alert. He'd taken Robin's word for it that the Dunnes were "good" people, not "bad" ones, but he was still on his guard.

"Well, come inside, then. Don't stand out in the cold." Aileen started waving them through the front door.

Robin was the first one through as the rest of the Dunnes surrounded Ruby and Michaela. It was almost as if all of the fae were protecting the two of them, the fragile human women. Even Akane was glancing around like ninjas were about to attack at any second.

Michaela rolled her eyes. Thanks to King Oberon, she could now kick ass with the best of them. Hell, maybe Robin would let her become a Blade.

Strong arms wrapped around her waist. "Not in a million years, my dear."

Michaela sighed. "I swear, sometimes I think you can read my mind."

Robin smiled mysteriously and kissed the side of her neck.

"Do I want to know?" Akane handed Michaela a cup of tea.

"I was thinking of asking Robin to train me as a Blade." Michaela took a sip. Mm. English Breakfast tea.

"It might not be a bad idea." Akane eyed Robin warily. "She'd be better equipped to protect herself, and even if she never got sent out on missions, she could keep herself alive until another Blade or you could reach her."

Robin tilted his head. "An excellent point. I will consider training, but Michaela, you will never be a Blade." He clamped his hand over her mouth. "No."

She licked his palm, hoping he'd be squicked out and let her go, but he merely chuckled. "Phmph."

"What?" Robin lifted his hand.

"Fine." Michaela slumped back against him, aware she was pouting.

Akane cleared her throat. "Jaden and I can train her when you can't, Robin. We'll make sure she's more than capable of defending herself."

"Thank you."

"I can take care of myself, you know." She wasn't made of glass. Not anymore, anyway.

"Uh-huh." Akane grinned. "Pardon me, but you're…you're…" The star in the center of her eye flared. "Holy shit." Her eyes rolled back in her head and she passed out at Michaela's feet.

Shane ran over, his face pale, and cradled Akane against him. "What happened?"

"Um. Sorry?" Michaela shrugged. "Her eye did something freaky, then she timbered."

Shane grimaced. "She took a look at you, huh? No wonder she passed out." He sighed deeply. "I wish Cassie were here."

"Cassie?"

Robin stroked her arm, probably hoping to soothe her. She didn't know what she'd done wrong, but she was getting the impression that she was responsible for Akane's condition. "Princess Cassandra Nerice of the Atlantean Court."

Shane just smiled while his family freaked out around him.

Michaela pulled free of Robin's arms and knelt by Shane. "Let me take a look at her. I'm a registered nurse."

Shane, that odd smile still on his face, laid his truebond flat on the ground. "You go right ahead."

Michaela reached for Akane's wrist and felt for a pulse. It was there, steady and strong. She lifted back her lids to check her pupils and immediately let go.

One eye was completely gold. The other was almost black, the star swallowing the pupil until it was no longer visible.

Right. Okay then. She could do this.

She felt compelled to place her hand across Akane's forehead. She took a deep breath and slowly let it out. There was a strange energy flowing through her, alien yet familiar at the same time.

She'd felt this once before. Oberon had used it to bring her back, to heal her body and restore her soul.

Michaela let the power trickle through her, afraid to let too much out. If just looking at her had knocked Akane out, Michaela was afraid of what would happen should she allow the torrent she could sense straining at her self-control free. She concentrated on healing whatever wound she'd caused Akane.

She's having twins.

She could feel them, living flames burning brightly inside their mother, frightened by her silence. Michaela reacted instinctively, reassuring the babies that their mother would be fine, that she would allow no further harm to come to her. Their restlessness settled, became sleepy unconcern, and she turned her attention back to Akane.

She carefully smoothed out the ragged edges she could see, laying a healing balm over them, bringing them back together into a single whole. Even the worn edges of an old wound were smoothed over, eased, the bright red flair of pain dying down into a serene green that had Michaela pulling slowly back, her job done.

She opened her eyes to find Akane staring up at her in shock. "It's okay. The babies are fine."

Akane licked her lips and sat up slowly. "So I heard."

Shane helped his wife stand up. "You all right, *mo chroí?*"

She nodded carefully. "I think so."

Shane helped her to the sofa. "You fell pretty hard. I think you dented Ma's floor with your head."

Akane's lips quirked up in a reluctant smile. "I'll pay for repairs."

"I'm glad she's okay. What happened, anyway?" Michaela looked around at the rest of the Dunne family, but they were all staring at her with a mixture of awe and shock. "Robin?"

Robin buffed his nails on his caramel silk shirt. The color really highlighted his fiery hair, and she loved it on him. "You're Tuatha Dè, my dear. Of course Akane had trouble looking at you with her inner sight. You glow far too brightly, beautiful."

"Oh." Michaela brushed her hair back from her face, aware the strands had grown silver. She'd lost her Seeming again, damn it. She hadn't quite gotten the hang of switching between the silver and gold coloring of the Tuatha Dè back to her human appearance. Where her hair and eyes had been brown before, they were now silver and gold, respectively. Her skin paled to a snowy white, giving her what Robin called an ethereal beauty and Michaela called her moon tan. She looked like she was in serious need of some UV rays.

"How? I thought all the Tuatha Dè were gone." Aileen slowly sat on a Queen Anne chair.

Michaela shrugged. "I died. I got better." She held out her cup with a hopeful expression. "More, please?"

Robin chuckled quietly as the Dunnes erupted with questions and comments. "That's my girl."

"This is all well and good, but Robin? You need to get back to the Gray Palace."

Michaela smiled at Ruby, who'd handed her another cup of tea.

"Oh?" Robin's voice was deceptively mild. They'd just left the damn palace, both of them needing to get away. Oberon had approved, so long as they returned within two days, Robin to resume his duties and Michaela to begin learning hers.

It wasn't much of a honeymoon, but it was the best they'd get, at least for a while. Oberon had been far too pale for Michaela's liking, and Robin's quick agreement had her worried.

He was just as concerned about Oberon's appearance as she was. He was just better at hiding it.

Shane nodded and stood up, bowing to Robin. "My Prince, you are needed."

Robin stilled. "Oh?" He took a deep breath, then let it out in a string of what she was pretty sure were curses from the look on Aileen Dunne's face. If so, they were the prettiest sounding curses Michaela had ever heard. "*Her* plan, I take it?"

Shane sighed. "All I know is he's not dead. But that's it. The vision was so murky I barely understood it until you arrived here."

"Show me."

The command in Robin's voice was usually reserved for his Blades. Michaela had heard it often enough in the two weeks since she'd been brought to Robin's Rocky Mountain paradise.

Leo picked up something covered in a blue cloth. Whatever it was, it was heavy. He was straining as he settled it on Mrs. Dunne's coffee table. "I've seen it, Robin, but..." He shrugged. "I don't know what to say."

"Lift the veil and let the piece speak for itself."

Robin was far tenser than he was letting on. His posture was relaxed, his hands easy, but the strain showed around his eyes as green fire danced across the blue. Michaela took hold of his hand and he let out some of the breath he'd been holding.

He loved Oberon. If something had happened to the High King, he'd be inconsolable.

The cloth was lifted to reveal a figure that was clearly Oberon. The long fall of silver hair was distinctive. He stood in front of a mirror, reaching out to touch its surface.

The mirror reflected nothing back.

How Shane had managed that trick, Michaela didn't know. "What does it mean?"

Shane shot Robin a grim look. "I have no idea."

Epilogue

Robin burst through the throne room doors, Michaela marching right by his side. The courtiers gasped, some in outrage, some in surprise, but all stilled as he came to a halt in front of the Gray Throne, his blue eyes glowing with green fire.

Oberon was missing. He hadn't been seen since he'd granted Robin and Michaela permission to visit the Dunnes. He'd disappeared into his chambers to sleep, and then simply disappeared. And when Robin found out who had taken his king, heads would roll.

"Harold."

More gasps, this time accompanied by cries of outrage, poured through the room like a tsunami as he took hold of Michaela's hand and settled her gently on the Queen's throne, a seat that had not been used in all the time the Gray Court had existed. Robin himself settled down on the High King's throne and threw his legs over the arm, swinging his left foot nonchalantly.

Robin's hair was bound in a tail at the nape of his neck by a titanium clasp with the symbol of the Court etched into it, the dark gray metal a foil for the symbol. A triple spiral triskelion, the bottom two spirals were white and black enamel, to represent the White and Black Courts. But the upper spiral, the one above them both, was done in pure, shining silver, the arms of the spiral reaching down to touch both the white and the black, blending into them.

The staff banged twice more. Harold cleared his throat in the sudden silence. "In light of the fact that the High King, His Serene Highness King Oberon, is missing, Lord Robin Goodfellow, Knight of Oberon, Prince of the Gray, appointed heir of the High King, now sits in his place. If, for any reason, the High King does not return to his throne within a year and a day, Prince Robin will be crowned High King."

Robin glanced around the room. Look at them squirm. How many of them had helped his king's kidnappers?

The majordomo stepped forward and tapped his staff against the floor twice, silencing the courtiers. "All hail the Prince Regent, Prince Robin Goodfellow."

Robin touched the clasp, one that would respond only to the rightful king or his appointed regent, enjoying the dismay on many a face as it became the crown of the High King.

Robin smiled, his teeth wicked sharp. "Call Lord Raven MacSweeney to us."

The court was stunned as the ex-Black Court operative swept into the room and bowed before the throne. "My liege."

Robin nodded at his son as he stood tall and proud. "Your oath, if it pleases you." There had not been time to bring Raven before Oberon as planned, therefore Raven would give his oath to the Regent. It would be equally binding, and the courtiers would be forced to accept it.

Raven gracefully knelt before the throne. "I hereby renounce all ties to the Black Lady, Queen Titannia, Queen of the Black Court, Lady of the Unseelie." The courtiers gasped as that name, anathema in the court for so long, rang out clear and true. "I declare myself Oberon's man from this day forth, in honor and in faith, having no other oaths to forswear. By the gods, I pledge my loyalty to the Gray Court, High King Oberon and his descendants. I declare myself the sworn servant of the Gray Lord, High King Oberon, King of the Gray Court, Lord over the Fae. I pledge my sword and my honor to uphold the laws of the Court. I and my house will abide by the laws handed down by the High King. I will faithfully perform all services required by Crown and Court. So swear I, Lord Raven MacSweeney."

Robin's eyes twinkled as Michaela nodded beside him, a serene smile on her face. "I, Prince Robin Goodfellow, the acting

Gray Lord, Lord of the Fae, hereby hear your oaths and accept them in the name of Crown and Court, and High King Oberon. I declare you our loyal servant, sworn to our bidding. From this day forth my sword shall defend you, my magic protect you, and my wrath be mighty should you fail of your duty. All former oaths to the Black are hereby null and void, by my power as Prince Regent. So swear I, Robin Goodfellow, the Hobgoblin."

Raven shivered as the weight of the oath's magic settled over him. He was now Gray Court, bound to Oberon, and thus to Robin.

"I hereby recruit you into the Blades, Lord Raven. Do you accept?"

"I do." Raven's blue eyes flashed green for a second. Robin wondered if any save Michaela and himself saw it.

"Very good. Now." Robin steepled his fingers together and continued to ignore the rising whispers of the courtiers. Michaela laid her hand on his knee, lending him her strength to do what needed to be done. "I have a job for you..."

He shivered as he made his way down the highway, the icy cold rain plastering what little clothing he had to his skin.

Something was very wrong. He needed to go somewhere. Be somewhere, but...

Why couldn't he *remember*?

The sum total of what he knew was this barren highway, this cold rain. Nothing, not even a glimmer of what he'd once been, lived within his mind.

Why? What had happened that he didn't even know his own fucking name?

Headlights cut through the dark, dreary night, slowing to a stop beside him to reveal a dark sedan. The driver's side door window rolled down, revealing a familiar face.

He gasped, stumbling back a step.

"*You.*"

About the Author

Dana Marie Bell wrote her first short story when she was thirteen years old. She attended the High School for Creative and Performing Arts for creative writing, where freedom of expression was the order of the day. When her parents moved out of the city and placed her in a Catholic high school for her senior year, she tried desperately to get away, but the nuns held fast, and she graduated with honors despite herself.

Dana has lived primarily in the Northeast (Pennsylvania, New Jersey and Delaware, to be precise), with a brief stint on the US Virgin Island of St. Croix. She lives with her soul mate and husband Dusty, their two maniacal children, an evil, ice-cream stealing cat and a bull terrier that thinks it's a Pekinese.

You can learn more about Dana at www.danamariebell.com or contact her at danamariebell@gmail.com.

Strike a match, light the candle…and fall into the spell.

Shadow of the Wolf
© 2012 Dana Marie Bell
Heart's Desire, Book 1

Christopher Beckett is from an ancient line of wizards, but with one aspect that sets him apart. His wolf. Right now that wolf is howling for a mate. Knowing it's only a matter of time before the wolf's needs override everything else in his life, Chris casts the spell all the Becketts have used to call their mates to them.

His wish list is short: She must be of a lineage at least as old as his own. And she must accept his wolf. When his mate appears, he realizes his list should have been one item longer.

Alannah Evans, a powerful witch of the Evans Coven, has no problem with Chris's wolf. It's the wizard part that sticks in her magical craw. Witches and wizards have always been at odds, so by rights, she and Chris shouldn't be striking sparks of attraction this bright. But Chris will not be denied, and gradually she finds herself trusting him—then falling into the fire of desire.

When it becomes clear an old enemy has targeted them both for death, Chris charges into a duel that could cost him his life. Or worse: Lana.

Warning: Product contains explicit sex, graphic language, magic, mayhem, and a wet, naked wolf shifter bearing hot chocolate. Mmm…chocolate.

Available now in ebook and print from Samhain Publishing.

It's all about the story...

Romance

HORROR

www.samhainpublishing.com

CPSIA information can be obtained at www.ICGtesting.com
Printed in the USA
LVOW06s2123270214

375499LV00004B/339/P